ISBN: 978-0-9766231-1-3
Published by Red Raptor Productions, Inc.
BLOOD LEGACY: HEIR TO THE THRONE Vol 1, 2009. FIRST PRINTING.
Office of Publication: Long Beach, California
BLOOD LEGACY it's logo, all related characters and their likenesses are ™ and © 2009
Kerri Hawkins and Red Raptor Productions, Inc.

What did you think of this book? We love to hear from our readers.
Please email us at: **khawkins@bloodlegacy.com.**

BLOOD LEGACY:
HEIR TO THE THRONE

RED RAPTOR PRODUCTIONS, INC.

Also available from Kerri Hawkins

BLOOD LEGACY: THE STORY OF RYAN
(ISBN: 1-58240-248-5)

BLOOD LEGACY: THE HOUSE OF ALEXANDER
(ISBN: 0-9766231-0-2)

THE DARKNESS: VOLUME I
(ISBN: 978-1-58240-797-5)

visit us on the web at
www.bloodlegacy.com

BLOOD

LEGACY

HEIR TO
THE THRONE

by **KERRI HAWKINS**

CHAPTER 1

THE BOY RAN SWIFTLY ACROSS THE TERRACED STEPS, his sandaled feet barely touching the smooth stone. The hem of his robe was embroidered in gold and stained with blood. The smell of smoke was acrid in his nose and his lungs burned all the more in his exertion and terror. The screams of the dying echoed throughout the city.

He saw soldiers ahead of him and felt a flicker of hope. But before he could start toward them, the soldiers were ambushed by barbarians. The marauders were huge, their size magnified by the pelts of animal skin draped over their shoulders, the filthy hair that ran down their backs and the wicked axes and clubs they wielded. The guards, armed only with pikes, offered little resistance and were beaten to the ground. One was impaled, the other beheaded.

The boy shrank back into the shadows. He knew the barbarians would not spare him. He had already seen them slaughter women and children; they were sparing no one. The fortunate died instantly before they could be tortured or raped. The cries of the less fortunate told him which fate he would prefer.

As the boy hid in the shadows, it did not occur to him to include himself in the category of "children" although he was but 12 seasons. He had been schooled for great responsibility since his birth and acted accordingly.

This thought gave the boy pause. He steeled himself, willing the trembling of his body to stop. He peered around the corner through the smoke and haze. The barbarians had moved on.

He darted from the shadows and sprinted down the corridor. He leaped the dead guards, skidding as he landed in a pool of their slippery blood. He regained his balance on the run and darted for the back stairway, one that was concealed to casual observation.

He took the stairs two at a time and was quickly at the parapet. He stood on the great wall and started across the walkway that led to his household. He glanced down into the city and stopped, stunned.

The city was on fire, the great statues toppled, the beautiful buildings defaced. The temple was defiled and the bodies of priests and guards were strewn about the steps.

The boy shook himself free from his horror. He had to get home. He hurried across the walkway, cautious lest anyone should see him. When he reached the other side, he pushed through the heavy wooden door.

A beautiful woman turned at the sound of his entrance, fear on her refined features. The fear was replaced with relief as she rushed toward him, pulling him to her breast.

"Ambrosius, I thought for certain you were dead."

The boy held his mother tightly, unable to speak of the horrors he had seen. When his mother finally loosened her embrace and leaned back to look at his face, he knew she was aware of the terror in the streets below.

The woman gazed down at her son, running her fingers through his silky black hair. People said he favored her, but she felt he possessed the beauty of Apollo himself. Her expression darkened. A beauty that could only hurt him in the present situation.

They both started as the door downstairs was smashed inward. They could hear the shouts of the barbarians as they began ransacking the house. It would be a matter of minutes before they found the stairway leading to the upper passageway, then their room. She withdrew a knife from her robes.

The boy took a step backward, gazing with resignation at the blade. He would accept his fate with bravery and honor. He was surprised, however, when his mother turned the blade in her hand and handed it to him hilt-first. She knelt down, holding him by the shoulders.

"There is a door at the base of the stairway. It leads to a hidden passageway that will take you away from the city. You must wait for me to distract these men, and then you must flee."

The boy shook his head. "Come with me. I cannot leave you behind."

The woman's expression was sad. They might have made it earlier, but now it was too late. Neither of them would make it without a diversion. She held the boy tightly.

"Listen to me. You must live, and you must grow to become the man I know you will be."

The boy felt tears begin to form and he fought them back. "I will stay here and protect you."

The beautiful woman shook her head. "No," she said, her jaw clenched, "You will leave here now." She felt her own tears threaten to flow. "And one day you will avenge me. Promise me that."

The boy angrily brushed the single tear that slipped out. His own jaw clenched and he nodded his head mutely, unable to speak. A loud noise in the hallway startled them both.

"Hide over there," the woman commanded, "and as soon as you are able, run."

The boy barely had time to duck behind the curtain when the door smashed inward and two burly, filthy men filled the doorway. The first came through the door bearing a bloody battle axe. The second was close behind.

The woman gazed at them fearfully, but with a proud tilt to her chin. She would not give these men the satisfaction of knowing her terror.

It did not matter to them The first glanced at the woman, noting her exquisite beauty. His gaze settled lewdly on her cleavage visible beneath her robes. He noted the purple color of her garments, and grinned broadly. He set his axe aside and reached for his belt, loosening his pants.

The boy tried to drown out the sounds, tried to block out the grunts of the man and the cries of his mother. His tears burned through his eyelids, and his breath came in ragged gasps as the air seared his throat. He clenched the dagger, wanting to rush from his place of hiding and impale it in the grunting man's back.

But he would not. He stood upright, his bitterness again nearly overwhelming his resolve. But he had promised his mother. He forced himself, just once, to look into the room, memorizing every detail of the horrific scene. And then he fled, his tears blinding him as he sought the hidden door.

He found it exactly where his mother had said it was and pushed it inward, smelling the welcome smell of fecund earth. He pulled the heavy door closed behind him, and although the passage was completely black, he began staggering forward in the darkness.

Ryan sat up in bed. The dreams were so frequent now, and so strange.

She stood upright, a lithe figure unfolding to six feet, if not more. She was a striking young woman, moving with preternatural grace as she pulled on a plain white shirt and a pair of simple cotton slacks. It was a testament to her extraordinary beauty that the outfit on her was stunning.

She brushed blonde hair from her eyes and did not bother to glance at the mirror as she left her room.

Ryan stepped down the elaborate staircase, absently running her hand along the smooth mahogany railing. She was somewhat surprised it was dark outside. It seemed as if it had just been morning.

She moved into the den, pleased to see the fire burning in the fireplace that took up the entire west wall. She settled into the chair before the flames, reaching for the glass of wine that was placed at her elbow.

"Thank you, Edward."

Edward bowed low. He had served his master for centuries now and although she needed little, he could anticipate most of what she might want. It was that familiarity which communicated to him her current mood, a certain preoccupation that although not unusual, was generally significant.

Edward cleared his throat. "Is there something troubling you, my lord?"

Although the masculine title should have seemed anomalous, somehow it did not. Although most of their Kind possessed a degree of androgyny, Ryan was the epitome of it. When Edward first met Ryan centuries before, she had been traveling as a handsome young boy, a deception she perpetuated without effort.

Ryan was thoughtful. "I am having odd dreams."

Edward nodded, settling into the chair across from her. Some might have been shocked at the casual way in which the manservant interacted with his liege, but he did so only because Ryan demanded it. And he engaged in such informalities only when they were alone.

Ryan turned to Edward, and to the casual observer it would appear a youngster seeking the advice of an older mentor. But a glance into Ryan's eyes told a different story, that of someone far older than Edward, one of immense power, one who in all likelihood needed little advice.

What Ryan did require, however, was a confidante, a role Edward had ably performed for centuries.

"I am dreaming through someone else's eyes."

Edward nodded again. It was not unusual for their Kind to see through the eyes of those they had Shared with, and no one possessed the gift as Ryan did. When two were locked in the act of transferring blood, it was possible for one to see through the mind of the other, not merely experiencing what the other had seen, but experiencing it as if it were firsthand.

Ryan continued slowly. "The eyes of someone I have never Shared with."

This gave Edward pause. It was possible for someone who was

extremely gifted to see the Memories of the one engaged in the act, and also the Memories that person had obtained through Sharing. In other words, someone like Ryan could see not only with the mind of those she Shared with, but with the mind of everyone that person had Shared with as well.

However, Edward had a sense that Ryan was speaking of something beyond that, and he had misgivings over what she would say next.

"The eyes of someone no one from our Kind has ever Shared with."

She said it matter-of-factly, belying the extreme import of the comment.

"Are you sure?" Edward asked, uncertainty in his voice. He was not one to doubt his master, but no one had ever described this type of event. "Perhaps they are just dreams?"

Ryan shook her head. "No, they are definitely Memories. Thoughts, emotions, events, just like the kind seen when Sharing. But they are of a time and place that I have never seen, a time that pre-dates even my father. And I do not know to whom they belong."

"Can you place the time period?" Edward asked.

"Not exactly," Ryan replied, "I see clothing that makes me think of the Roman Empire, but having no direct experience of that time, I cannot confirm it."

Edward nodded his understanding. Historians rarely got common garb correct, having so little to go on. Someone like Ryan, however, had firsthand experience of the last 1500 years. She had direct experience from the time of her birth in the 14th century, and the indirect experience she had from Sharing with the Others, the most ancient being her father. A question occurred to Edward.

"Do you know when Victor was born?"

Ryan shook her head again. "No, he does not even know."

This surprised Edward and Ryan explained. "There seems to be some type of 'event horizon' in the Memories of the Old Ones. The most ancient, Victor, Abigail," a complex mix of emotions flitted across Ryan's face, "Aeron—nothing in their minds gives hint of where they came from."

"Is it possible they are hiding it from you?"

Ryan nodded. "I have considered that possibility and I do not believe it to be true. I get the sense they do not know how they came to be."

Edward wished to continue the fascinating conversation but he sensed a presence in the hallway. He stood and moved to the entry, pulling the heavy door inward.

Ryan smiled, Edward did not have to say anything. She, too, had sensed the approaching presence. Edward made the announcement with formality, anyway.

"You have a gentleman caller."

Ryan did not turn around. "Please send him in."

Edward glanced down at the tiny figure grasping his pant leg. The toddler looked up with earnest blue eyes, and when Edward nodded to him, the boy ambled into the room toward the chair.

Ryan felt the presence at her elbow and reached down. She grasped the small boy by the back of his shirt, lifting him with one hand, much like a lioness would grasp a cub by the back of its neck. She dangled the small boy in front of her, gazing at him in mock seriousness.

"And what do we have here?"

The little boy gazed at his mother in adoration. He could not yet speak, but shared a mental bond with her so great he did not need to. A mischievous smile played about his lips, a smile so much like Ryan's that, if that were the only similarity, it alone would give his lineage away.

Edward watched the pair. That was far from the only similarity. Although the boy had jet-black hair and deep blue eyes, he looked so much like Ryan it was astonishing. In fact, it was probably good the boy had the slight physical variations because otherwise it would appear Ryan had cloned herself.

The dangling boy giggled and Ryan relented. She settled him onto her lap and he immediately pressed against her, curling into the curve of her arm. As Edward watched them, the analogy of the lioness and the cub returned to him. Ryan was not even close to a traditional maternal figure, rather she cared for the boy with a combination of fierceness and tenderness that evoked the image of the great cats. The boy, for his part, responded in kind. He was fearless, full of spirit and limitless curiosity.

Edward hated to disturb the familial scene, but he did have a job to do.

"Has the boy eaten?"

Ryan smiled to herself. Edward knew full well that Drake had not eaten. It was just his way of reminding her that the boy did in fact need to eat. Requiring no food herself, she occasionally had to be reminded. She gazed into the blue eyes of her son, eyes far warmer than those of his father.

"It is not as if you will let me forget, hmm?" She bunched the back of the boy's shirt and again lifted him with one hand, sending him into giggles once more. She handed the dangling boy to Edward, who took him with far more caution than Ryan displayed.

"Come along, young master Drake," Edward said. His aristocratic demeanor masked his affection for the boy, but the toddler knew him too well. Drake peeked over Edward's shoulder at Ryan, who winked at him as he was carried off. The boy giggled again.

"I will be upstairs, Edward."

"Very well, my lord." Edward said. He knew she would be in the room adjacent to her own, returning to her ceaseless vigil.

Ryan pushed through the double doors, stopping for a moment to stare at the prone figure on the bed.

It was a man, dark-haired and devastatingly handsome, his fine features in quiet repose. His long form covered the length of the dais he rested upon, and although his chest neither rose nor fell, he appeared to be peacefully sleeping. He had slept so for months, neither dead nor alive, neither corruption nor animation touching him.

Ryan went to the fireplace, kneeling down to neatly stack the wood. She arranged the kindling, then expertly lit the flame with a flint. In less than a minute, the wisps of smoke had turned into a blazing fire.

Ryan settled into the chair near his bedside where she had spent hours that had turned into weeks that had turned into months, all the while willing his consciousness to return. She stared at her father's handsome visage, aching at his absence, tortured by the thought that she had contributed to his condition.

Ryan sat back, rubbing her eyes. The last few years seemed a dream. She had only been recently reunited with Victor, having thought him dead by her own hand centuries before. She had been tried for his murder, but he had reappeared at her trial, revealing for the first time that he was her biological father as well as her mentor. Ryan had known, but the Others had not. The revelation of her birth explained much about her that had puzzled the Old Ones, her unique gifts, her unusual power, and the fact that Victor had been able to Change her long after his blood should have been poison.

Ryan remembered her first introduction to her Kind, to the hierarchical web of power and position that held them all. Three things determined the strength of each One. First and foremost was the power of the One who initiated the Change. Under normal circumstances, there were limitations that regulated this advantage. Young Ones, by definition, were those whose blood was not powerful enough to initiate Change. Old Ones were those whose blood had grown too powerful and would kill any human. Only those occupying the middle ground could initiate Change, so there was a narrow window of reproductive potential.

Under normal circumstances.

Victor had proved the extraordinary exception, able to Change Ryan when he was already an Old One and the most powerful of their Kind.

This brought Ryan's thoughts to the second determination of power. One gained strength by Sharing the blood of someone more powerful. Sharing was always pleasant, and the seduction even more so.

As a result, the more powerful were occasionally willing to Share with those younger than themselves. These unions were extremely dangerous to the younger of the pair, however, because Sharing to the point of death was a great pleasure, and their Kind was an inherently predatory species. Most Young Ones did not survive because their mentors lacked the desire or self-control to keep from killing them, or merely failed to protect them.

Again, Victor had proved the exception. Although his desire for his child was great, he had protected Ryan and kept her from the Others when she was a Young One. There were those who said Ryan had never truly been a Young One, so powerful had she been even as a child. Although their Kind eventually moved beyond the point of death, there were those who said Ryan had never been vulnerable to that fate.

And so Ryan had Shared with the greatest of their Kind for centuries, every union making her stronger. And those centuries only added to her power, because the final contribution to strength was age. The older one lived to be, the more powerful one became. Although Ryan was seven centuries old, her power rivaled that of those twice her age.

Ryan was thoughtful. She had once wondered why there were not more of their Kind if all eventually became immortal. She now understood the deadliness of the Change, the irresistible, predatory urge to kill one another, and the limitations on reproduction that served to check their population.

And then there was the purge.

Ryan frowned. That had been barbaric, even for their Kind. Until very recently, Ryan had been unaware of the purge. It was a tradition amongst their Kind, a kind of "thinning of the herd" in which the weak and unacceptable were destroyed. Ryan had been tasked with the last millennial purge. She had not wanted to obey the Grand Council, but at the direction of her father, she accepted the undertaking and proceeded to wipe out their Kind in staggering numbers. Most of the smaller purges concentrated on Young Ones, but Ryan had moved into the ranks of the middle, and even into the ranks of the Old Ones, an art once thought impossible.

This line of thought brought her to Aeron, and she felt a cold satisfaction at his fate. Aeron had been her father's greatest enemy, and hers as well. He had attempted to assassinate both Ryan and Victor by turning their unique anatomies against them. Ryan's body had fought off the genetically-induced virus, but her father had not been so fortunate. As Ryan recovered, Victor remained in his suspended state, neither alive nor dead, but showing no signs of decay.

Aeron had poisoned Victor with a genetically modified virus. But the virus had been made from Ryan's blood, and she felt it was her negligence that allowed the blood to fall into Aeron's hands. Ryan also felt she had weakened her father in an earlier attack and did not think he would have succumbed otherwise. Victor was more powerful than she was, yet she had fought the illness off sufficiently to take revenge on Aeron.

Ryan rubbed her eyes again. All of this led her to her son. She would have a fine time explaining to him one day why she had destroyed his father.

Ryan grew reflective once more. No one had ever been able to explain how Victor was actually able to sire a child, because none of their Kind had reproduced outside of the Change. Nor could she explain how she had replicated the feat with her son. Well, Ryan thought wryly, beyond the obvious mechanics of the act, which had been quite human.

Ryan grew restless. She stood, taking a moment to rest her hand on Victor's chest. She then started downstairs. Drake should be finished eating and she wanted to take him out riding. It was late, but his sleeping patterns were as odd as hers. And he certainly was not afraid of the dark.

CHAPTER 2

RAPHAEL STARED AT THE SOLID ROCK WALL before him. He had never been in the chambers of the Grand Council before, and it was overwhelming to contemplate the fact that he was six stories beneath the surface of the earth. It was more overwhelming to contemplate that few of their Kind had ever seen this place, and none as young as he had been invited here before.

Raphael swallowed. He had been "invited" here for a very specific reason, a task he dared not fail to accomplish. Failure would surely mean his death, as well as the death of the young woman in the next room, the latter paining him more than the former.

"Judging by your demeanor," came the sultry voice from the shadows, "I would almost say you were nervous."

Raphael caught his breath. The magnitude of the presence caused him to take a step backward.

The darkness seemed to shift as a raven-haired woman materialized from the shadows. Stunningly beautiful, everything about her spoke of seduction. From the tilt of her head, to the set of her perfect lips, to the sardonic glint in her eye.

Raphael went to one knee. He had met the mother of his line only once, and she had passed by him with barely a glance. Now she was in front of him, her power emanating outward and filling the confined quarters, wrapping itself around him until he could not breath. Although he had no physiological need for oxygen, he felt the loss keenly all the same. He stammered out a greeting.

"My lady, I am honored. I had no idea to expect you."

Marilyn stared down at the ebony-skinned young man, entertained by the effect she had on him. He was indeed handsome, a worthy addition to her line, even if he was little more than a Young One.

Not that young, Marilyn reminded herself. The youngster was about to prove that.

Raphael stood, but kept his eyes down-cast in respect. Marilyn was slightly taller than him and placed her finger beneath his chin to raise his gaze. She stared at him a long moment.

Raphael was lost the minute he made eye contact with her. Power and promise were in that sultry gaze, the promise of unimaginable pleasure coupled with death. Raphael suddenly understood why so many of their Kind were killed in the act of Sharing. He would willingly give his life for even a moment with this woman.

Marilyn smiled, revealing perfect teeth that made Raphael want to moan. He wanted those teeth at his throat. Marilyn released his chin, smoothing the front of his shirt as she lowered her hand.

Marilyn turned from him. "I thought it best if I supervise this little venture." She glanced around the room, then turned back. "I understand this is your first time. As a member of my line, I can't have you fumbling about like a school boy."

Raphael could not hide his embarrassment. "I will not harm Sus—, Dr. Ryerson."

"Hmmm," Marilyn said, examining him. "We shall see. But I cannot leave such an important act to chance."

Raphael understood her concern. Changing a human to one of their Kind was intensely dangerous, and even those that survived the initial transition often did not survive the complete Change. And this particular human was very special to the most powerful of their Kind.

Marilyn was thoughtful. "A pity I cannot Change Dr. Ryerson myself." She glanced at Raphael. "But I believe you will serve as an adequate conduit."

Raphael was uncertain. "Your blood is far too powerful my lady. You would kill Dr. Ryerson instantly."

"Hmm, yes." Marilyn's tone was entirely casual. "And as enjoyable as that might be, I hardly think Ryan would forgive me."

Raphael found his courage, even in the face of such overwhelming force. He was instantly protective of the young woman in the next room. "I cannot let you harm Susan," he said firmly.

Marilyn was amused, flicking him a glance. "You could hardly stop me, boy." She settled onto the couch. "But that is not why I am here." She glanced at him beneath long dark eyelashes. "Come here."

Raphael swallowed hard but could not have resisted if he wanted to. And he did not want to. He settled near her on the couch and that sultry gaze imprisoned him.

"My blood is too powerful for Dr. Ryerson, but I do not believe it is too powerful for you."

Comprehension at last dawned on Raphael, but he could not believe what she was suggesting.

"You are going to Share with me?"

"Yes," Marilyn said simply, "I am."

Raphael now understood completely. Marilyn could not change Susan Ryerson herself, but potentially could affect the outcome of her transition. The older the One who initiated the Change, the more powerful the offspring would become. With Marilyn's blood flowing through his veins, her mark on Susan would be powerful.

Raphael stared at the Old One before him. There were very few of their Kind more powerful than the seductress before him. He knew he might die in the act of Sharing with her. And he knew that she chose to Share with him for political reasons that had nothing to do with him.

At that moment he cared very little, and in subsequent moments, did not care at all.

CHAPTER 3

THE BOY WATCHED THE BUCK FORAGE in the undergrowth of the forest. He carefully removed the bow slung over his shoulder. The weapon, made from a combination of wood, horn, and sinew, was bound together with hide glue. He had learned to make it as a child when he had graduated from the bow made solely from wood.

He pushed thoughts of his childhood away and carefully removed an arrow from the quiver slung across his back. He fitted the arrow and pulled the string rearward, anchoring it skillfully close to his eye. He aimed at the deer's chest, lowering the arrow slightly so that if he missed, he would miss cleanly.

He did not miss. The arrow flitted through the air with such great force and accuracy that the buck took two sideway steps, then fell to the ground, impaled through the heart. Although the boy rushed forward to slit the deer's throat, it was not necessary. He knelt by the great beast's side, placing his hand on the still-warm body. He offered thanks to the Goddess of the Hunt, but also thanked the local forest god just in case. He did not wish to anger any deity, and extra thanks could not hurt.

Although still young, perhaps 15 seasons at the most, the boy was extremely strong. Even so, he would not be able to carry the carcass so he settled down to butcher the animal. He was proficient, carefully removing the pelt and hanging it to dry over a nearby tree branch.

He then removed every internal organ, setting them aside for different uses. In the end, he would use every part of the deer. Hollow organs would become pouches, sinews would become cords or glue, the meat would be served fresh or dried and salted for preservation.

The boy was thoughtful. He would take some of the fresh meat to the local forest dwellers. Although they thought him strange, a solitary figure living alone among the great trees, he had earned a grudging respect from them. In turn, he had learned much from them in the three years he had been on his own.

The boy's expression darkened. He had been taught as a child that the forest dwellers were pagans, inferior creatures in comparison to the advancement of the great Empire. But it was not the forest dwellers that had fallen when the barbarians came. They had wisely slipped away into the safety of their ancient trees. The boy had followed them, turning his back on the great civilization that crumbled like a dried leaf in a clenched fist.

Although it would take him several trips, the boy eventually moved all of his kill to his permanent campsite. Strategically located at the base of a hill, there was a small cave in which he stored his few possessions and where he slept when the weather was poor. When it was clear, he slept outside beneath the stars and the sweeping canopy overhead.

Finished with his chores for the day, the boy debated heading over to the forest dwellers camp. He opted for a swim first and headed toward the river. His favorite spot was a deep pool formed by a small but perfect waterfall. There were flat rocks on the shore, excellent for sunning chilled skin after bathing.

As attuned to the forest as he was, he nearly missed the figure standing upright in his pool. He stopped abruptly, ducking into the underbrush and hoping he was being quieter than he thought. He pushed aside a branch and peered out from his hiding place.

There was a woman bathing in his pool. She was facing away from him, but he could tell she was completely naked. Long, dark hair flowed down her back, clinging to her wet skin. She turned toward him.

The boy caught his breath. She was magnificent, the most beautiful woman he had ever seen. Statuesque, flawless skin, perfect breasts, a flat stomach…

He could see no lower because the rest of her was underwater. And when he raised his eyes once more to those faultless features, he was greatly embarrassed to realize she was looking at him.

The woman, however, did not seem the least bit embarrassed and made no move to cover herself. Dark eyes flashed with mocking amusement, and although it would seem he had the upper hand, the boy wanted nothing more than to flee.

"Are you spying on me?" she asked.

"No," the boy stuttered, trying to defend himself, "I was just–"

The boy's words trailed off as the woman made her way toward shore, each step revealing more of that perfect body. Although he knew he should look away as a matter of courtesy, he could not take his eyes from the faultless skin. She was coming right toward him, and he entertained all sorts of projected intentions until he realized her clothing was on the rock in front of him. He lowered his eyes in humiliation, willing the hardness between his legs to disappear.

The woman took her clothing and began dressing, still watching the boy. He was a gorgeous specimen, dark hair and dark eyes, a perfect mouth. He was at that age where he was just beginning to fill out, his chest and shoulders broadening, his back widening, his stomach taut and hard. She examined him quite unabashedly and he blushed beneath her scrutiny.

"You are not of the forest people," she commented.

The boy realized she was speaking to him in Latin, a fact his mortification had caused him to miss. She spoke the language strangely, though, and although he was familiar with many of the local dialects, he could not place her accent.

"My name is Ambrosius," the boy said, as if that offered some sort of explanation.

"Hmm," the woman replied, "My name is Ravlen."

"Ravlen," Ambrosius repeated, the name unfamiliar to him in any context. Everything about the woman was unfamiliar, the way she looked, the way she carried herself, the way in which she interacted with him. Although he did not much believe in the local gods, or in fact any god, he almost wondered if one of the forest goddesses had come to him.

Even her garments were strange, which Ambrosius noted now that she was fully clothed. The flowing gown fit snuggly in flattering locations, doing nothing to diminish the tightness of his trousers.

"Are you alone?" the boy asked, his voice a little hoarse.

Ravlen smiled. "Not really," was all she said.

Ambrosius glanced around into the forest. As the woman spoke, there seemed to be sudden movement all around them. But he could see nothing, and the forest settled once more into peaceful quiet. He did note, however, that there were no birds chirping. He was not certain if he should be afraid. He turned back to the woman, who was gazing at him with a look that bordered on predatory. He gazed at her uncertainly, then unconsciously squared his shoulders and straightened to his full height. Even though she was a full head and shoulders taller than him, he stared her directly in the eye.

"Are you hungry?" he asked, "because I have food."

Ravlen gazed at the beautiful little creature, impressed.

"Yes," she replied, "that would be very nice."

Ambrosius busied himself with preparations around the fire. He periodically rotated the spit of meat that hung over the flames. The woman was content to simply watch him with an unnerving gaze that did not seem to waver or require blinking. Ambrosius from time to time glanced into the surrounding forest, certain they were not alone. But he could see nothing.

Because he spent so much time by himself he was not adept at conversation, and thankfully, the woman did not seem to desire it. Finally, the meat was prepared and Ambrosius served her with what manners he could remember. He settled opposite her across the campfire, watching to see if she was pleased with the meal.

She eyed the meat curiously, as if it were something she had never seen before. But she bit into it without hesitation, and after a moment of thoughtful chewing, a look of pleasure spread across her face.

"It is delicious," Ravlen said.

Ambrosius was greatly relieved and settled to eating his own meal. Under normal circumstances, he would gnaw on the bone like some savage, but this evening he was trying to remember the graces his mother had taught him. The woman watched him, entertained, and he had the uncomfortable feeling she could read his thoughts. There were so many things he wanted to ask her, but something made him hold his tongue.

Impossibly, the woman finished the entire chunk of meat he had given her. It was three times a normal portion, but apparently she had been hungry. He started to offer her more, but realized the hunger in her gaze was probably not for food. He shifted uncomfortably, then swallowed hard.

"You are a warrior," she said.

"What?" Ambrosius asked, surprised. He was not feeling very valiant at the moment. "No, my father was a military man. I have had but a few years training."

The unblinking gaze held him captive. "Yes, I realize you are still a child."

Ambrosius was not going to agree with this statement, either, but she continued before he could object.

"But I believe you to be a warrior nonetheless."

Ambrosius could not look away from those perfect features or that magnetic gaze. Nor could he resist any command she gave him.

"Come here," she said.

Ambrosius stood, then walked stiffly over to where she sat. He was mortified that once again his arousal was in full display. He hoped his trousers were loose enough that his desire was not evident, but he had no such luck. His waist was on level with her line of sight, and she glanced with curiosity at his pants. To his intense embarrassment, she reached up and placed her hand flat on the front of his trousers. He certainly could not hide the hardness of his member with her hand on him.

She again had a curious expression on her face, as if assessing the experience. It was a dispassionate look, as if she were collecting scientific evidence. A look of enlightenment crossed her features and she smiled.

"Ah," she said, glancing at him knowingly, "I understand." With one hand she grasped a nearby pelt and snapped it outward, creating an instant bed. She pulled him downward on top of her.

Ambrosius had the strangest feeling this had not been her first choice of events, but he could not fathom what the alternative would have been. It did not matter as he began passionately kissing her, wanting to feel every part of that magnificent body he had seen in the river. She helped him by disrobing them both, an act so practiced it made Ambrosius hesitate.

"I–" his voice cracked with embarrassment. "I've never done this before."

The woman pulled him back towards her, enjoying the hardness of his young body. "Neither have I," she said with some amusement.

Ambrosius did not see how that was possible, but instinctively knew that on some level she was telling the truth. For the rest of the night, the two were intertwined, coming to passion more times than seemed humanly possible.

Many hours later, Ambrosius awoke to find himself alone. There was no sign of the woman, nor any indication she had ever been there. As he rinsed his mouth, trying to rid himself of a strange metallic taste on his tongue, he was quite certain of one of two things. Either he had been visited by a forest goddess.

Or he had dreamed the entire thing.

Ryan awoke with a start. She was seated in the overstuffed chair in her den. How strange. Not only was she dreaming through the eyes of some stranger, now it seemed she was dreaming his dreams.

She sat upright and slowly turned her head to the side, cracking her neck. She turned it the other direction, and it gave another satisfying crack.

That had been quite the adolescent fantasy, Ryan thought. The dark-haired boy seemed familiar somehow, although Ryan knew she had never met him. And the woman she definitely had no recollection of.

A phone rang off in the distance. Although it was clear across the mansion, her hearing was so exceptional she could hear Edward's side of the conversation from the den. She heard his footsteps, purposeful in her direction, and felt his presence as he stood in the doorway.

"What news?" she asked, staring into the fire.

Edward paused, then said simply "She lives."

Ryan found herself releasing the breath she had been holding. She had maintained certain human gestures long after they had no purpose, and this sign of tension relief was no exception.

"And her condition?" Ryan asked, her tone deliberately casual.

Edward was not fooled. "Dr. Ryerson is well."

Ryan turned to look at him. "No complications?"

Edward cleared his throat. "No more than might be expected from Marilyn's presence."

Ryan raised an eyebrow. "Marilyn was there?" She then answered her own question. "Of course she was." She turned back to the fire, settling back into the chair. "Send a summons and my plane. As soon as Dr. Ryerson is well enough to travel, I wish her to return here."

"Oh, and Edward?"

Edward stopped and turned.

"I am sensing we will have a visitor very soon."

Edward frowned. He was not aware they were expecting anyone.

Ryan cocked her head to one side, her gaze focused on a very distant point. She appeared to be listening to something only she could hear. Her focus returned to the room, and then to Edward.

"You will need to prepare the entire east wing."

Edward's frown increased. There was only one person who traveled with such an entourage. He nodded stiffly.

"Very well, my lord. I will have the staff prepare quarters immediately."

CHAPTER 4

RYAN STOOD AT THE TOP OF THE STAIRS watching the caravan approach. Were she so inclined, she would have counted the limousines, but it seemed something close to twenty, which was as precise as she cared to be. The lead car pulled around the circular drive, stopping just forward the stairs. The car second in line came to a stop directly at the bottom of the stairs. Ryan steeled herself as doors began opening.

Men and women began pouring from the vehicles. Mostly male, all were attractive and moved with an elegant athleticism. They glanced up at the figure at the top of the stairs, bowing in respect if they had previously met Ryan, and standing dumbfounded if they had not.

Ryan was oblivious, her eyes on the car at the foot of the stairs. A manservant opened the door and extended his hand. The hand was accepted, although this occupant needed no assistance.

A strikingly beautiful older woman stepped from the vehicle. Regal and mesmerizing, she flowed with a grace that was hypnotic. She raised her eyes to Ryan, and Ryan felt the gaze pierce her to her core. The wave of power emanating out from the woman washed over her, bringing her both pleasure and discomfort. Ryan knew she displayed none of this outwardly, and knew just as surely Abigail was fully aware of it.

Those in the entourage watched the scene, astonished. Even

those who had seen the crown prince and the matriarch together were surprised at the currents flowing between them. The interaction between Old Ones was always intense, and these two were arguably the most powerful of their Kind.

Ryan started down the steps. Abigail watched as the girl approached, noting the same careless, boyish sense of fashion Ryan had possessed for centuries. She also noted the girl wore it with the same devastating effect. Abigail extended her hand as the girl neared.

Ryan grasped the fingers and bowed, brushing her lips across the hand in a chivalrous gesture. Abigail felt the shock of electricity flow through her arm and inwardly smiled at the girl's impudence. Ryan ever was one to tempt fate.

Ryan raised her head and offered her arm. "Welcome, my lady. Your usual accommodations have been prepared."

Abigail took the arm and they started up the steps. "I appreciate your hospitality, as always, my dear."

They passed Edward at the top of the stairs, and he bowed low. Abigail glanced at him.

"Edward," she said with something close to disdain.

"My lady," he replied. He stood upright and watched as Ryan and the matriarch entered the great doors. He was not so foolish to display any disrespect, but he was also very protective of his master. This One was exceedingly dangerous.

Ryan glanced backward over her shoulder at him, a look of mischief on her face. Then again, Edward thought, his master generally did not require any protection.

Ryan led Abigail to the stairway. "Would you like me to show you to your quarters?"

Abigail tilted her head, extending her senses throughout the estate. She turned to Ryan.

"I think I would like to pay my respects to your father first."

Ryan bowed, perhaps a bit stiffly as the mention brought her pain. Abigail watched the reaction knowingly.

"Of course," Ryan said, "I will take you to him now."

Ryan led Abigail into Victor's chambers, and the beautiful

matriarch moved to his bedside. Although Abigail was always tightly in control, Ryan sensed a moment of genuine emotion in her, a deep sadness and sense of loss. Abigail laid her hand on Victor's chest.

Ryan moved to her side, looking down at her father.

"There has been no change?" Abigail asked, although it was more of a statement than question.

Ryan swallowed, another distinctly human and unnecessary gesture.

"No, no change. I have sent word for Dr. Ryerson to return as soon as she is well enough to travel."

Abigail glanced at her. "That is wise," she said, "for many reasons."

Ryan turned to her, sensing her disapproval. She knew Abigail would elaborate and was not disappointed.

"Dr. Ryerson is a liability to you," Abigail said. "There are those who would strike at her to strike at you."

Ryan felt her anger rise, but maintained her composure. "I find it difficult to believe there are those foolish enough to risk the consequences of harming her."

Abigail was calm, but unyielding. "Perhaps not by harming her. But there are also those who would court her to curry your favor."

Ryan was unyielding as well. "Then let us hope Dr. Ryerson possesses better judgment than that which you attribute to her."

"Yes," Abigail said smoothly as she turned away, "let us hope."

Ryan took one last look at her father, briefly touching the hands folded on his chest, then joined Abigail at the doorway. "Allow me to show you to your chambers."

Ryan led Abigail down the hallway and through double doors that opened inward into a brightly lit room. "I trust you will find this to your liking."

Abigail surveyed the suite, noting it was decorated in the pale blues and whites she preferred. There was a coolness to the suite that perfectly fit her demeanor.

"It is ideal. Thank you." She turned to Ryan, her gaze lingering on the girl. "Would you care to join me for some tea?"

Ryan noted that Abigail's servants had already completely taken over the wing and were setting up tea service. The irony of being invited to tea in her own house was not lost on her.

"Of course," Ryan said.

Abigail settled onto the couch and Ryan sat down across from her. A handsome young man brought tea, then just as quickly vanished. Ryan inhaled the fragrant scent of the leaves, not recognizing them. Apparently Abigail's staff had not trusted her selection of tea and had brought their own. She took a drink of the scalding liquid, enjoying the burning heat.

Ryan became aware that Abigail was watching her with the unblinking gaze of their Kind. Ryan took another drink, then replaced the cup in its saucer. She sat back and returned the unblinking gaze.

"I seem to have somehow displeased you."

Abigail watched the girl intently. "You have never failed to please me, my dear."

Ryan shifted uncomfortably on the couch, the innuendo targeting her with great precision.

Abigail reached for her cup, took a sip, then continued.

"But perhaps what you sense is my impatience."

Ryan held her gaze as Abigail placed the cup down.

"Ryan," Abigail said firmly, "it is time."

Ryan could hold her gaze no longer and looked away. Abigail could see Ryan's jaw clench, and pressed her attack.

"The hierarchy has been without a leader now for almost two centuries."

"Most of which has been my fault," Ryan interrupted.

"That is of no matter," Abigail said. "With your father unable to fulfill his duties, and your defeat of Aeron, you stand unchallenged. You have the full support of the Grand Council."

"And why do you not take this position yourself?" Ryan asked quietly.

Abigail did not hesitate. "It is not my place."

Ryan looked at her. Abigail had left it unsaid, but it was not unknown, and Ryan would not let it pass.

"A King can dominate subjects," Ryan said with a tinge of sarcasm, but no trace of bitterness, "but the One who dominates the King rules all."

Ryan sensed the very dangerous shift in Abigail, although outwardly the matriarch's demeanor did not change. When Abigail responded, she did not speak aloud, but Ryan heard her voice quite clearly.

Do not tempt me, little one.

Ryan knew she had overstepped. It took a moment, but she apologized.

"Forgive me," Ryan said, "that was unnecessary."

Abigail gazed at her intently. "But not untrue."

A smile tugged at the corner of Ryan's mouth. Abigail was incorrigible, not to mention incredibly dangerous. The elegant woman was capable of a maternal seduction that Ryan had no defense against.

Abigail was also perhaps the only one capable of swaying one so stubborn.

Ryan's posture changed as she sat upright. Her shoulders squared and her tone became suddenly business-like. She addressed what appeared to be empty space behind her.

"Edward–"

Edward materialized.

"Send word to the members of the Grand Council to convene in two weeks time." Ryan's eyes were on Abigail. "We will gather here."

This surprised Edward, but he quickly recovered. "Of course, my lord. I will send word immediately."

Ryan was not finished. "Also send word to the keepers of the Grand Council chambers."

Edward paused, waiting for instruction.

"Tell them to begin preparations for a coronation."

Abigail gazed at her expectantly, and Ryan turned to Edward. "Mine."

Edward was stunned, although his patrician manner did not reveal it. He could not, however, conceal his pleasure at the announcement.

"Very well, my lord. I will coordinate the preparations myself." He backed from the room, disappearing as quickly as he had appeared.

"So he is capable of smiling," Abigail said dryly.

Ryan stood, bowing from the waist. "If there is nothing else that you require of me," she said with just a trace of sarcasm, "I will take my leave." She turned, but had not made it a step when Abigail's words stopped her.

"There is one more thing," Abigail said, "that I require."

Ryan froze, then slowly turned. There was little doubt as to Abigail's meaning, but in case there was any misunderstanding, Abigail gestured to the empty place at her side.

"Won't you sit with me a moment?"

It was less a request than a command, and Ryan could not refuse either from Abigail. She slowly moved to the couch, then settled next to the stunning woman. Abigail's influence settled over her, the immense power forcing her to relax. The feeling was both discomfiting and intensely pleasurable. As powerful as Ryan was, she felt her head grow heavy; the desire to rest her head on Abigail was overwhelming. Abigail adjusted a pillow, guiding Ryan's head and facilitating that desire. She leaned down, her teeth very close to Ryan's neck, and whispered in her ear.

"I require," Abigail said softly, "to know what you are hiding from me."

If the statement was meant to surprise Ryan, it did not. She knew Abigail far too well. She shifted slightly, but Abigail's grip on her was steel.

"You know I can conceal nothing from you," Ryan said quietly.

"Then why," Abigail said, pausing to brush her razor-sharp teeth across the vein in Ryan's neck, "must I find the truth this way?"

Ryan arched upward at the pain and the intense pleasure that accompanied it. Abigail's lips covered the wound as she began to take the girl's blood, and within seconds she had forcibly invaded Ryan's mind.

Do not hide from me.

Ryan could not resist the whispered mental command and relaxed her thoughts. In an instant, Abigail had complete access to her mind.

And so stunned was Abigail by what she saw, she actually broke contact in her feeding, something that had not occurred in a millennium. She gazed down at the girl in her arms.

"You have a son."

Ryan tried to push Abigail's influence from her, not to escape but rather to speak coherently.

"Drake Alexander," she murmured, "he is a year old."

Ryan felt a myriad of emotions from Abigail, emotions she had difficulty processing in her disoriented condition. She sensed Abigail's disbelief, her incredulity, and beneath it all, her calculation as she quickly considered the implications.

But above all, Ryan sensed Abigail's overwhelming pleasure. Abigail was truly delighted at the news. She leaned down to whisper in Ryan's ear once more.

"You are truly amazing, little one."

Ryan gazed up at Abigail. In their strange, erotic world, Abigail had become a motherly figure for Ryan, although their relationship had a distinctly predatory and sensual nature. It was clear that Abigail, by extension, now had a grandson.

God help the boy.

"You will pay for that," Abigail said, amused by the girl's thoughts. She sliced deeply into the other side of Ryan's neck, causing the girl to arch upward once more. Abigail held her without effort as she took her blood, and it was not long before Ryan slid into the wondrous lethargy that allowed Abigail to feed to her heart's content.

Many hours later, a knock on the door caused Abigail to look up from her book. She glanced down at the unconscious form on her lap. The girl had satisfied her completely. Ryan had a consummate ability in Sharing, taking only enough blood to relieve the unbearable pressure of her partner's veins, allowing the one feeding on her to consume even more.

Abigail was thoughtful. The girl was not a fool. She controlled the act of Sharing as much by giving as she did by taking, perhaps even more so. And when the girl did take control by feeding...

The repeated knock on the door interrupted her very pleasant thoughts.

"Come," she said with a trace of irritation.

The door opened and Edward took a step inward. He held a small bundle, a small bundle with its thumb stuck in its mouth and piercing blue eyes that glanced down at his mother, then at her.

Edward was deeply apologetic. "Forgive me, my lady. But he is inconsolable without her."

Abigail gazed at the boy.

"Aren't we all," she said with uncharacteristic candor.

Edward stared at her, stunned at the admission, then quickly dropped his eyes. He did, however, feel somewhat more charitable toward the she-dragon.

Abigail regarded Edward with cool amusement, then returned her attention to the boy. "Let him come."

Edward set the child down. He waited long enough for the boy to start toward his mother, then removed himself from the room.

Abigail watched the boy toddle across the room with far more grace and assurance than one his age should have. When he reached the couch, he grasped Ryan's shirt and pulled himself up onto her with little effort. Ryan shifted slightly, and even in her unconscious state, wrapped her arm around his waist and pulled him close.

He settled in, returning his thumb to his mouth. He shifted slightly so he could look up at Abigail, then shifted again so he could comfortably maintain her gaze. He somberly sucked his thumb, assessing her.

Abigail stared down into the blue eyes. She had not known Ryan as a child, but she would guess this boy could have been her twin. He had the same fine features, the same perfect mouth, the same high cheek bones and slightly arched eyebrows. He even had the twinkle of mischief that was ever-present in Victor Alexander's wayward child.

She gazed down at him, and there was one thing Abigail knew with certainty.

"You," she whispered quietly to the boy, "are going to be as dangerous as your mother."

CHAPTER 5

AMBROSIUS SWUNG THE CRUDE AX with skill, carefully splitting each log with a single blow. The maidens giggled nearby, watching him work, but he was oblivious to their presence, as usual lost in thought.

Weylin also watched Ambrosius. As chief of their tribe, he welcomed the boy's presence, although in truth the boy was clearly a man now. Perhaps 17 seasons, he had reached his full six foot height and was still putting on muscle, filling out his slender frame. Weylin hoped his frequent visitor would choose a wife from the clan and make the forest village his permanent home. He had even hinted that his own daughter was available and interested, but Ambrosius had merely smiled, perhaps a little sadly, and continued his work.

That sadness seemed to permeate Ambrosius' demeanor. Weylin had heard rumor the boy's family had been killed by barbarians when he was very young. The story went that his parents were of Roman nobility and had been murdered during one of the Saxon incursions. It would not surprise him if Ambrosius was of noble birth; he carried himself with quiet assurance and dignity. And the handsome, aristocratic features that attracted so much feminine attention added to the probability of that patrician birth.

But as Weylin watched, the boy glanced up, peering off into the forest as if looking or waiting for something. And the longing in his expression was a melancholy that came from only one source: a woman. Weylin sighed. Whoever she was, she held Ambrosius tightly.

Still, he could try.

"Ambrosius!" Weylin called out.

The boy glanced up. "Yes?" he said politely.

"My daughter is down in the meadow gathering flowers for the festival. Would you be so kind as to check on her?"

Ambrosius smiled, sensing the chieftain's intent. "Of course," he replied.

He set off through the forest and in moments was at the edge of the clearing. The chieftain's daughter, accompanied by several other young girls, was cheerfully picking flowers. Their carefree laughter drifted across the grassy plain. His blood froze, however, at the sight just past them, a group of men on foot. The girls were unaware of the rapidly approaching threat.

Ambrosius' expression grew dark. From the long, scraggly hair, the thick beards, and the dirty pelts the men wore, he was certain they were barbarians, a group of Saxon raiders out looking for easy plunder.

Ambrosius broke into a sprint, calling out to the girls as he began running towards them. They glanced up, all smiles when they saw who it was. But their smiles disappeared into looks of alarm when they realized Ambrosius was gesturing behind them. They turned, saw the group of raiders, and began screaming and running toward Ambrosius.

Unknown to any of those on the field, a group of horsemen watched the scene at the far edge of the clearing, hidden beneath the canopy there. The horses stepped nervously, sensing the tension of their riders. Still, the leader held his hand up for patience. Under normal circumstances, he would already have ridden out to save the women, but he was quite astounded at the dark-haired boy running across the meadow. He had never seen anyone move that fast.

Ambrosius was unaware of the scrutiny of the horsemen. All of his attention was on the band of raiders. There were eight, perhaps nine, all bearing weapons, either swords or battle axes. He himself was unarmed, having left the wood ax back at the village. It did not matter; his wrath would be his weapon.

The lead barbarian grinned savagely. He was happy to have outrun his comrades, knowing he would get the pleasure of killing the whelp running toward him, then the pleasure of running down the slowest maiden. He raised his axe to slice the dark-haired youth in two.

He would get no such satisfaction. With a great cry of rage, Ambrosius leaped in the air and hit the barbarian feet-first in the chest. Impossibly, although the barbarian was much larger than him, the Saxon was not only stopped in his tracks, he actually went backward. The boy snatched the ax from the stunned man's hand and with one great blow, cleaved his head off.

The remaining barbarians slowed at the sight of their leader being beheaded. But the pause was only momentary as they screamed in fury and began running toward Ambrosius once again. The boy hefted the great ax and with a massive heave, sent the weapon end-over-end until it embedded itself in the new lead barbarian with a loud "thunk." This again slowed the Saxons, who were not quite certain how this was happening.

Ambrosius was preparing himself for another charge when he heard stampeding hoof beats. A group of horsemen was approaching from the east, heading for the horde of Saxons. The horses quickly engulfed the band of would-be-raiders and the air filled with cries of pain. As the dust settled, the horses wheeled around, then slowed to a trot. There were no barbarians left standing

The leader of the horsemen guided his steed toward Ambrosius. The boy was not certain if the men were friend or foe, but anyone who fought barbarians would at least get the benefit of doubt.

"I did not think you were going to leave any for us," the horseman said, dismounting. He approached and removed his heavy leather glove. He extended his hand to Ambrosius. Ambrosius eyed the hand, then clasped the other man's forearm in the traditional greeting of his childhood. The man noted the gesture with approval.

"My name is Tristan," he said.

"My name is Ambrosius," the boy replied.

This surprised the horseman. "You are Roman?"

The boy shook his head. "Not anymore."

Tristan nodded, understanding. It was difficult to swear allegiance to an Empire that had withdrawn all support from these lands, leaving the remaining Britons to the mercy of the Angles and Saxons.

"Well, then, Ambrosius who is not-a-Roman, tell me this." He glanced down at the dead, beheaded Saxon at his feet. "Can you ride a horse?"

CHAPTER 6

SUSAN RYERSON WAS STARING with total fascination at the color of her son's hair, the same reddish hue of her own. But she had never quite seen it this way before, with a thousand subtleties of color that achieved their own subtleties as the light shifted. She was quite enamored with the experience and realized she had been staring at his head for quite some time.

"What's wrong, mom?"

Susan shook her head. How embarrassing. She was acting like some drug addict on a hallucinogenic free-for-all. "I'm sorry, Jason. I'm a little out of sorts."

Jason stared at her suspiciously. She had been acting very strange lately.

"It takes a little getting used to, doesn't it?"

Susan glanced up at Raphael in the doorway, smiling. "That is the understatement of the year."

"Raphael!" Jason yelped, jumping up and running to the dark-skinned man. Raphael caught him, and even though Jason was in a growth spurt, easily swung him so that he was upside down. He held the laughing boy for a moment, then turned him upright, gently setting him down.

Susan watched the two with her new, preternatural senses. Ryan had tried to explain to her what she felt and saw, but Susan now had the extraordinary experience firsthand. She could see colors that previously had not existed for her, colors she did not even have words for because humans could not see them. She could also see colors that did exist, but which previously she had not had the ability to perceive. The sky now looked far more violet to her because she could see further into the ultraviolet spectrum, perceiving wavelengths of light that had been invisible before.

All physical feeling was heightened. The slightest touch, the movement of her shirt against her skin, the feel of flannel against her cheek, all served to endlessly distract her, as if she could no longer filter out any sensation. The simplest feeling such as the sun upon her face was so wondrous it could cause her to lose hours. It was a good thing Ryan's Kind were immortal; they probably lost years in the transition.

As ecstatic as the sensory bombardment was, Susan could not relinquish the scientist in her. She found herself continually running small experiments, such as holding her breath to assure herself she no longer needed to breathe. It was difficult for her to process that she no longer needed to sleep or eat, and she became aware of how much the ebb and flow of her life was constrained by such physical needs, especially now that it was so unconstrained. She felt unmoored, but it was not an unpleasant feeling.

Susan could not wait to return to her medical equipment so that she could begin running all sorts of experiments on herself, studying the ongoing change to her system. Although she had access to the penultimate research subject in Ryan, she was often too embarrassed to ask Ryan to continually subject herself to testing. Additionally, Susan now had the opportunity to test the Change itself, the transition from human to immortal. Ryan was one of the most advanced of her Kind, and now Susan had the opportunity to study the more "primitive" version: herself. The anticipation was killing her.

"You will be leaving within the hour," Raphael said, interrupting her reverie, "Madame has traveled ahead." Raphael smiled to himself. He was too young to read Marilyn's thoughts and would not have so intruded were he able. But he knew whom the dark-haired one wanted to see.

Susan was relieved. It was difficult enough being around Marilyn; the intensity was incredible. But in her newly vulnerable condition, sensitive to every nuance, every sensation, it was impossible.

Raphael watched his protégé with a mixture of pride and protectiveness. Marilyn's "interference" had definitely had an effect, and Susan was aware of much more than most Young Ones. But Raphael was uncertain if that would be helpful, or a great hindrance, in what she was about to face.

CHAPTER 7

RYAN PUT THE BOOK DOWN and extended her senses to see if her son was awake. He was sleeping soundly, and she found herself somewhat disappointed. From what she understood, he slept far less than a normal infant, but still far more than her.

This made Ryan smile. Finally, someone who slept more than she did. Many of the Old Ones had commented on the amount of time she spent sleeping. Although she had no normal pattern and could go weeks if not months without sleep, she could also sleep for weeks and months at a time. She had once slept for 14 years straight.

Ryan's expression darkened. That had been after her Change, the transition from human to their Kind. Ryan's Change had been particularly horrific because Victor had been so immensely powerful when he Changed her. It was only the fact that she was not fully human that had allowed her to survive. She wondered if her son's Change would be as difficult.

Ryan stood, restless. The restlessness was not unusual for her, but it generally had a cause, one which she could not quite identify at the moment.

She started down the darkened hallway. She could sense all sorts of movement throughout the mansion, mostly from Abigail's staff. Ryan wondered if that was the source of her restlessness. Somehow she did not think so. It seemed as if there was something else, something very familiar…

Ryan was slammed backward into the wall so hard that the marble caved inward in an outline of her body. Her assailant held her against the wall as bits of stone fell to the ground, making little clinking noises as the dust settled. Surprisingly Ryan did not appear angry, nor did she struggle. If anything, she appeared faintly amused at the attack.

Marilyn gazed down at the girl, their lips nearly touching. "I have missed you, little one."

The endearment, as always, was slightly mocking and tinged with intimacy. Few would dare address Ryan so, but Marilyn had always had her way. Marilyn further had her way by bending down and planting a lingering kiss on Ryan.

"I can see that," Ryan said as Marilyn leaned back, still maintaining her hold on the girl.

"You have been so distant from us these days," Marilyn said, slightly scolding.

"Yes," Ryan said, "I have already received that lecture from Abigail."

Marilyn smiled, and her teeth were brilliant in the darkness. "And did she discipline you in her usual way?"

Only Marilyn could make Ryan blush so. It was a physiological throwback Ryan wished she did not have, one Marilyn took every opportunity to exploit. Marilyn enjoyed the girl's obvious discomfort, a discomfort that grew at a noise from the doorway.

"Ahem," Edward said, clearing his throat.

Ryan glanced over, conscious of their very indelicate positions. Marilyn did not release Ryan, and merely glanced in his direction before returning her attention to Ryan.

"Edward," she said dryly over her shoulder.

Edward's reply was as dry. "Will you be assaulting my master in the corridor, or may I show you to your chambers?"

Marilyn gave Ryan another lingering look. "You are right, assaulting her in my chambers is a much better idea."

Marilyn stepped back, releasing Ryan. She turned to Edward, beginning to speak, then went utterly still. Ryan was aware of the stillness, and also of its cause.

"Mon Dieu," Marilyn said, disbelief evident in her voice, "Ce n'est pas possible."

Ryan looked over at her son who stood in the doorway, Edward's pant leg clutched in his tiny fist.

"Many things are impossible," Ryan began.

"And now you have done them all," Marilyn finished for her. She stared at the tiny creature in the doorway.

If there was a candidate for less maternal instinct than Ryan, it was Marilyn. Which was why Ryan was surprised when Marilyn stooped to the boy's eye level and motioned for him to approach. Ryan was more surprised that the boy immediately complied, toddling to Marilyn as if he knew her well. He gazed up at the raven-haired beauty intently. Marilyn clasped his hand to steady him, then reached and ran her hand through his silky dark hair. He gazed at her with warm blue eyes, then reached up to touch her own dark hair.

"Edward," Ryan said with mild exasperation, "my son is a flirt."

"Hmm, yes, my lord" Edward said in his driest tone yet, "I have no idea where he gets that from."

Ryan threw him a sharp glance. He was of no help to her when it came to Marilyn.

Marilyn released the boy and stood. Drake looked up at Ryan, then ran back to Edward who picked him up. Marilyn watched the boy, then turned to Ryan. There was wicked amusement in her eyes.

"I now understand why your father kept us from you when you were a child." Marilyn said, her eyes lingering on Ryan's lips. She abruptly turned. "If you would be so kind as to escort me to my chambers."

Ryan watched the dark-haired beauty disappear. "Edward," she said, her misgivings evident, "do not let anyone eat my son."

"Yes, my lord," he paused, but could not resist a parting comment. "I am sure you will find a way to keep Madame otherwise occupied."

Ryan threw him one last, dark look, then started off down the hallway after Marilyn.

"I trust these accommodations are acceptable."

Marilyn glanced around the room. It was furnished to her taste, warmly luxurious with sensual colors and soft light. She frowned slightly, tilting her head.

Ryan glanced around the room, trying to diagnose what had displeased her. "If there is something that is unsatisfactory…"

Marilyn looked around the room as if trying to place what had displeased her. She turned to the couch, then to the bed. A look of enlightenment crossed her face. "Ah, that is it."

Ryan turned to identify what had offended Marilyn, and was shoved halfway across the room and headlong into the bed. She went face-down into the soft comforter, barely able to roll over before Marilyn was upon her. In an instant, Ryan was pinned to the mattress, gazing up at the dark-haired woman. Marilyn examined the girl's position, her amusement evident.

"Ah yes, that is much better."

"Why is it," Ryan asked, trying to think clearly, "that I can defeat any enemy in battle, yet have no defense against you?"

Marilyn smiled and leaned down towards the girl's neck.

"Because I am not your enemy," she whispered in her ear.

Although Marilyn was immensely hungry, she so enjoyed toying with the girl. She brushed her lips across Ryan's cheek, then gently bit Ryan's lip. She stared at the drop of blood for a moment, then stole it with a kiss. It was her undoing, however, because the instant the girl's blood touched her mouth, her urgency increased a thousandfold.

"You will make an excellent King, ma cherie," Marilyn whispered, returning to her ear, "because you have an incredible ability to satisfy your subjects."

Her perfect teeth sliced into Ryan's neck, and Ryan tensed from the pleasantly agonizing sensation. Marilyn held her tightly, and it was not long before the lethargy forced her to relax in the grip of her irresistible assailant.

Marilyn's hunger had fore-shortened her usual seduction, but she would get her full gratification by prolonging the act through the night.

In the east wing, Abigail sat sipping a cup of tea while she embroidered. She cocked her head to one side, then smiled to herself. Her lead consort approached, then bowed low.

"As always, you have won your wager, my lady."

Abigail treated the announcement as if it were no matter. "I have known Marilyn for a very long time."

The consort bowed again. "Indeed." He disappeared as quickly as he had appeared.

Abigail took a sip of tea, then returned to her embroidery. It had not been a wager of "if," only "when." And the immediacy of Marilyn's act had clearly been Abigail's prediction.

Abigail smiled to herself again. The girl was going to have a difficult week.

CHAPTER 8

RYAN CHECKED THE SADDLE BAG one last time, ensuring she had sufficient food and water for Drake. Satisfied, she reached down for her son. Edward handed him upward and Ryan settled the small boy on the horse in front of her.

"Are you sure you do not wish accompaniment?"

Ryan shook her head. "Thank you, Edward. But I really wish to be alone for a few hours."

Edward understood. Just being in the presence of the Old Ones was exhausting. He could not imagine having to satisfy them as well. He glanced at the small boy. He did not know what effect the presence of the Others was having on the child, but it could not hurt to spirit him away. Ryan's estate was so large that she could disappear on her steed for days.

Ryan had promised him she would not do so, and reiterated the promise.

"I will return before nightfall."

She wheeled the mount around with masterful horsemanship, then set out a breakneck speed. The velocity likely would have terrified a normal child, but Edward could hear the boy's laughter even above the fading sound of the hooves.

Jason jumped out of the limousine and ran up the stairs. He nearly ran headfirst into Edward, who stepped onto the landing as he approached.

"I'm, I'm sorry, Edward," Jason said, trying to catch his breath. "Is Ryan here?"

"I am dreadfully sorry, young sir," Edward said formally, "but Ryan is out riding for the day, and I am afraid she will not return before evening."

Jason could not hide his disappointment.

"And Drake?"

"He is with Ryan as well."

This statement took all of the wind went out of his sails. As Susan approached, she could see the disappointment on her son's face. That meant Ryan was not here. She tried to hide her own disappointment.

Edward stared at the young woman, enchanted. The transformation in her had been remarkable. She had been a lovely young lady before, now she was stunning. There was high color in her cheeks, and Edward realized she was blushing because he was staring. He bowed low, offering his hand.

"Welcome back, Dr. Ryerson. And may I congratulate you on the success of your Change."

Susan took his hand, still unused to the slight shock she received when touching Ryan's Kind.

Her Kind, she reminded herself. Her Kind.

Edward examined her carefully. "You definitely bear Marilyn's mark."

Susan fully blushed now. She was not certain that was a good thing. Ryan had chosen her mentor, and specifically chosen one from Marilyn's line. Susan was not exactly sure why, although Marilyn was extremely powerful.

"Speaking of which," Edward continued, "Marilyn is here, and Abigail as well."

A wave of anxiety swept over Susan, feelings she tried to hide unsuccessfully. She would have to get used to this inability to hide anything. When she had interacted with the Others as a human, they knew much of what she thought and felt. Now they knew everything, and she felt positively transparent.

Edward felt sorry for the young doctor. Most Young Ones would never have to deal with what she would soon face. Then again, he thought, most Young Ones would never call Ryan Alexander a friend, so the reward far outweighed the penalty. He gestured for them to enter.

"I have prepared your usual quarters in the southern wing," Edward said, "you and master Jason have adjoining suites."

Susan felt relief wash over her. She was staying in the same wing as Ryan, who liked to sit upon the balconies watching both the sunrise and sunset from the unobstructed views. Edward could sense her unasked question, and answered in a lowered tone.

"Abigail is in the east wing, and Marilyn in the west."

Susan put her hand on the older man's arm. "Thank you, Edward," she said, truly grateful.

He patted her hand. "Do not mention it."

Susan settled into her familiar quarters, pleased to see her computer and all of her research exactly as she had left it. Well, not exactly. She could tell the staff had been in here tidying up. She changed clothes, feeling oddly as if she were home. She glanced out the window. Jason was heading across the yard toward the stables. He would probably wait there all day until Ryan returned.

Susan folded her sweater. Jason had worshipped Ryan from the very day they had met, and Ryan, as imposing a figure as she could be, was remarkably gentle with the boy. Susan smiled. She remembered when Jason had asked Ryan to be her dad. Ryan had been slightly bemused until Jason explained to her with a child's logic that he already had a mom.

A strange look passed over Susan's features as a jolt of electricity traveled through her. She found herself sharply exhaling out of habit. The electricity did not seem to fade, however, but rather seemed to grow, creating a pulsating heaviness in her that was not without pleasure.

"What now?" Susan murmured aloud.

The feeling grew, and Susan tried to suppress her concern because she realized what the source of energy was.

It was an Old One. A very Old One.

The air around her seemed to hum, filled with the power of the One approaching. Susan tried to assess the experience clinically, but was having difficulty because the feeling was intensely pleasurable and intensely terrifying. It was a primitive, instinctive response, as if some ancient, untapped part of her brain were springing to life. Or, she thought to herself, some entirely new, untapped part of her brain.

The feeling built to a crescendo until it was nearly unbearable, and it grew even more so as the doors opened.

Abigail stepped into the room, and although Susan had seen her many times, she realized she had never truly seen her before.

Her cool gaze rested upon Susan and Susan felt it penetrate to the deepest part of her soul, to every cell of her body. Abigail gracefully settled into the settee before Susan, examining the red-haired woman.

She continued to examine her at some length and then spoke at last. "So you are now of Marilyn's line."

Susan blushed. She knew Marilyn had given Raphael her blood prior to Changing Susan, and it was apparent Abigail knew it as well. A slight smile flickered about Abigail's lips as she casually continued. "I am surprised her offspring did not kill you in the act."

Susan's chagrin deepened. Raphael had nearly done so and had barely regained his self-control in time to keep Susan from dying. Abigail's slight smile increased.

"I trust you are now well, Dr. Ryerson?"

Susan nodded, finding it difficult to speak. Being near this woman brought a level of discomfort that was hard to fathom. It was as if every nerve-ending in Susan's body were firing simultaneously, creating a sensory overload that was both enjoyable and extremely discomfiting.

Susan had experienced a much milder form, having been around Raphael and his companions, and she was already having difficulty dealing with the dark desire that would uncoil so frequently and at the most inopportune times. Being around Abigail amplified that feeling exponentially, making Susan feel completely out-of-control.

Susan glanced down, forcing the clinical scientist in her to come forth. She tapped into the cold, hard, factual part of her, relying on years of discipline and empirical truth. This was nothing more than a physical manifestation of her new, extraordinary senses, and she could command them with the same iron will and intellect that had mastered her human desires for so many years.

Abigail was entertained by the doctor's struggle, knowing it was about to get much worse. Susan, with her new, untried abilities sensed this subtle shift in Abigail's demeanor, but was unable to interpret it. Abigail saved her the trouble, however, by giving a slight nod rearward, and Susan followed the glance.

Ryan stood in the doorway.

Abigail smiled, feeling the shock of the young woman across from her. To have known Ryan as a human companion was quite different from knowing her as one of their Kind.

Ryan stared at Susan. She had changed remarkably, in ways both subtle and not. She had always been beautiful, with titian hair and blue-green eyes, but now there was a luminance about her that reminded Ryan disturbingly of Marilyn. Although Susan had always been slender, her cheekbones were now pronounced, as were her faultless lips. She was extremely attractive, even for one of their Kind, and Ryan noted it was good that Susan was under her protection. Otherwise Susan probably would not survive her youth, so often did desire translate to death in their Kind.

Ryan approached, and Susan was held captive by the casual examination that burned through her. It was a surreal experience, as if someone she had known for years was now someone she did not know at all. The power that flowed outward from Ryan was staggering, and Susan could see it even with her infantile preternatural eyes. The magnetism that had manifested itself as mere charisma when Susan had been human now manifested itself as the elemental physical force it actually was.

Abigail watched the silent exchange with amusement, forever entertained by the interaction of their Kind. Ryan sensed Abigail's thoughts and her subtle torture of Susan. She turned to Abigail, holding her gaze for a moment, then allowed her eyes to drift downward to her décolleté, the pale white skin above the breast which Ryan often fed from. The insolent act had the desired effect. Outwardly, Abigail revealed nothing, but inwardly was completely aroused.

The girl would pay for that later.

Ryan turned back to Susan.

"I apologize for my absence." Ryan said, "I was not expecting you today and returned as soon as I heard word of your arrival." Ryan held out her hand.

Susan hesitated. The air of sensuality between Abigail and Ryan was almost unbearable, creating longing that rippled outward, catching everything that could sense it in its wake. Against her better judgment, she took the hand.

It was like grasping a hold of lightning, or what she imagined lighting would feel like. It shot through her arm up into her brain, back down through her spinal column and out every extremity and pore of her body. Ryan held the hand, as if she, too, were assessing the experience. She finally released it, and Susan felt the loss intensely.

"You bear Marilyn's mark," Ryan said. She then frowned slightly. "I have yet to determine if that is a good thing, even after centuries."

"You did make that decision, my dear," Abigail reminded her.

"Hmm," Ryan said thoughtfully, eyeing Susan, "yes, I did." She examined Susan far more clinically, and Susan imagined this is what a bug under a microscope felt like. "You are well?"

Susan nodded. "Yes, I am fine." She tried to appear businesslike. "I am looking forward to getting back to my research."

"There is time enough for that. Please feel free to get settled."

Susan glanced at Abigail, then back at Ryan. "Where is Drake?"

Ryan shifted uncomfortably, and she could feel Abigail's unblinking gaze on her. It would not sit well with her that Susan had known about her son first.

"He is in the yard with Jason, playing"

Ryan stole a glance at Abigail, who spoke to her mentally.

You will pay for that as well.

Susan moved to the window where she could see the two boys. Although Jason was always gentle with Drake, she was concerned.

"Are you sure they are alright? Drake is still so small."

Ryan smiled, watching the two boys play below. "Drake is already nearly indestructible."

Susan turned to her, an eyebrow raised. "I'm not certain I want to know how you know that."

Ryan cleared her throat uncomfortably. There had been a few mishaps.

"I am certain Edward is no more than a few feet away, he is quite devoted to the boy." Ryan turned to Abigail, who was still watching her with the gaze one would reserve for an unruly child. Ryan extended her hand, half in courtesy, half in surrender.

Abigail took the hand, rising gracefully. She nodded to Susan, then turned to Ryan. She leaned close, speaking in a conspiratorial whisper, but loud enough that Susan could hear.

"I realize you will have many duties to perform this week, my dear," Abigail said with deceptive gentleness. "And that the Others will make great demands of you." The underlying softness in her voice became steel. "But if you keep toying with me, I will have you confined to chambers."

Abigail released Ryan's hand, and turned to the door. In case there was any misunderstanding, she turned to Ryan once more.

"My chambers," she said with emphasis.

Abigail disappeared, leaving Ryan to stare at the empty doorway. She could feel the heat rise in her face. She turned to Susan, who was trying to maintain a straight face.

"And I am supposed to be King," Ryan said with self-mocking.

CHAPTER 9

SUSAN WAS SEARCHING FOR RYAN. She could not sense her presence in the house, and wondered if Ryan was purposely concealing it. Regardless, she had a pretty good idea where Ryan could be found. She paused before the heavy double doors, pressing her ear against the wood. She felt foolish for doing so, realizing Ryan had probably heard her approach.

She raised her hand to lightly knock, but was unable to complete the act because the door swung inward, causing her to pitch forward off-balance. Ryan caught her by the shoulders, muffling laughter as she did so.

"If you are trying to skulk about, you are going to have to be a good deal more quiet than that."

Susan pushed away indignantly. "I was not skulking about. I just didn't want to disturb you."

Ryan relented from her teasing. "You are not disturbing me," she said, stepping aside. She motioned for Susan to enter.

Susan's indignation slipped away as she stepped into the room. Her eyes immediately went to the dark-haired man in unmoving repose.

"There has been no change?" Susan asked.

Ryan's expression sobered. "No, his condition is the same."

Ryan returned to Victor's side, and Susan joined her. Susan's manner became brisk, professional.

"I would like to do an updated examination as soon as possible," Susan said, "to see if there are any changes that are not outwardly detectable."

Ryan bowed slightly. "Of course. I am grateful, as always, for your assistance." She glanced down at the paperwork Susan held in her hand, and at the lab coat she wore over her clothes. "I see you have wasted no time in returning to work."

Susan was mildly embarrassed. "I don't know if what I'm doing will be of any help to your father, but this is an opportunity I could not pass up."

One arched eyebrow moved slightly upward. "Let me guess, you are experimenting on yourself."

Susan could not contain her excitement as her words began to pour forth.

"This is a researcher's dream, an opportunity without equal. I am devising so many experiments in my head that I literally cannot keep up with them. Every time I find something new, it opens up a different avenue of investigation. I could spend a lifetime just studying the genetic differentiation that is occurring in my body."

"Good thing you have more than one lifetime," Ryan reminded her.

Susan caught her breath, realizing she must sound ridiculous. The act of breathing reminded her of one of her preliminary findings, and she immediately returned to her exposition.

"For example, I could never figure out why your heart beat at times, and other times did not. Or why sometimes you appeared to be breathing, and other times had no need to do so."

Ryan was curious. "I have wondered that myself."

"Apparently the autonomic nervous system still functions, although it is no longer necessary. Many of the activities the autonomic system performed have either ceased or been taken over by the somatic nervous system. In other words, previously involuntary actions are now under conscious control."

"And yet my body remembers how to do these things," Ryan

mused, "so sometimes it still does?"

"Yes, as far as I can see. That doesn't mean your heart never needs to beat. There might be times when there is still some physiological purpose..." Susan paused, clearing her throat, "For example, when Sharing blood."

The thought flustered Susan, and she focused her attention on the papers in her hand, shuffling through them loudly in the silence. Ryan graciously did not point out that Susan's autonomic nervous system was shunting blood to her cheeks. Susan found something to focus on in her printouts.

"I discovered the composition of my blood has changed, and I'm beginning to find traces of some of the attributes I found in your blood when I first examined you."

"For example?" Ryan asked politely.

Susan read from the paperwork. "I have identified L-gulonolactone, an enzyme that converts glucose to Vitamin C, not normally found in human beings. My growth hormone levels have dramatically increased, with no attendant negative side effects." Susan shuffled the papers again, peering over an MRI printout.

"My digestive system has begun to reroute itself, merging with the circulatory system. The aorta and esophagus are now connected. My heart is beginning to enlarge." Susan shook her head. "It was difficult enough to note these changes in you. It is bizarre to watch my own anatomy change this way."

She flipped through a few more pages. "Some of the most exciting findings have to do with the changes in my DNA."

"Wait a minute," Ryan said, "how exactly are you able to make comparisons?"

Susan cleared her throat again. "Well, I kind of anticipated these experiments."

"Ah," Ryan said, "you took samples of your own blood and tissue before you were Changed."

Susan felt the heat rise in her cheeks once more. "I extensively documented my physical condition before my Change. My concern was that I could not anticipate all of the experiments I would want to conduct, or that something would arise later and I would need some type of control measure. So, yes, I saved a little bit of everything."

Ryan smiled. Susan Ryerson was probably the only human in history that had undergone the Change primarily out of scientific curiosity. "Okay, so go on."

Susan shuffled the papers once more. "We've had numerous discussions regarding the changes in your DNA, relative to a normal human's. However, you and your father are so unique that I have had to study the Others to get a clear picture of what might be normal for your–, I mean, our Kind. This is really the first chance I have had, though, to conduct a controlled experiment of the transition."

"So do you have 46 or 92 chromosomal pairs?" Ryan asked.

Susan was surprised and pleased at the question. It indicated Ryan actually paid attention to her often complicated and complex explanations.

"I have 46 pairs, like the Others. The only two I have tested with 92 are you and Victor."

"I wonder if Drake has 92," Ryan speculated aloud.

Susan saw her opening. "That brings up something I wanted to ask."

Ryan already knew the request. "You want to test Drake as well."

"Well," Susan said with hesitation, "if you wouldn't mind."

"Lucky boy," Ryan said to herself. She returned to the subject at hand. "How about the extra nucleotide? I believe you designated it with an 'I'. Do you have that?"

In her research, Susan had identified the strange nucleotide with an "I," which she had labeled in exasperation as "I have no idea." It was an addition to the normal four of human beings. She had never seen the compound in any human, nor in any of the Others besides Ryan and Victor.

"No," Susan replied. "I do not have the 'I' nucleotide. I believe that chromosomal variation is something unique to Victor that he passed down to you through sexual reproduction with your mother. And perhaps it was the act of sexual reproduction which resulted in the double set of chromosomes. Again, it is something I would like to test Drake for."

"Lucky boy," Ryan repeated.

Susan returned to her paperwork. "You were right about DNA being overwritten."

Ryan stared at her blankly. "You will have to refresh my memory on that one."

"When we were first discussing Victor's illness, you speculated that DNA might be rewritten in the Change, and possibly in the very act of Sharing. I have not had the chance to examine the before and after of Sharing…"

Ryan smiled again. Every time Susan tried to speak clinically of Sharing, she choked on her words like a pre-teen discussing sex.

"But I have documented the alteration in my DNA from pre-transition to the present. I don't really understand the affects of the changes yet, but they are extensive. Under normal circumstances, this type and level of mutation would cause immediate death, but contrary to all known science, it seems to be doing nothing of the kind. When I am able to sit down and process the data, I assume there will be numerous favorable mutations in chromosomal areas dealing with strength, endurance, stamina, etc. Again, I could spend an entire lifetime just examining this aspect of my anatomy."

"Well," Ryan said, her attention returning to her father's prone form, "I am glad you are making progress."

Susan set the paperwork aside. "This is not a priority. With your permission, I would like to examine Victor to assess his current condition. And I would also like to examine Drake in the hopes that he is as genetically similar to you as you are to your father. It will give me one more control measure to work with."

Ryan bowed once more. "I will return with my son."

Ryan returned a short time later carrying Drake. Susan was still examining Victor's prone form, so Ryan settled into a nearby chair with her son. The small boy watched with interest as Susan hovered over his grandfather.

"She's going to poke and prod you like that in a moment," Ryan said, nudging the boy in the ribs. Drake grinned at Susan, then buried his face in Ryan's shoulder.

Susan paused in her ministration. "He is a doll."

Ryan brushed the hair at the nape of Drake's neck. "Do you regret not being able to have more children?"

Susan paused, and her silence was telling.

Ryan ruffled Drake's hair again. "You saved your ova as well."

"Well," Susan stammered, "it seemed like a good idea. With the technology available to preserve the eggs, it seemed foolish not to maintain that as an option."

"I think it was a very wise decision," Ryan commented, and Susan relaxed. "I wonder if more of my Kind will take advantage of these medical procedures as time goes on. Think about it. You can continue to have children after your Change. You could have a child born a thousand years after Jason."

This thought was as awe-inspiring as it was frightening. Susan was still adjusting to the sense of timelessness that Ryan took for granted, and really did not want to think about it. Ryan continued her casual conversation.

"You seem to have been very clinical about your Change."

Susan thought back to the passionate exchange that sparked her transformation, to the times she had ventured into the dark eroticism of Sharing, to the dangerous, sensual currents that swirled about her constantly.

"No," said Susan, "not exactly."

Ryan merely smiled.

Susan turned back to Victor, resuming her examination. "Actually," she said over her shoulder and under her breath, "I still keep looking in my mouth for fangs."

"You won't get any," Ryan reminded her.

Susan quickly finished her assessment and set her instruments aside. She brushed her hands on her lab coat.

"Okay, if you want to just hold him, I'll get a blood test."

Ryan shifted Drake onto her knee as Susan approached with a needle. He gazed at the needle somberly, then looked askance at his mother.

"It might hurt a little," Ryan said, "but only for a moment."

Susan took his tiny arm as Drake locked his blue eyes on Ryan's. Ryan reached out mentally to soothe him, and he did not flinch when Susan inserted the needle. Nor did he take his eyes from his mother.

As the blood began to pour into the vial, Susan felt the inopportune stirring of desire and inwardly cursed herself. All sorts of recriminations began to fill her head: her lack of professionalism, her lack of control, an appetite that had obviously turned to pedophilia.

"Don't be so hard on yourself," Ryan said. She had not turned her gaze from Drake, but she was evidently aware of Susan's internal struggle. "There was a reason my father kept me from the Others when I was a child." Her eyes drifted down to the blood pouring into the vial, "and a reason why he kept me from himself."

Ryan returned her gaze to Drake's. Susan watched the two, fascinated. There was clearly the gentle devotion customary in a mother/child relationship. But there was also an underlying current of sensuality between the two of them. It was hard to define, a way of interacting that was non-sexual but intensely intimate.

Susan withdrew the needle and a small drop of blood appeared on Drake's arm.

"Do you want me to kiss that for you?" Ryan asked him, dark amusement in her eyes.

It seemed Drake knew full well the game they were playing, and Susan swore there was dark humor in his eyes as well. He lifted his arm to his mother. Ryan leaned down and kissed the small puncture wound. It stopped bleeding immediately. Ryan gazed at her son for a long moment, then glanced up at Susan.

"He's going to be a handful."

Susan tucked the vial of blood into the pocket of her lab coat. "It seems to me he already is." She had a sudden thought, and pulled a swab stick from her other pocket.

"Hold on a moment," she said. "I don't even know if you still have saliva, but I want to check something." The swab hovered near Ryan's mouth until Susan said with exasperation, "Open your mouth."

Ryan obeyed the order patiently and Susan took her sample. Ryan then turned to Drake.

"This whole 'king' thing does not appear to generate any additional respect."

Drake grinned.

CHAPTER 10

RYAN ENTERED THE LOWER COURTYARD and stopped for a moment. She closed her eyes, listening to the clank of metal on metal. The sound brought back so many memories it was momentarily overwhelming. She opened her eyes and rounded the corner.

Two of Abigail's staff were sword-fighting on the main terrace. Ryan identified the blades as rapiers, 17th century European, not a preference of hers but solid weapons. Jason was seated on a nearby bench, avidly watching the pair. He was rarely separated from Drake, but Edward had just put the boy down for a nap so he was on his own at the moment.

Ryan approached, watching the two combatants. They were very skilled and fought with ferocity and preternatural speed. The rapier was actually a good choice of weapon because it would flex with the force of their blows. The ting-ting-ting of the metal was accompanied by the laughter of the men watching. It made Ryan think of other times, times which seemed to belong to other worlds.

"Hey Ryan," Jason called out. He was obviously excited to see her. "Why don't you show them how it's done?"

The men stopped, suddenly aware of her presence. Her "presence" was normally unmistakable. But Ryan was unused to the constant attention from the Others and the commotion her approach caused. She found herself creating a mental shield just to avoid the continual stares.

She nodded to the men, who all bowed respectfully in return. She was surprised when one of the combatants called out to her. Although not a Young One, he was not particularly old either, perhaps born in the same century as his weapon.

"I understand you are a great swordsman," he said, "would you care to spar?"

A much older man, both in appearance and in actual age, quickly stepped forward. "I beg your pardon, my lord." He gave the younger man a scathing glance. "He forgets himself."

Ryan recognized the older man as one of Abigail's chief consorts. She glanced at they younger man. "It is of no harm," she said, amused, "fortune favors the brave."

The man sent another scathing glance to the youngster. "But not the stupid."

Ryan smiled. "Again, it is of no harm. Under other circumstances, I might accept, but I am not fond of the rapier."

Abigail's consort bowed low. "Very well, my lord. Thank you for your understanding."

Ryan turned and began to walk away. The younger man raised his eyes to Ryan's departing back. Perhaps her skill with the sword had been exaggerated.

The thought had no sooner coalesced than the young man felt the air next to his ear part as an object passed by at tremendous speed. The object was not even a blur so great was its velocity, leaving only the instantaneous impression of something sharp and lethal. It split the crowd of men with deadly precision, flying through the air directly at Ryan's retreating back.

In an impossible move and seemingly without effort, Ryan shifted her head slightly to the side, allowing the sword to pass by her ear, catching it in full flight by the hilt. It was frozen, stopped cold by the casual gesture, levitating by the grasp that held it level.

Ryan lowered the sword, her back still to the men. She glanced at the weapon's beautiful curve, the extraordinary workmanship, the deadly sharpness of the blade, and then slowly turned around. The men were astonished, not only by the incredible maneuver, but by the smile that played about Ryan's lips.

"Is this a challenge?" Ryan asked, amusement in her voice. The men were uncertain whom she was addressing.

"It is a gift," came the reply.

The crowd of men turned, parting to reveal the One Ryan knew was standing there.

An extraordinarily handsome Asian man stepped forward, the intensity in his gaze mirroring that of his protégé.

Kusunoki drew his own sword. "And a challenge," he added, his eyes gleaming.

Ryan did not hide the fierce joy she felt at his presence. Kusunoki leaped forward, covering the distance between them in single bound. Ryan took one step back and brought her sword up to parry, and the weapons locked. The combatants stared at one another across the immobile blades, their delight in the battle evident.

"Do not break my gift before I have had a chance to use it," Ryan chided him.

Kusunoki smiled, a gesture that would surprise most who knew the stern warrior.

"It will not so easily break, I forged it specially for you."

Kusunoki stepped rearward, then forward on his attack. The blades began flashing in the sunlight, barely discernible as two distinct objects. The athleticism of the combat was matched only by the grace of the contestants. The two appeared to move as one in a deadly dance, lethal choreography honed over centuries. The blurred swords seemed to sing as they sliced through the air, their song increasing in tempo until there was only a single, prolonged note in the air.

The intensity of the battle increased until neither combatant could be clearly seen, only a smeared impression of where they had just been. The intensity grew until the very air hummed with electricity, sparks flying from the deadly blades. Finally, as the battle seemed to approach a climax, hurtling toward some unknown conclusion, both combatants went to strike a killing blow.

And all went still.

Ryan stared across at Kusunoki, and Kusunoki at Ryan. They were frozen in a dangerous embrace. Each had trapped the blade of the other in the palm of their free hand, and each now gripped the other sword tightly.

Ryan smiled, and Kusunoki smiled in return. Each slowly began to withdraw their sword from the grip of the other, slicing deeply into the skin. Neither flinched, nor showed any sign of pain. Ryan appeared to enjoy the incision.

Kusunoki raised his bloody palm and Ryan mirrored the gesture, pressing her palm to his. The mingling of the blood sent shockwaves through both, but it was Kusunoki who closed his eyes at the sensation. He reopened them and gazed at his most beloved student.

"I have missed you," he said simply.

Ryan smiled. It was rare for the taciturn warrior to express any emotion.

"And I have missed you, my master." She held his gaze, "And I have not forgotten my debt to you."

Kusunoki nodded, and removed his hand. Both felt the loss of contact keenly.

Ryan lifted the katana up, examining it in the sunlight. It was beautiful.

"It is perfectly balanced, a true work of art." She gave it one last experimental swing, then lowered it.

"Jason," she called over her shoulder.

Jason ran up quickly, his eyes wide. Ryan handed the sword to him, and he took it gingerly.

"Take this in the house and give it to Edward."

Jason could not believe his good fortune. He held the sword as if it were made of gold and began carefully working his way back to the mansion.

Ryan turned to Kusunoki. "Let me show you to your quarters. I must say," she said thinking of Abigail's requirements, "that you were the easiest to prepare for."

Kusunoki smiled. He knew his room would be simple and spare, decorated in an ascetic style that would make him comfortable. He put his hand on his most favored student's shoulder and the two started toward the stairs.

The group of men watched the two leave, none having moved since the battle began. The older of the group finally shifted, and it seemed to break the spell. The others began moving about, although slowly. The younger man who had so boldly addressed Ryan was still frozen. He stared dumbfounded at Ryan's retreating back. The consort leaned over to speak in his ear.

"Lucky for you," the older man said to him with sarcasm, "she doesn't like the rapier."

Ryan entered the mansion with Kusunoki at her side. Edward met them at the door, bowing deeply to the ancient samurai.

"Kusunoki Masahige," Edward said, utilizing his full name, "welcome." He glanced at the blood on Kusunoki's hand. "Would you care for a bandage, sir?"

Kusunoki shook his head. "Thank you, Edward. It will heal in a moment."

Marilyn chose that moment to sail into the room. "Ah, Kusunoki. No wonder Ryan is in such high spirits. I imagine you two have already been off beating each other to death?"

Kusunoki bowed to the dark-haired beauty, offering his intact hand in greeting. "It is a pleasure, as always, Madame."

Marilyn caught sight of the blood on his other hand. Ryan quickly put her damaged hand behind her, but Marilyn caught the gesture.

"Oh my," she said, "you two wasted no time."

Abigail chose that moment to make her entrance. She had watched the fierce sparring from her balcony and welcomed Kusunoki's presence. He was an extremely stable influence on Ryan, and one of the few among their Kind who lacked political ambition.

Kusunoki bowed to the matriarch. "It seems I owe you great

thanks, my lady."

Abigail was curious, unable to discern his meaning. The aloof Asian was one of the few of her Kind she could not read well.

"And what have I done to earn such gratitude?"

Kusunoki glanced at Ryan. "I am guessing you are the one responsible for forcing our crown prince's hand."

Abigail nodded her understanding. Kusunoki was fiercely loyal to the Alexanders, serving Victor for centuries. He had spoken most forcefully for Ryan to assume leadership of the hierarchy when it became apparent Victor was unable to serve.

"I believe it has been a coordination of efforts," Abigail said diplomatically, "Ryan has been subjected to many types of 'persuasion' of late."

Ryan turned to Edward, exasperated. "Why is it that whenever the Old Ones gather, I am suddenly a child and they speak of me as if I am not here?"

Edward was not placing himself in the midst of this battle. "Hmm," was all he said noncommittally.

Kusunoki settled into his spare room. It was perfect. A simple bed, a small table at floor level, an oil lamp, and an ancient Japanese tea set. A bookshelf with a few books including an original manuscript of the "Art of War."

Kusunoki extended his senses throughout the mansion. He could feel Victor faintly, his spirit still present, but just barely. He wished to pay his respects to his lordship. He sensed that Ryan was with her father and hoped he would not disturb her.

Kusunoki paused in front of the double doors. Ryan sensed him and bid him welcome, but there was something else that made him hesitate, a presence that seemed very familiar, yet unknown. He pushed through the double doors, still trying to assess the feeling.

Ryan sat at her father's side, her back to the door, and it was not until Kusunoki approached that he identified the source of the feeling. Identified it, but had difficulty comprehending it.

A tiny boy sat in Ryan's lap, cradled in her arm. The child sat quietly but was very alert. Big blue eyes examined the approaching stranger with a very direct gaze. The boy glanced up at Ryan, as if assessing her reaction to the stranger, then returned his gaze to Kusunoki. Apparently Kusunoki passed muster because the child's eyes twinkled.

"I hope you are prepared to train another Alexander."

Kusunoki sat down slowly, his eyes on the boy. His resemblance to Ryan was astonishing. Kusunoki turned and then casually put his feet up on the footrest.

"Will he be as difficult a student as you?"

Ryan shrugged, glancing down at the infant. "Probably not. He seems to have a much better temperament than me." A look of wicked mischief came into her eyes as she addressed her former master.

"But then again, he is my son."

CHAPTER 11

TRISTAN AND GAVIN LEANED OVER the crude map, discussing strategy. The Saxon encampment was cleverly placed, uphill and surrounded by rough terrain. The Saxon forces were also numerous, outnumbering Tristan and his men nearly two to one. Still, it was the best chance they were going to get to attack before winter set in.

"Where is Ambrosius?" Tristan asked.

Gavin glanced about him. "I think he is sparring. I will go find him."

Tristan nodded his thanks and turned back to the map.

In the two years that Ambrosius had been with his men, he had become one of Tristan's most trusted advisors. The boy had proven not only excellent on a horse, but astonishing with a sword, not to mention possessing near mystical accuracy with a bow. He had become greatly beloved of the men, who respected and admired his quiet strength. In his younger life, Tristan's greatest regret was that he had no son to carry on his name. His wife had died in childbirth with his sole progeny, who did not live long afterward. Tristan now felt he had a worthy successor, if not of his blood, then of his spirit.

Gavin approached with Ambrosius at his side and Tristan stood upright. He gestured to the map.

"Ambrosius, do you have any suggestions?"

Ambrosius glanced at the map, orienting himself. "I am familiar with this country. It is good land for hunting." He was silent for a moment, in deep thought. He finally placed his finger on a spot near the Saxon encampment. "I would attack here."

Tristan and Gavin looked at one another. As intelligent a tactician as the boy had proven, apparently even he could have a bad day.

"That is extremely rough terrain," Gavin suggested delicately, "rocky and choked with briars."

Ambrosius nodded. "Exactly. I would position the archers here and the infantry here," he said, tapping the map. "If the attack occurs in the morning, the sun will be behind the archers and in eyes of the enemies. If the prevailing winds hold, they will be at the archers back, aiding the arrow's flight while hindering the Saxon's. Any dust from the battlefield will be blown toward the barbarians."

Tristan cleared his throat. "That does not change the fact that you are attacking over very unfavorable ground."

Ambrosius nodded, still examining the map. "Which is why the attack is not an attack, but a feint. The real attack," he said, moving his finger to the south of the Saxon encampment, "will come from the heavy cavalry from this direction. The Saxons will hold position, the cavalry will split their forces, then regroup for a flank attack." Ambrosius again pointed to a feature on the map. "The approach for the cavalry is narrow, but the ground is favorable for a quick strike."

Tristan began nodding slowly. The plan was brilliant. He turned to Gavin, who also nodded his approval. Gavin smiled.

"Is this more of your childhood schooling?" Gavin asked. "Julius Caesar perhaps?"

Ambrosius was still staring at the map. "No, not Julius Caesar, but nor can I take credit for it." He was still calculating every eventuality, but seemed satisfied the plan was sound. "This is very much like the Battle of Issus." He looked up at Tristan. "I would like to lead the feint, with your approval."

Tristan started to object. It would be by far the most dangerous part of the battle and the men involved in the feint were likely to be killed. But Tristan knew that if anyone could survive, as well as protect his men, it was Ambrosius.

"Very well," Tristan said reluctantly, "but you will hold there only as long as you need to."

Ambrosius nodded. "With your leave, I will prepare for battle."

Gavin watched the young man depart. He turned back to Tristan. "The Battle of Issus?" he asked.

Tristan, too, watched the young man depart, noting he carried himself with the bearing of a General.

"Our young friend is not merely a student of Roman tactics," Tristan said, "but of classical ones as well. The Battle of Issus was fought and won by Alexander the Great."

Ambrosius sat on his horse in the early morning light. The steeds surrounding him all stepped nervously, but his horse was steadfast, unmoving. The shadows in front of him were shortening as the sun rose behind him. He could feel the gentle heat on the back of his neck in the cool morning air.

Tristan had given him command of the entire initial force, infantry, archers, and cavalry. Ambrosius wondered how the more seasoned commanders would respond, but they seemed cheered by his presence and his responsibility. It was a responsibility that weighed heavily on Ambrosius. It was one thing to risk his own life; another to risk that of his men.

Ambrosius glanced down. He had placed a stick in the ground and marked a line in the dirt when the attack should begin. The shadow now touched the line. Ambrosius raised his arm, and the infantry began marching toward the Saxon line. They seemed to be struggling over the rough terrain, causing great hilarity to echo down from the Saxon soldiers. Ambrosius had directed his men to exaggerate the difficulty of their progress, and he was pleased to see that many of his soldiers had a second career in drama if they so chose.

As predicted, the Saxons could not wait to attack the struggling, vulnerable infantry, and charged down the hillside. The infantry immediately dropped to their knees, shields up, and Ambrosius raised his other arm. The archers let loose their first volley of arrows, arrows that flew straight and true, lifted by the favorable winds. Waves of Saxons went down beneath the blanket of death.

The infantry was immediately back on its feet, now charging up the hill with far less difficulty than they had portrayed, catching the Saxons off-guard once more. There was instant chaos, the sights, sounds, and smells of death in the air. The world became a whirling mass of severed limbs and spattered blood, accompanied by screams of rage and pain.

Ambrosius waited as long as he could, then sent the cavalry charging up the hill. Many of the cavalrymen were certain their horses would never make it over the rough terrain, but somehow their steeds seemed to be following the horse of their commander, which never missed a step. In a surprisingly short time, Ambrosius was in the midst of battle, his sword swinging and slicing through metal, flesh, and bone.

At some point, he was unhorsed, but it was no matter. He would just as soon slaughter the barbarians face-to-face. He lost track of time, and certainly lost track of how many men he had slain. All he knew is that he was continuing to move forward and although covered in blood, had barely sustained a scratch.

After what seemed an interminable amount of time, Ambrosius heard the horn signaling the flanking attack had begun. As expected, the Saxons were completely unprepared for the secondary assault, perhaps because the "feint" had been so lethal and effective. Surprisingly, Ambrosius and his men had nearly split the Saxon defenses up the middle, so successful had their advance been. The flanking attack and subsequent regrouping annihilated any remaining discipline of the barbarian troops, and the Saxons turned to run.

Ambrosius whistled for his horse, and the steed ran across the battlefield toward him. He mounted the horse while it was still on the move, swinging upward with amazing athleticism. Drawing his sword, he charged after the fleeing Saxons, joined by any of his men still standing. He began to chase the barbarians back into the sea and his men eagerly followed. In fact, at this moment, his men would have followed him to the very edge of the world.

Many hours later, Ambrosius, accompanied only by his horse, picked his way back through the forest. He had killed every last Saxon he could find, and he had long ago outrun every one of his men. It was possible he would not be able to return to the battlefield before the sun rose again and although he did not want to concern Tristan, he was considering stopping for the night.

The fatigue of his horse finally made the decision for him. He dismounted and led the animal to drink in a nearby stream. It was a very peaceful setting, and the stream flowed by so gently the reflection of the full moon was barely disturbed. He glanced down at his clothing and armor. He was covered in blood and the stream looked inviting.

Ambrosius disrobed, leaving his sword within arms reach, and waded into the chilly stream. He let the cold water run past him, then lowered himself fully to wash the blood from his arms and torso. He dunked his head, cleansing the crusted blood from his hair. He stood upright, enjoying the sensation of the cool night air on his bare skin. A chill passed through him, one that had nothing to do with the cold air. He had the distinct feeling someone was watching him.

He turned, reaching for his sword, but it was no longer where he had placed it. Instead, it was held by an exquisitely beautiful woman with long dark hair and flashing dark eyes, eyes that examined his nakedness quite openly. What she saw obviously gave her pleasure, and she glanced down at the sword she held in her hands.

"They will return," Ravlen said casually.

Ambrosius, too, looked at the bloodied sword.

"–and in greater numbers." Ravlen added.

Ambrosius knew she was referring to the Saxons. "I know," he said simply.

She set the sword down. "But still you will fight them."

Ambrosius nodded. "Yes."

She smiled as she stepped into the water. "I told you that you were a warrior."

He gasped as she placed her hands on his chest, running her fingers along the ridged muscles of his body. She did it with that same sense of simple curiosity, as if exploring some strange new world with every touch. He did not move, patient beneath her exploration. He watched her, trying to memorize every feature, every expression, every gesture, every mannerism.

"I have missed you," he said, his voice thick with emotion.

She smiled as one would smile at a child, then gestured toward the bank of the stream. "Show me how much you have missed me."

CHAPTER 12

KUSUNOKI INHALED THE FRAGRANT, GRASSY SMELL of the tea. It was green tea, made from a line of plants he had bred for centuries. He cultivated and plucked the buds himself, experience having taught him the ones that would give the full but light, slightly sweet flavor for the tea.

He rose at the slight knock on the door and moved to let Ryan in. She stopped in the doorway, taking a deep breath.

"Gyokuro," she said, assessing the aroma.

Kusunoki nodded, pleased.

"Picked in May."

Kusunoki smiled, even more pleased "So you did pay attention to your lessons."

Ryan smiled as well. "Yes, even the ones that did not involve slicing something in two."

Ryan moved to the table and kneeled. It was not a formal tea ceremony, but Kusunoki still served the beverage with great ritual and reverence, a reverence Ryan emulated as she sipped the tea.

Kusunoki gazed at the wisps of steam that rose from his cup. "So what is it that has finally forced your hand?"

Ryan glanced up, a wry expression on her face. "You mean other than the constant pressure from you and Abigail, as well as the Others?"

Kusunoki's tone was mild. "We have not even seen you for almost two years."

"You do not need to be here for me to feel your presence," Ryan replied.

Kusunoki smiled. So she had sensed his meditations.

The two were silent for a long moment, and Ryan was deep in thought. When she finally spoke, there was no trace of her previous playfulness.

"My hand was not forced. I believe it is what my father wishes."

Kusunoki looked at her sharply, uncertain of her meaning. "You can sense Victor?"

"No," Ryan said, hesitating. "Well, maybe yes. I am not certain." She paused again, searching for the words. "I do not know if I am truly sensing him or if it is just that I wish I could sense him."

Kusunoki thought it was probably the former. If anyone could maintain contact with Victor in his current stasis, it would be Ryan. It was, however, immaterial to the discussion at hand.

"Either way, you are correct."

Ryan turned to him, an eyebrow raised in question.

"Assuming command is what your father would wish."

Ryan stood, unfolding to her full height in one supple movement. Kusunoki watched his beloved pupil. She had always moved with a deadly grace, giving the impression of surface relaxation with tautness beneath. She moved to stare out the window, resting her hands on the windowsill.

Kusunoki stood, as graceful as his pupil. He moved behind her and gently placed his hands on her shoulders. She surprised him by leaning back into his chest, and the shock of contact caused him to sharply inhale.

Ryan smiled. "I see I am not the only one who maintains irrelevant human gestures."

Kusunoki lowered his arms, encircling her waist in a relaxed embrace. Ryan leaned her head against his shoulder, enjoying the comforting sensation. It reminded her of her father.

Ryan's mind was open to him, and Kusunoki was amused. "Is

that how you think of me? As a father-figure?"

There was a playful sensuality in Ryan's reply. "Not entirely." She turned her head slightly and glanced up at him. "But then again, that is not entirely how I think of my father, either."

Kusunoki's eyes drifted downward to the vein running along the tendon of Ryan's neck. His eyes caressed the skin that covered the blood.

"I remember the first time I saw you," he said, "wild, unruly, impossibly powerful for one so young." He raised his eyes to hers once more.

"You have not changed much."

Ryan did not speak, merely smiled. There was a sudden, quiet, intensity in Kusunoki's voice as he added, "Except you are much more powerful."

Ryan turned her gaze forward, still leaning her head against his shoulder. "Time makes us powerful. The circumstances of my birth have made me powerful."

Kusunoki shook his head. "No, those are insufficient causalities. Your training and discipline have made you powerful."

It was an extraordinary compliment from her master, and it pleased Ryan greatly. But she would give credit where it was due. "The blood of the Others has made me powerful." She turned to him and spoke with quiet emphasis. "Your blood has made me powerful." She was silent for a moment, then added, "A debt acquired and a debt unpaid."

Kusunoki glanced down at the girl in front of him. "And would you Share with me only to satisfy a debt?"

Ryan turned forward again, the playful smile returning as she repeated herself. "Not entirely."

Her sensual teasing amused him, and he leaned forward to whisper in her ear. "It is difficult to believe you are even more dangerous without a sword."

Ryan tensed as he sliced into her neck, but she did not pull away. Kusunoki's influence was immeasurable and she did not resist it in any way, welcoming his warmth and strength.

Kusunoki, on the other hand, nearly lost his grip on the girl at first contact. He was astonished at the power present in her blood, and as it began to flow through his veins, his system staggered under the onslaught. He brought all his mental discipline to bear and focused, simultaneously adjusting his grip on Ryan. He had the sudden insight that all of his predictions regarding Ryan's future abilities had one thing in common.

They had all been markedly underestimated.

Kusunoki broke his feeding just long enough to guide Ryan to the couch. He lifted her and held her much like one would hold a child, cradling her head so that he could maintain contact with that flow of life. As he sat, the blood spread to his every extremity, creating an intense flush that was unbearably pleasurable. And Kusunoki, master of discipline, felt his will dissolving into a chaos that made him desperately want to relinquish control. It had been centuries since he had felt the bloodlust so intensely, and never had he such a desire to kill.

Ryan sensed his thoughts but they caused her no concern. She herself was caught in the dance, that wondrous place where inhibition was a quaint notion with no standing. She felt her heart slow, felt that wonderful lethargy that made death seem a welcome option, a release that had no equal.

She distantly felt Kusunoki's growing distress, the thought that he might not be able to maintain control as his frenzy increased. And it was this distress that caused her to act.

Kusunoki was startled to find himself sitting on a precipice in a blood-red world, peering into black depths without end. He turned to Ryan, who sat shoulder-to-shoulder with him, her legs dangling over the ledge. She seemed very amused by their positions on the edge of the infinite abyss. He glanced around him. He had seen this place dimly, when she had fed upon him, but without the clarity he had now. He was amazed at her mental control.

"What is this place?" he asked.

Ryan glanced around. It was different every time, yet always the same.

"This is my playground," she said, "I believe it is the edge of death."

Kusunoki looked around again. They seemed in some great chamber, a half dome with a blood-red sky and walls that pulsated. He leaned forward, staring into the infinite darkness. He glanced down, realizing he had a death grip on Ryan's wrist. Ryan looked down as well.

"And are you going to toss me into that great blackness?" she asked, still amused.

He stared at the wrist, uncertain of his response. Ryan then offered him an even greater temptation.

"Or perhaps we could just jump together."

Kusunoki closed his eyes, and slowly released the wrist.

"No," he said quietly, it the most difficult word he had ever spoken.

Ryan glanced down into the darkness, unconcerned. "Perhaps another time," she said.

Kusunoki struggled, knowing that in the real world he was still feeding upon Ryan. But he suddenly understood that he could drain every drop of blood from her body, and she was in no danger of dying.

Ryan was content to sit on the edge, staring into the blackness, but a sudden tension filled her. She peered into the darkness. There was a presence in the depths, something unspeakably malevolent and ancient. She had felt this presence before, the hint of something reptilian and monstrous. She had the sense that claws were snaking upward from the blackness, and she heard the terrifying voice, one that spoke with the faintest sibilant hiss.

"I AM COMING–,"

Ryan stood pulling Kusunoki away from the edge as she did so.

"–FOR YOU."

Kusunoki raised his head. They were back in the mansion and the blood red world had disappeared. He glanced down at Ryan, his concern evident. She was pale and nearly unconscious, but that was not what concerned him. He had sensed tremendous agitation from her, and if not mistaken, genuine fear. He cradled her in his arms, and she buried her head in his chest. For a long moment, he was at a complete loss.

"I am sorry," Ryan said at last.

Kusunoki brushed her hair from her eyes, not understanding. "Why are you sorry?"

"I did not mean for you to be dissatisfied."

Kusunoki stared at her. Although normally reserved, he could not hide his incredulity. She had just given him the most extraordinary experience of his immortal life, and she was apologizing. He cleared his throat.

"I have never felt such fulfillment in all my centuries," he said simply, "and all other acts pale in comparison. Trust me," he said with emphasis, "I am completely satisfied."

This seemed to reassure Ryan, and she relaxed in his embrace. He could sense she was still troubled, and he had to ask.

"What did you see that caused you such dread?"

Ryan shook her head. "I am not certain. It is a vision of some sort. One I have had before." She shook her head again. "I cannot explain it."

Kusunoki realized the subject troubled her and decided to speak no more of it. He concentrated and allowed his influence to settle over Ryan, calming her. Ryan felt the reassuring presence and relaxed. Only her father had a similar comforting effect on her.

The samurai was again aware of the comparison, and admitted to himself that this time the association gave him great pleasure. It made him realize the great love he had for his pupil was returned because Ryan loved no one more than Victor. Kusunoki smiled, well, perhaps that blue-eyed little creature he had met earlier.

Kusunoki settled into the couch, willing to let the girl sleep for awhile. The thought of Victor returned him to Ryan's vision, and a drop of concern rippled through his tranquility.

Victor was known to possess a degree of clairvoyance. He had once described it to Kusunoki as a general sense rather than a detailed description of future events. Kusunoki glanced down at the sleeping girl. He wondered if Victor's child possessed her father's gift as well.

Abigail watched the two figures in the courtyard below. Both wore blindfolds over their eyes, but it was apparent neither needed eyesight to perform the elaborate, ritualistic martial art form. Kusunoki and Ryan were side-by-side but moved as one. It was an ancient dance, both beautiful and deadly.

Marilyn approached and Abigail nodded in greeting. Marilyn joined her at the balcony railing, also watching silently. The form ended and the two participants turned to one another, bowing. Kusunoki removed his blindfold, then stepped forward and removed Ryan's. Some sort of silent communication passed between the two. In a surprisingly tender gesture, the handsome Asian leaned down and gently kissed Ryan's forehead. The two then parted.

"This displeases you far less than I would think," Marilyn commented, watching the girl disappear into the house.

Abigail smiled her cool smile. "It is not my place he takes," she said simply.

Marilyn nodded, and Abigail continued. "A place I have no doubt he will relinquish when Victor returns."

Marilyn was not fooled. Abigail's motives were always multiple and complex. Marilyn's response was casual, but her words edged. "And until then, he assists you in keeping our little crown prince in check."

Abigail again smiled her icy smile, her cool demeanor unwavering. "A task which you yourself perform with enthusiasm."

The barb may have been intended as an accusation but it had no such effect on Marilyn. Instead, it brought forth the image of the girl in her bed, which immediately and pleasantly preoccupied her.

"Hmm, yes," was all she said. She enjoyed the reflection for a moment longer, then grew serious once more.

"Ryan has grown immensely powerful."

It was Abigail's turn to be noncommittal. "Hmm, yes," she said.

Marilyn turned to face Abigail. For a moment there was a dangerous intimacy between the two, currents of sensuality that swirled around them, threatening to sweep away all in their path.

"And what will you do," Marilyn asked her softly, "when the girl discovers how powerful she truly is?"

For the briefest moment, Abigail's eyes lingered on Marilyn's lips, a hint of past and present seduction that had always existed between the two. The moment stretched outward, both women enjoying the sensation. Abigail smiled, ever-present amusement flickering in her cool gaze as she turned from the raven-haired beauty.

"When she discovers her power," Abigail said over her shoulder, "I trust you will be there to help me hold her down."

CHAPTER 13

SUSAN SMILED AS SHE FELT A WAVE of warmth wash over her. It was an intensely enjoyable sensation, like the heat of the sun on cool skin. She turned as Ryan walked in the room.

"It is not as easy for you to sneak up on me now."

Ryan gave a mischievous grin. "Not without trying." She glanced around at the various test tubes and charts. "Hard at work, I see."

"Yes, I have interpreted some of your father's results, and found some interesting things."

Ryan moved to Victor's side. "That sounds promising."

"Well," Susan said, pulling out one of her numerous charts, "I don't know if it's promising or not, but at least it's a change. Do you remember when we discussed the rise of histamine in Victor's system just prior to him going unconscious?"

Ryan thought back to the conversation. "Yes. You proposed that his histamine levels rose to put him into a state of hibernation, to protect his body while it attempted to fight off the virus."

"Right," Susan said, "a theory that was given credence by the fact that Victor's hippocampus has continued to exhibit activity even though he shows no traditional life signs. Although histamine is generally thought of as an arousal molecule, it does seem to have a depressive function as well."

"So what has changed with my father?"

Susan looked at the chart. "His histamine levels are beginning to fall."

"Is that a good thing?" Ryan asked.

"I'm not certain. This still seems more science fiction than science. Victor's levels of histamine were stratospheric to begin with, so they are not dropping down to what could be considered 'normal' levels. But the decrease may be a sign he is preparing to come out of stasis. At least it is some type of change."

Ryan was not satisfied. "But you are not certain it's a good change."

"No, I'm not. And there is one additional variation to factor in. The rate of mutation of his mitochondrial DNA has slowed as well. Again, I am uncertain if this is a positive or negative change. It could be negative, an indication his system is failing and he is no longer able to fight off the attack."

"Is that what you believe?"

Susan shook her head, much to Ryan's relief. "No. Actually I think it is probably a positive sign. There are no symptoms indicating his condition has worsened. My guess is that his system is beginning to repair itself. And I found something incredible that may be aiding your father, and I have confirmed it exists in both you and Drake as well. "

"You have analyzed Drake's results?"

"Yes," Susan said, "it is amazing how much I can accomplish now that I no longer have to sleep. Drake, unsurprisingly, has 92 chromosomal pairs, just as you and Victor. And you will be relieved to know he also exhibits considerable uniparental disomy, just as you do."

"So most of his chromosomes come from me, not Aeron."

Susan smiled at the wry tone of voice. "Yes, just as most of yours come from Victor, an extremely unusual occurrence in nature, one that generally produces fatal results. But that's not what I found so interesting."

Susan spread out a chart on the table in front of her. "Drake also has the 'I' nucleotide, leading credence to the theory that it is something specific to your family. It seems to be passed on only in sexual reproduction and not through Sharing, because I have not identified it in anyone else. I do not know if it can be passed by the Change because Victor has Changed only you, and you have Changed no one."

Susan stood upright. "Anyway, this fifth nucleotide is acting in a very favorable way right now."

"How is that?" Ryan asked.

"This fifth nucleotide has created an RNA strand that is acting similar to a Dicer or Argonaut protein."

"And this is good because?"

Susan explained. "One of the purposes of RNA transcription is gene silencing. In other words, the ability to turn off the production of certain genes that might be harmful. That is exactly what Dicer and Argonaut proteins do in both animals and plants, in a very precise way. And that is exactly what this new RNA strand is doing. It might be why your system is easily able to accommodate the extra set of chromosomes you have. And it is probably how you fought off the virus."

"It acted as a master switch," Ryan said reflectively, "and shut down what was causing damage."

"Exactly," Susan said, "and my hope is that this is what is slowing the rate of mutation in your father's system, as opposed to any type of organic failure."

It was not a definite finding, but it was at least hopeful. "Thank you, as always," Ryan said, "is there anything I can do at this point?"

"I think we just continue to wait," Susan said. She wished she had more definitive news for Ryan, but she wanted to err on the side of caution. At least now she was cautiously optimistic. She picked up a nearby folder.

"Oh yes," Susan said, "in an unrelated matter. I got the results back from the swab I took after we tested Drake."

Ryan glanced at the paperwork in her hand. Susan seemed very pleased with herself.

"I found traces of thrombin, which is an enzyme which aids in coagulation. I have seen you several times stop bleeding by touching your lips to the wound, and now I have an explanation for it."

"It wouldn't suffice just to say a kiss made it better," Ryan said. She stood. "Well, I am taking Drake riding. Jason has asked to go as well. Would that be acceptable to you?"

Susan stared at her a long moment, and Ryan shifted uncomfortably. "What?"

Susan was mildly flustered. "Nothing, it's just—"

"What?"

Susan set down her chart. "I just appreciate your asking."

Ryan gave her another wicked grin. "Just because I am going to be King doesn't mean I will start ordering you around." She flicked an imaginary piece of lint from her shirt, then continued under her breath. "I couldn't even get away with that when you were human."

A deep blush crept up Susan's cheeks, which caught Ryan's eye. "I am so glad I am not the only one who still does that."

Susan shuffled paperwork, desperately wanting to change the subject. "Yes, you may take Jason out riding. I would never hear the end of it if I didn't let him go."

"You could go as well."

Susan stopped. She had not been riding for years, but had done so avidly as a child.

"I don't know," she said uncertainly, but Ryan could hear the wistfulness in her voice. Ryan jumped to her feet.

"I insist," she said, heading toward the door, "that's an order."

The three horses picked their way through the forest, content to amble at something less than Ryan's usual breakneck pace. Drake sat comfortably in front of Ryan, holding onto the saddle. Jason was handling his horse well, a gentle mare Ryan had chosen, and Susan was pleased to see her own riding skills were quickly returning on the steed Ryan had chosen for her.

Ryan commented on this fact. "You ride well."

The compliment pleased Susan, but her horsemanship paled in comparison to Ryan's. "And you ride as if the horse is part of you."

Ryan smiled, revealing perfect teeth. "You have to remember, dear doctor, that when I was born this was the only form of transportation available." She gave her stallion the slightest nudge, and he moved into sync next to Susan's horse.

"I was originally too poor to own a horse, but I was sent packing on one after spending the night in the stockade."

Susan glanced over at her. "And what did you do to deserve a night in the stockade?"

Ryan's tone was casual, but she lowered her voice so that Jason could not hear. "I killed a priest."

Susan's glance was sharper this time, but Ryan did not seem inclined to elaborate. Upon Susan's insistent stare, Ryan relented. "Trust me. He deserved it." She reached down to adjust Drake's position, pulling him into the fold of the kilt-like throw across her shoulder. He relaxed in the sling, gazing up at his mother in adoration. He glanced over at Susan, giggled, then returned to his inspection of Ryan.

Susan looked up. Jason had gotten quite a bit ahead of them on the trail. "Jason, why don't you hold up and wait for us?"

"That's probably a good idea right now," Ryan said, a little too casually.

In that instant, Jason's horse spooked. It whinnied once, then bolted through the forest, Jason clinging to its back. Almost before the horse bolted, Ryan was after it, leaning forward on her steed, guiding the horse with one hand while holding Drake with the other. Susan kneed her own horse and joined the chase. She could not keep up with Ryan, but she was doing a fine job of keeping them in sight. That was until Ryan veered from the path and disappeared into the forest.

Susan kept after Jason, steadily gaining on him. To his credit, he was maintaining his balance and doing what he could to regain control of the horse. He might actually have succeeded except the horse again spooked, this time braking to a sudden halt. Susan felt her heart leap into her throat as she watched Jason vault over the horse's head, arms and legs flailing.

The next events happened in slow motion for Susan. Out of the corner of her eye she saw Ryan's horse approaching Jason's at a sharp angle. But Ryan was not on the horse anymore, she was already in the air, having leaped from its back the moment Jason was launched forward. In an improbable move, she caught the back of his shirt in mid-air, holding him like a much larger version of her son. In an even greater impossibility, she did so while still casually cradling Drake in her arm. She twisted, and all three went tumbling into a pile of leaves, Ryan breaking the fall of the two boys.

Susan rode up, breathless although she no longer needed to breathe. She dismounted, thinking she heard Jason crying, but then realized he was laughing. He was buried up to his neck in leaves, and Ryan herself to her waist. Ryan could barely contain her mirth and Drake was in high spirits. The three quieted as Susan stood there with her hands on her hips.

Ryan nudged Jason. "I think you're in trouble."

Jason looked up at his mother, then back at Ryan. "I don't think it's me she's looking at."

Ryan glanced up at Susan, noting the exasperated expression. "I think you may be right."

Ryan stood, still grasping the back of Jason's shirt and bringing him easily to his feet. He brushed himself off, plucking a few leaves from Drake as well. Ryan also brushed a few leaves from Drake, who seemed greatly entertained by the entire incident. Ryan glanced up at Susan.

"Please stop looking at me like that. It reminds me of my father." She brushed a few more leaves off, then said under her breath, "Or even worse, Abigail."

Susan's expression softened, but Jason did Ryan no favors.

"You didn't need to worry mom, Ryan can run faster than that horse. Last time that happened—"

Jason's voice trailed off at Ryan's pained expression. Susan raised an eyebrow.

"The last time?"

Ryan glanced down at Jason. "Thanks." She turned to look down at Susan, who had stepped closer.

"Nothing will happen to Jason, Dr. Ryerson," Ryan said, gazing at her intently, "or to you."

Susan realized she had made a tactical error in moving so close to Ryan. It created all sorts of sensations she was incapable of dealing with. As logical and dispassionate as she tried to be, her Change had created desires in her she could not reconcile with her former life as a scientist.

It was also blocking her ability to sense anything else, a difficulty her son did not have.

"Um, Ryan?" Jason asked uncertainly. There was a trace of fear in his voice.

Ryan showed no concern. "I know, Jason, they've been here for quite some time." She turned, apparently addressing the empty forest around them.

"If you're quite through terrifying my guests, please show yourselves."

Her words were gently mocking but without anger. If anything, there was a trace of pleasure in her voice. Susan looked around, suddenly able to sense what Ryan had so easily perceived.

The forest appeared to shift and move, then figures began to materialize from the shadows. Susan was quite certain she would have been frozen in fear had Ryan not been present, and Jason shifted closer to Ryan as well. Only Drake looked on without fear, taking his cue from his mother.

The figures were all ebony-skinned, some black as night, all clean-shaven. As a whole, they possessed piercing dark eyes above strong jaws, beautiful princely features. Although they wore contemporary clothing, the cloth seemed barely able to contain the bulging muscles and rippling sinews of their bodies.

One particularly handsome man stepped forward, his dark eyes intense, his face expressionless. Ryan gazed at him a long moment.

"You're not going to crucify me, are you?"

Kokumuo gazed at her. "You're not going to let me forget that, are you?"

"Not in this lifetime," Ryan replied. She flicked her gaze up and down his strong form. "I think I prefer you in your traditional garb."

Kokumuo returned the rather insolent inspection. "I rather preferred you in at as well."

Ryan smiled. They had both been wearing next to nothing when they had met before. "You forget, my friend. That was your garb. Mine would be a full suit of armor."

"Hmm," was all Kokumuo said. He then barked a command in Swahili to his men, and went to one knee. All of his troupe followed, bowing low. Jason watched the scene with wide eyes.

"That will be enough of that," Ryan said a little uncomfortably. "I think I'd prefer the crucifixion."

Kokumuo and his men rose to their feet as one. Kokumuo's tone was respectful with just the slightest trace of lecture. "You will have to get used to that, my lord." He changed the subject. "Ala has requested your presence." He turned a pointed glance to the child she held in her arms, "and she wishes to see your little one as well."

Ryan cocked her head to the side. "She knows of my son?"

Kokumuo nodded. "She has known for quite some time."

Ryan smiled to herself. That did not surprise her. Ala had gifts similar to Victor's, ways of knowing that went beyond time and space. And if anyone would have sensed the boy's presence, it would have been the primordial nature mother herself.

Ryan made a clicking noise, and all three horses obediently approached. Ryan gave Jason a leg up, noting that several of Kokumuo's men elbowed one another to assist Susan to her mount. Ryan mounted her own horse effortlessly, Drake still cradled in one arm. She wheeled the stallion about.

"Then I will not keep Ala waiting."

Ryan took the steps to the mansion two at a time, Drake balanced on her shoulders. She could feel Ala's wonderful, earthy sensuality and greatly desired to see her. She glanced down at herself. She also greatly needed a bath. Jason's rescue operation had left her somewhat muddied.

Edward materialized at the door. "Ala—" he stopped short, noting her soiled appearance. "—can wait until you are more presentable."

Ryan did not break stride. "Please forward my apologies and tell Ala I will be with her momentarily."

Ryan took the indoor stairs two at a time as well, still balancing Drake on her shoulders. The boy held on to her head as she disappeared upward with breathtaking speed.

Edward watched his master disappear, his patrician features stern with disapproval. "Indeed."

Ryan pushed through the doors of her chambers and onto the open baths beyond. Victor had been a great admirer of the Turkish baths and for centuries had designed his manors with elaborate bathing areas. This one was no different, with steps down into a gradually sloped ledge that dropped into a deep pool. The pool was fed by an underground hot spring and steam filled the room. There were seating areas beneath the surface where one could relax neck-deep in the water. A waterfall/shower bordered the far wall, sprinkling cool water for a post-bath rinse.

Drake clapped his hands in excitement. The baths were one of his favorite activities.

"We don't have a lot of time today," Ryan said to him, quickly stripping him down. She set him down in the shallow water at the pool's edge, then quickly stripped her own clothing. She dove into the steaming hot water, then re-emerged next to the ledge where the boy sat.

"Come on, let's get you clean."

Drake could sense his mother's urgency, but would have none of it. He slapped the water around him, then kicked his feet, spraying water in Ryan's face. She gazed into her son's twinkling eyes with mock seriousness.

"Oh, is that how you want it. Well fine."

She gently slapped the water as well, creating little sprays that sent him into a paroxysm of giggles. He reached out and placed his tiny hands on her cheeks, pulling her to him.

"Look, little mister. I have responsibilities. I cannot keep the Old Ones waiting so you can play in the bath."

"Please do not hurry on my account."

The voice had a deep, melodic quality to it, mellow and caramel-smooth. An immense, ebony-skinned woman stood at the top of the stairs, magnificent in both size and beauty. She possessed an elemental magnetism, ancient and irresistible. If Abigail was the matriarch of their Kind, then Ala surely was the earth mother. Ala settled gracefully onto the top steps, raising the hem of her elaborate robe in order to place her bare feet in the warm water. She was quickly surrounded by several of her escorts, whom she waved off.

Ryan smiled and greeted the Old One. "Habari mama."

Ala eyed the small boy who was watching her intently from a few feet away. He gave a few hesitant slaps to the water while contemplating this newcomer. Ala assessed him for a moment, then motioned for him to approach. Drake stood, the water coming only to his ankles on the shallow ledge, and toddled over to the woman's open arms.

Ryan was unsurprised, and less so when the boy curled up on Ala's lap, resting his head against her breast. He settled in, a look of deep contentment on his face. Ryan thought for a moment he was going to go to sleep. She sighed aloud.

"I know just how you feel, little one."

She knifed back into the water, swiftly finishing her bath without the distraction of the boy. She pulled herself from the water, quickly rinsing and drying off. She disappeared for a moment, reappearing in her usual casual attire.

"I trust Edward showed you to your chambers?" Ryan asked, toweling her hair.

Ala nodded, still gazing down at the little boy. Ryan watched the scene, touched. Ala could be an extremely imposing figure, terrifying if she chose to be. And yet she held the boy as gently as if he had been a newborn. Ryan made the snap decision that if anything ever happened to her, she would entrust the boy to Ala.

Ryan stopped. That was an odd thought.

Ala looked up, and Ryan was not certain if Ala had read her thoughts or merely felt her emotions. Either way, Ala understood exactly what Ryan meant.

"I do not believe anything will ever happen to you, my liege."

The significance of the statement as well as the title hung in the air. Ala had only used that designation with her father.

"But," Ala continued, "if the need should ever arise, I will protect the boy with my life and care for him as my own."

Ryan nodded, deeply grateful for the loyalty and allegiance to both her and her son. But she could not shake the strange disquiet the earlier thought had created. On cue, Edward appeared and collected Drake. Ala handed the now sleeping boy to the manservant while her gaze remained upon Ryan. Ryan approached and settled beside her, enjoying the warmth, both physical and spiritual, that emanated from Ala.

"You are still having your visions," Ala said.

Although Ryan had only known Ala a few years, Ala often had more insight into her than those who had known her for centuries. Ryan knew that Victor possessed the first sight, an ability to sense future events, although he claimed he could see them only dimly. Ala had a different gift, an ability to sense things as they occurred, regardless of distance. Many of their Kind possessed the ability to sense one another from afar. But Ala's abilities went beyond that.

"I am seeing many strange things these days," Ryan said, "and I am not certain why." She thought about the strange, reptilian creature that seemed to lurk just beyond the edge of the netherworld. A symbolic figment of her imagination she was certain, but one whose meaning she could not determine. The fear the creature inspired was definitely real, an emotion that was deeply unfamiliar to Ryan.

Ala felt the wide range of the girl's emotions, allowing them to drift through her without contact so that she could experience them fully. Ryan continued.

"I actually feel as if I am seeing through someone's eyes, someone who is not of our Kind, and someone I believe predates even my father."

Ala's eyes widened. She had always been fascinated by the fact that none of their Kind had any knowledge of where they came from. Even Victor's mind was completely blank concerning his origins. The fact that the girl might be sensing some trace of that beginning was enormously significant. It was extremely exciting to Ala, whose traditions of her native culture placed great emphasis on ancestry.

"None of it is clear," Ryan said, shaking her head. She seemed frustrated. "And I don't know that any of it means anything."

Her thoughts on the matter quite different, Ala held her tongue. It was better not to influence the girl at this time, rather better to let the visions continue until they coalesced. She rose to her feet effortlessly, proffering her hand to Ryan.

"I understand you have spent the week satisfying the Old Ones."

Ryan took the hand, also rising to her feet. She smiled at the remark as Ala continued.

"And yet you yourself have not fed."

There was slight scolding in the remark, and a trace of curiosity.

"I was running an experiment," Ryan said mischievously, "I wanted to see how much my system could bear."

Ala's rebuke was gentle and without sting. "I fear Dr. Ryerson is a bad influence on you." Her tone lowered to a conspiratorial whisper as the two started toward the door. "So how is your experiment coming along?"

The invitation in that low, melodic voice was unmistakable. Ryan closed her eyes as the warmth of Ala settled over her.

"I think it's over now."

Many hours later, Ala watched as the girl slept. Kokumuo fussed over her a bit, making certain she was comfortable in her near-unconscious state. Ala inwardly smiled. Kokumuo was not one to fuss over anyone, but he did so now over a creature who was indestructible and invulnerable. Astonishing the effect this girl had on all of their Kind. Ala wondered if that blue-eyed youngster would have a similar effect, and somehow knew that he would.

There was a brief knock at the door and Kusunoki entered. Kokumuo excused himself, nodding respectfully as he departed. Kusunoki settled beside Ala, and the comfortable silence that ensued bespoke of the long companionship they had enjoyed.

It was Kusunoki who finally broke that silence.

"And so the pieces are moved about the board once more."

Ala contemplated his words before replying.

"Yes, but is it a chess board or are we playing Go?" Ala asked.

It was a wise question, and Go was perhaps the better answer. Both were games of strategy and tactics, but unlike chess, where the objective was the absolute defeat of the opponent by capturing the King, the objective of Go was to control the largest part of the board. Stones were placed on a grid and were captured when surrounded on all sides by stones of the opposing color. The goal was to form territories that could not be captured by an opponent. The game ended when neither player could move. It was perhaps a better metaphor for the endless stratagems of their Kind.

Kusunoki watched the sleeping girl. Although Ryan had been Changed at the age of nineteen, she generally had an ageless quality about her that could make her appear much older. Right now she did not even look nineteen. He returned to the metaphor thoughtfully.

"At least in Go, the stones remain the same color. In our version, the colors seem to change at whim."

Ala carefully thought of Abigail, careful in that her thoughts were shielded. She knew how powerful the matriarch was, and her proximity made her even more so. Ala would not resist a barb, however.

"Yes," she agreed, "and some of those stones don't seem to be black or white."

Muffled laughter came from her companion. Kusunoki appreciated Ala's caution, but her fearlessness even more. He again grew contemplative.

He had spent hours playing Go with Ryan. She always chose the black stones; he always played the white. In her youth, he had beaten her often. Now, those victories were far less frequent. He was as proud of her skill at the game as he was her skill with a sword, and he had taught her both.

"I don't know," Ala said thoughtfully, "even if those stones keep changing colors, somehow I see Ryan sitting with a board full of black stones at the end of the game."

Kusunoki silently agreed.

CHAPTER 14

AMBROSIUS STARED INTO THE FLAMES of his fire. His hill fortress was secure, but he had a sense of foreboding at the moment, a sense he had learned to pay heed to. These many years since Tristan's death had brought great responsibility to him, and although the warlords were numerous, none were as powerful as he.

Some, however, were far more destructive, intentionally or not. Ambrosius raised his head as the Welsh messenger arrived.

"Let me guess," Ambrosius said, "Infaustus has struck again."

The messenger hid a smile. "Infaustus" was not Gwrtheyrn's name, but it was how the great commander referred to him. It meant "unlucky" with a connotation of great incompetence.

"My lord, the Saxon mercenaries Gwrtheyrn allowed to settle are beginning to cause trouble. There is even rumor that his actions have created a perception of weakness and cowardice, and the Saxons are planning a full invasion."

"That would not surprise me," Ambrosius said, sighing. If anything, the Saxons were consistent. They respected only force. "And where might this invasion force be staging?"

The messenger swallowed hard. "It is rumored that troops are gathering at Mynydd Baddon."

"Mons Badonicus," Ambrosius murmured to himself. An interesting choice. It was terrain that would favor a large attacking force. The Saxons must be coming en masse.

"Send words throughout my lands," Ambrosius said, "any man who will follow me should gather before the full moon."

The messenger nodded, grateful for the commander's quick action. And every man he knew would follow this one.

Ambrosius walked through the camp, respectfully greeted by all he passed. It was the night before battle and there was much tension in the air as last-minute preparations were made. Seasoned veterans spoke quietly amongst themselves while checking their battle-gear one last time. Novice youths who days before had bragged to one another of their future exploits now sat nervously in silence, somberly gazing into the campfires. The presence of the commander brought calm and reassurance to both the veteran and the raw recruit as he made his way through the camp.

Ambrosius himself was not afraid. He had been in too many battles now to feel fear. Instead, he felt a tension that was almost pleasant, an anticipation to engage in the activity for which he had been born.

As was his custom after making his rounds, Ambrosius walked into the forest alone. He would remain in solitude for the next few hours, at first mentally rehearsing his battle strategy, then calming his mind to stillness. His senior officers knew not to disturb him.

Ambrosius settled on a large rock. The moon shone brightly enough that he could clearly see the forest around him.

"I told you they would return."

Ambrosius leaped to his feet, sword in hand. He whirled toward the voice, his instinct causing him to react before his memory took hold.

Ravlen gazed at the menacing sword without fear, entertained as always. She pushed the point away, unconcerned by the deadly blade.

Ambrosius lowered the sword, stunned. He had not seen her in almost two decades, and yet she had not changed at all. She was still dazzling, a flawless goddess.

He, however, Ravlen noted with pleasure, had changed significantly. He was truly a man, now, broad through the shoulders and chest, with strong, muscular arms and legs. He wore his dark hair to his collar with a short, neatly trimmed beard on his chin. Time had turned the beautiful boy into a ruggedly handsome man. There was an intelligence and melancholy in his eyes that was irresistible.

"Oh, my handsome warrior, do not look at me that way."

"You left me," Ambrosius said, unable to hide his emotion. "All my life I have been a hollow shell."

Ravlen stepped away from him, examining the leaves on a nearby tree. "You should have taken a wife," she said, "it is unseemly that one such as yourself has no offspring."

Ambrosius took two steps toward her and grabbed her by the shoulders, turning her around. He had the sense that what he was doing was very dangerous, and that he was able to do so only because she allowed it. Although Ambrosius was one of the tallest men in the land, they were easily eye-to-eye.

"You are my wife," he said, his voice hoarse, "while you exist in any form, even in memory, I can have no other."

She smiled at him, again that smile one would reserve for a child. Not condescending, but rather gently admonishing, as if he simply did not understand.

"Well then, my husband," she said, "perform your marital duty."

Ambrosius crushed her into an embrace and took her to the ground. His passion for her was all-consuming, a passion she easily matched. Although Ambrosius was incredibly strong, he felt this woman could have crushed his bones if she so chose.

It would have been a death he welcomed. And for the next several hours, he welcomed that death again and again.

Ambrosius stirred, reaching out to his side. The space was empty but the ground was still warm. He sat upright, and was relieved to see that Ravlen was still there standing at the edge of the trees. She had her back to him as she stared out into the meadow below. He took a moment to examine her lithe form, memorizing every line and curve of her body.

Ambrosius felt a great sadness settle over him. He stood and quickly dressed. Ravlen did not move, nor turn toward him.

He finally cleared his throat. "I am not going to see you again, am I."

Ravlen turned toward him, an unfathomable look in her eye. It was difficult to say if she was sad, or relieved, or if in fact, she felt anything at all. The only sense Ambrosius had was that, as always, she seemed mildly amused.

"No," she said, the slightest trace of regret in her voice, "you will not."

Ambrosius looked down at the ground in front of him, struggling with his emotions. His throat ached with words he would not say, and his heart throbbed painfully in his chest. He felt hot tears gather beneath his eyelids, and blinked quickly to drive them away.

It did not matter, however, because when he looked back up, Ravlen was gone.

He clenched his jaw, turned on his heel, and began striding back to camp.

The men watched as their leader strode from the forest, trying to gauge his mood. He was solemn, his dark eyes filled with some deep emotion they could not assess. But he was not afraid, that much was evident. If anything there was a pronounced lack of fear, the fearlessness of one who had nothing to lose. His bearing was confident, as if the outcome of this day had already been determined, yet now meant very little to him.

As the barbarian horde began to stage, the men continued to glance toward their leader. Ambrosius watched the Saxons gather, their numbers staggering, the mass extending across the entire horizon. Yet still he showed no fear, and his demeanor gave his men comfort and assurance. He knew the well-armed barbarians would attack first, possessing ferocity but little discipline, and he was soon proved correct.

Ambrosius led the counter charge and although his men had seen him fight in many battles, they had never seen him fight like this. He appeared as one possessed, his strength, skill, and endurance unmatched by any on the field. Barbarians fell by his sword, first a dozen, then scores, and as the day wore on, hundreds. All would agree that the general fought as if neither life nor death had any hold on him.

Legends were born at Mount Badon on that day. Ambrosius went into battle as one already dead, and many say for that reason he could not be killed. A thousand Saxons fell before his blade and before the day was done, he had turned the barbarian invasion back into the sea.

Although the Saxon conquest of the British Isle would one day succeed, it was stopped entirely in the lifetime of Ambrosius Aurelianus.

Ryan awoke, a great heaviness upon her. The dream had seemed so real, and the sadness of the man so deep it physically pained her. She had no idea who the man or mysterious woman were, but somehow she had the feeling that she would not dream of them again.

CHAPTER 15

THE DOOR TO ABIGAIL'S SUITE WHISPERED OPEN upon her approach. The servant who held it bowed as Ryan strode into the room. Abigail was seated on the pale blue couch reading a book. She looked up as Ryan entered the room. The servant quickly excused himself and Ryan stopped a few feet from Abigail, her manner both formal and polite.

"You requested my presence?"

Abigail examined the girl, an inspection that went far beyond merely physical. Ryan was patient beneath the assessment, having undergone it many times over the centuries.

"And will you," Abigail asked with steel gentility, "respond to my requests so willingly once you are King?"

Ryan settled into the chair across from her. "I am not certain my response is 'willing' even now. But," she added, "I do not see my level of compliance changing."

Abigail set the book aside, pleased with the answer. She enjoyed the girl's cleverness as much as her more physical talents. She did not, however, delay making her point.

"Although it was little more than a formality, the Old Ones were unanimous in their acceptance of you as new leader of the hierarchy."

Ryan absorbed the news. It was not really a surprise, but it did provide some relief as another step completed. "I wonder," she said, no trace of regret in her voice, "how unanimous the vote would have been were Aeron still here."

Abigail's response was firm. "Aeron is not here." When Ryan did not appear satisfied, she added, "And a four-to-one vote would still have been binding."

"And would it have been four-to-one?"

The response would have blind-sided a lesser adversary. But Abigail was no ordinary opponent and she was unfazed by the question.

"Do you think I would vote against you, having gone to so much trouble to bring you to this point?"

Ryan contemplated her words. Although it was not the most reassuring response, the reasoning was sound and consistent with Abigail's usual calculating manner. It did not provide her any ease. Abigail sensed the girl's continued pensiveness. She leaned forward slightly. Her tone was quiet but her words were intense.

"Do you not trust me even now?"

The clenching of her jaw was visible as Ryan struggled to resist the magnetism of the woman across from her. When she responded, however, it was with complete honesty.

"I don't know."

The answer did not displease Abigail nearly as much as Ryan thought it would. It actually seemed to entertain her more than anything.

"And is that upon the advice of your father?"

The reference to her father surprised Ryan, not only because it was out-of-place, but because it was completely accurate.

"Victor told me," Ryan said slowly, "to trust no one."

Abigail stared at her with her unblinking gaze. "Yes that sounds like him." She leaned back into the couch. "Then it might surprise you to know that your father did in fact trust me."

With mild skepticism, Ryan asked, "In what way?"

Abigail appeared to be enjoying herself. "He entrusted me with that which was most dear to his heart."

Knowing what she was referring to, but disbelieving what she was hearing, Ryan waited for Abigail to finish.

"You."

"My father," Ryan said doubtfully, "entrusted me to you?"

The girl's uncertainty entertained Abigail even further. "Yes, he left me with two very simple instructions. I was to safeguard your welfare–"

Ryan wondered how Victor would assess the success of that edict.

"–And see that you assumed leadership of the hierarchy. And in two weeks time, I will have accomplished both."

Her brow furrowing, Ryan struggled to grasp what she was hearing. Although she could not fathom his reasoning, it sounded exactly like something Victor would do. He had to have known Abigail was the most dangerous of the Others, both in a general sense and very specifically, to her. To task her with Ryan's care was both a brilliant and exceedingly perilous tactic. One that apparently had been successful.

"What," Ryan asked slowly, repeating a question she had asked years before, "did my father offer you in return for your assistance?"

She received the same answer.

"You," Abigail said simply.

Ryan settled into a stunned silence. The machinations of the Old Ones, including her father, never ceased to amaze her. She had not the patience nor the guile to involve herself in such subterfuge, and certainly not the desire. She had no idea how she was going to be King over such an assembly.

"Actually my dear," Abigail said softly, reading her thoughts, "that is exactly why you will make such an excellent King."

She continued, deeply thoughtful. "Sometimes I envy your lack of ambition, it makes you extremely powerful."

If Ryan was taken aback by the earlier revelations, Abigail's words now utterly silenced her. Such a confession from the matriarch was unheard of. But if Ryan interpreted the admission as a sign of weakness, the predatory gleam in Abigail's eye made her think otherwise.

"But it also leaves you open to manipulation by those who do possess ambition."

"And is that what you do to me?" Ryan asked quietly, "manipulate me to further your own ambition?"

Abigail's gaze rested on the girl's lips, then moved to the vein that ran alongside her throat. "You forget, my dear," she said leisurely but with emphasis, "I already have everything I want."

This at last forced Ryan to complete silence. She sat in the chair for a long time, a look of distraction on her face. Abigail watched the range of emotions flit across the girl's features, and as always, was enamored by the unconscious display.

She gently broke the silence. "I made an observation about you centuries ago, when you were but an infant."

Ryan looked up at her.

"I said the most dangerous thing about seducing you was not knowing who was seducing whom."

Ryan held her gaze. "And do you now have an answer for that conundrum?"

"No," Abigail said simply with a smile. "I do not."

The exchange seemed to release the tension in Ryan. She let the confused thoughts drift away. A few moments later, she changed the subject entirely.

"Were there any other matters from the Grand Council?"

"Just one," Abigail replied as Ryan steeled herself, "you must designate a Second at your coronation."

Ryan tried to assess Abigail's tone, to see if there was anything underlying her words. But the matriarch was being purposely enigmatic. Unwilling to play any more games, Ryan asked her outright.

"And do you have a suggestion?"

Without hesitation, Abigail replied, "Kusunoki."

Both surprised and pleased at the response, Ryan was wary.

"And your reasoning?"

"Kusunoki is extremely powerful," Abigail said casually, "and utterly loyal to you. He would make an excellent Second."

And he is no threat to you, Ryan said inwardly, doing nothing to hide her thoughts.

Abigail did not respond, merely smiled her cool smile. She leaned over to retrieve her book from the end table, and Ryan knew she had been dismissed.

CHAPTER 16

RYAN STOOD IN THE SHADOWED ALCOVE. The last time she had stood in this position, she was about to stand trial for her father's murder and her failure to take his place in the hierarchy. The irony was not lost on her.

The Great Hall had been significantly modified for this occasion. Its standard structure was unalterable, for it was many stories under ground, possessing impossibly high ceilings supported by walls of solid rock. Alcoves were carved in the rock walls and balconies hung from extraordinary heights. These features were unchangeable. But it was now decorated in a formal style with finery that covered centuries. Ancient, priceless tapestries hung with renaissance artwork. Golden statues mingled with irreplaceable marble carvings. Candles, lamps, and torches cast a warm glow, flickering light in all directions. The enormous chamber was lit entirely by flame.

Susan Ryerson sat toward the front of the assembly in what she was certain was a place of honor. She wished she had been sitting in the back of the room. She and Raphael were attracting an inordinate amount of attention. They were by far the youngest in the room, probably by several centuries. And she was definitely the only Young One. Her newly acquired senses were only making things worse because she could hear the varied whispers and speculations regarding her presence. The proximity of so many of the Others would have been agonizing under normal circumstances, the heightened expectation and excitement due to the ceremony made it unbearable.

Susan felt an immense presence and looked up to find Marilyn standing in front of her. This attracted even more attention as the eyes of nearly everyone in the room followed the dark-haired beauty. She was wearing a stunning, blood-red gown that somehow would have been just as appropriate in the year 1350 as it was at the present. Desire and longing trailed her like some great, invisible veil, complementing the outfit.

Marilyn's dark eyes flashed with enjoyment; she was obviously in high spirits. She was quite aware of the doctor's discomfort. "It is interesting, is it not, the currents that flow between our Kind?"

Susan glanced around her. That was a huge understatement. It was as if some great web of sensation bound them all together, each movement, thought, and emotion sending vibrations throughout, felt and experienced by all the rest. Some, like Marilyn, had the ability to influence the entire web, collecting strands by mere movement, slicing through filament as she pleased, leaving a swath of pleasure and destruction in her wake.

To Susan's chagrin, she felt the presence of another One who had such ability in even greater measure. She turned at Abigail's approach, realizing that now, for certain, everyone in the room was watching them. The pressure of so many eyes was now inconsequential compared to the power of the two standing in front of her. She had the sudden impulse to stand, then regretted the act when she realized how much shorter she was than both Marilyn and Abigail.

Abigail was dressed in her own stunning finery, a gorgeous pale blue gown that accented her smooth skin. Susan tried not to stare at the graceful neck. Abigail observed Susan's discomfort with her usual cool amusement. She turned to Marilyn.

"This reminds me of the first time Victor brought Ryan to the Others, when she was a Young One and quite oblivious to our Kind."

Marilyn assessed the memory fondly. "Yes, when she came in late and was dressed like a stable boy." A thought occurred to Marilyn. "You did dress her today, didn't you?"

The remark further amused Abigail, although there was a trace of concern in her reply. "No, I did not. I hope that was not an oversight."

Marilyn was trying to picture what Ryan might show up in. "I certainly hope she's not wearing jeans." Whatever vision she had of Ryan's attire obviously gave her pleasure, and Susan did not want to ask.

Another presence entered and Susan turned to see Ala and her closest consorts take their places. This redirected some of the attention away from them as Ala possessed her own massive gravitational pull. Susan took the opportunity to quickly retake her seat. Some unknown signal seemed to have passed as both Marilyn and Abigail began drifting towards their assigned places, Marilyn's in the front row, and Abigail's on the raised dais in the front of the room.

The energy in the room suddenly and dramatically increased, although to Susan's eyes nothing had happened. She tried to assess the feeling clinically, trying to compare it to something she knew. It reminded her of the sharp drop in atmospheric pressure right before a major thunderstorm, the kind that made every living creature's hair stand on end. The murmuring and movement in the room settled into utter stillness, oddly duplicating that strange calm right before a storm.

Ryan stood in the alcove, eyes closed, perfectly composed. She was utterly still, utterly controlled, in a near-perfect meditative state. No trace of her presence could be felt, even to Kusunoki who stood right next to her. He was astonished at her mental control. It was perhaps his proudest moment with his pupil.

Ryan opened her eyes, but still did not move. Edward felt the tautness in his master, like a bow string drawn to its extreme and then held motionless for an eternity. Although he had not drawn a breath in centuries, he found himself holding his now.

"It is time," Ryan said simply.

Kusunoki and Edward stepped forward to open the great doors. Ryan took a single step through the open doors and stopped.

Abigail, the only one facing the doorway, smiled. Slowly, one by one, people in the Great Hall began turning around, more to see what the matriarch was looking at rather than sensing anything themselves. They began to get haphazardly to their feet, some out of respect, some so they could get a better view. Ryan simply stood there, fully composed, as murmurs went through the crowd at her appearance.

She wore the breastplate of the ceremonial armor of the House of Alexander. As much a work of art as a method of protection, the black plate was elaborately etched with medieval design. It flared outward at the shoulders, giving an already formidable figure a terrifying size. A black tunic was worn over the armor, drawn at the waist, then divided down the front below the waist to the knees. The tunic was emblazoned with the gold dragon crest of the Alexander line. A blood-red cape draped around the shoulders flowed rearward, and a gleaming broadsword was attached to the waist belt. Ryan had foregone the gauntlets and greaves, opting instead for a simple black shirt, pants, and boots which offset the dramatic half-armor to perfection. The darkness of the outfit was in stark contrast to her light hair, which appeared almost white in the illumination of the Great Hall.

It was arresting, it was awe-inspiring, it was the clothing of a Warrior King, one as much from some alien future as from the past.

Abigail was greatly pleased. Every once in awhile, the girl took her completely by surprise. She herself could not have picked more perfect attire. And some present would remember it was exactly what Victor had worn to his coronation, albeit with some minor adjustments for space age materials.

Ryan still stood in the center of the aisle, Edward and Kusunoki flanking each side. No one seemed to be able to sense her presence, and she was exhibiting the same tautness in her body she had in the alcove. Edward, completely against protocol, actually glanced around him at the spectators. The fact that Ryan was capable of this always astonished him. He could feel as the Others began to reach out to her.

The tension in the room grew to excruciating levels. Some actually appeared distressed at the unyielding pressure they could feel but not fully perceive. All were now extending their senses in the direction of the One standing in the doorway.

Abigail watched the scene, entertained by the high drama. This was the equivalent of having someone stare into an unlit lamp, bemused as to why it would not illuminate, then having the light suddenly blind them. Only in this case, the intensity of the light was closer to that of an imploding star. Abigail sensed the girl was waiting for something, something from her. It pleased her.

Show them, she said silently to Ryan.

Ryan made a slight movement of her shoulders, a gesture so subtle it seemed little more than a shrug. But it had a spectacular effect. A tidal wave of sensation swept forward through the hall, striking each person to a greater or lesser degree. Susan nearly fell and was caught by Raphael, who himself stumbled at the blow. Marilyn caught her breath as the pleasurable heat passed through her. Ala closed her eyes at the wondrous feeling, and Abigail herself allowed the vibration to hum through her system. But she knew the girl was capable of more.

No, she directed silently, show them everything.

Ryan focused her concentration to a single point, then gave another shrug, a barely perceptible shift of her shoulder that caused the cape to flutter. Before she had merely released her perceptual veil; now she displayed her full power. A shockwave slammed forward through the assembly, not the kind emanating from a violent disturbance but rather the kind generated from a steady supersonic flow. If the Old Ones had the ability to influence the entire web, Ryan had the ability to shatter it entirely through pure harmonic vibration.

Which she chose not to do. Instead, she began striding forward with Kusunoki at her side. A slightly-numbed Edward snapped back to the matter at hand and quickly caught up. There was murmuring amongst the crowd, but beyond that, only the rhythmic clank of the sword at Ryan's side made any noise in the Great Hall. Ryan appeared serious and solemn, her eyes on the dais ahead, fully mindful of the weight of the moment. But as she approached Susan, she glanced left and gave a quick wink, turning her head back forward without pause. Susan hid a smile. King or not, Ryan was still incorrigible.

Ryan started up the steps towards Abigail. She sensed the older woman's great pleasure in her right now. Ryan normally cared little for ceremony but she understood the significance of this event, and whether or not it mattered to her did not matter. She stopped at the top of the stairs, facing the current leader of the Grand Council.

Abigail examined the girl. She was magnificent in every way. Possessing such remarkable androgyny, the garments she wore did not make her more masculine or less feminine, largely because such terms were both insufficient and meaningless for her. Strikingly beautiful, she could have modeled for the archangels of Renaissance paintings, although the angel she most epitomized was perhaps the fallen one.

Ryan was very aware of Abigail's thoughts, and although fully cognizant of the reverence of the moment, could not resist insolently lowering her eyes so that they lingered on Abigail's throat, then on the décolletage of her dress. Edward caught his master's glance out of the corner of his eye and looked over, loudly clearing his throat. Ryan obediently raised her gaze, the corner of her mouth twitching.

Abigail forcibly suppressed the desire that coiled upward. The girl truly was impossible and would certainly pay for that later, King or not.

"Let's get this over with before the situation degenerates entirely," Abigail said dryly, loud enough for only those on the stage to hear.

With great formality, Kusunoki held out the cushion which held the ceremonial crown of the leader of the hierarchy. It was a beautiful piece, pure gold with little adornment other than its intricate design. Ryan went to one knee so that Abigail could place the crown upon her head. She, too, spoke just loud enough for those nearest her to hear.

"I don't suppose this will be the last time in this position, crown or not."

Kusunoki, despite himself, chuckled. Abigail ignored him, responding to the barb with her own. "I rather prefer you on both knees, my dear, if not flat on your back."

Ryan stood upright, and although she and Abigail were nearly the same height, she appeared to tower over her for the moment. Her eyes twinkled with mischief. "I guess I deserved that."

Abigail's gaze lingered on her throat for a moment. "That and much more, my dear."

Those in the audience could see what was occurring on the stage, but had the feeling there was far more going on than met the eye. Still, a great cheer went up in the hall as Ryan turned to face her Kind. After centuries, the hierarchy was complete once more.

As Ryan raised her hand, the hall fell into expectant silence. She spoke in normal tones, but her voice carried clearly over the expanse of the room.

"As is my right and prerogative, I name Kusunoki Masahige as my Second, to act in my behalf should the need arise."

A pleased murmur greeted this announcement as Ryan continued.

"Although it is also my right to dissolve the Grand Council as a ruling body, I would ask that the Council remain assembled and available in an advisory capacity." Ryan looked to Ala, then to Marilyn, then nodded respectfully to Abigail. "With the permission of the Old Ones, of course."

It was a gracious and humble request, one that was also met with pleased murmuring from the crowd. Many had entered with preconceived notions of the powerful upstart who had upended the chain of command by her strange birth. Ryan Alexander was already proving to be a surprise as a leader.

Abigail was now even more pleased with the girl. Ryan had acted with perfection on this date. Abigail nodded at the request. "The Grand Council would be honored."

Ryan gave a short bow, then turned back to the assembly. "Then, as we are now whole once more, let us move from ceremony to celebration."

Susan moved about the room, clinging to Raphael's arm. After the intensity of the ceremony, she would gladly have foregone this part of the festivities.

Or so she told herself. She had to admit it was incredibly exciting being around the Others. Although she was trying to maintain her detached professionalism, it was impossible. The air was filled with a pleasurable tension, a tension that felt like sexual desire in overdrive.

It was as if everyone in the room was evaluating everyone else as a potential suitor. Which, she realized, was exactly what they were doing with no attempt at subtlety. Everyone was categorizing and being categorized, assessed in normal classes of attractiveness and desirability, but also by the unseen qualities of power and ability.

Susan glanced around. There truly was no one unattractive in the room, and some were absolutely stunning. Her glance brought unexpected attention as she inadvertently made eye contact with a handsome young man whose invitation was obvious in his eye. But the predatory aspect to his smile sent a chill down her spine, and she quickly looked away.

She could feel others reach out to touch her, and Raphael's hand on her arm was bringing her no comfort. She could feel the dangerous desire begin to rise in her, a certain recklessness that was foreign to her nature. She could feel Raphael struggle to protect her, but he was no match for the power in this room. She could hear the murmurs of those around her, some sympathetic, some merely entertained at her plight.

Susan felt a hand caress her face, but there was nothing there. She felt other hands on her body and looked down, but again, there was nothing there. Some of the caresses were nearing inappropriate areas. The invisible hands began to pull at her, and she actually took an involuntary step before she fought off the sensation. Her heart began to beat rapidly, her fear activating a vestigial human response. The murmurs grew louder, reaching a crescendo in her ears although she was certain they were at normal conversation levels. Her fear increased, both for what she was feeling and the dangerous, self-destructive reaction it was provoking in her. She needed to leave right now, but her resolve was crumbling.

The murmuring was deafening now, surpassed only by the thunderous beating of her heart. She was both terrified and humiliated, and turned to flee.

And ran into a brick wall.

"Shhh," Ryan said softly in her ear, instantly calming her. Her arms were about the young woman, having caught her in an embrace as she turned to run. Susan was never more thankful to see anyone in her entire life, and for a moment simply buried her head in Ryan's shirt.

There was stunned silence about the room. No one had expected Ryan's presence at so informal a gathering; it was unheard of. Nor were they expecting any of the Old Ones, so they were equally surprised when Marilyn slipped up beside Ryan, placing her hands about the girl's waist. She pressed against her back, whispering in her ear.

"Do not be angry, ma Cherie. You know they cannot help themselves. It is our way."

Ryan felt her anger teeter on the edge of fury. She just as strongly felt Marilyn's soothing presence settle forcefully over her. No one in the room had any illusions that anyone other than Marilyn was capable of controlling the events of the next few seconds.

Ryan turned her head to the side to address the raven-haired beauty. "I know," she said quietly, tightly controlled, "it is the only reason why I have not killed everyone in this room."

Marilyn reached up to caress Ryan's cheek, turning the girl's chin slightly so that Ryan was looking at her.

"See, I knew you would make a good King, capable of such restraint."

Ryan felt her anger dissipate entirely, completely distracted by Marilyn's flirtation. Her eyes settled on Marilyn's lips. "And since when do you value restraint?"

Marilyn smiled, knowing she had successfully dampened Ryan's explosive temper. She adjusted her position, now merely enjoying her proximity to the girl.

"Under most circumstances, I don't value it at all."

"Hmm," Ryan said, turning her attention back to Susan as the young woman raised her head and took a step backward. She was obviously embarrassed. Ryan grasped her by the shoulders and looked her deeply in the eye.

"You will be fine, now."

"I'm, I'm sorry," Susan stammered, "I don't know what happened."

Ryan smiled mischievously. "I do." She turned as Kokumuo approached, resplendent in the native attire he had changed into. He bowed low to Ryan.

"Is everything all right, my King?"

"Everything is fine," Ryan said. She nodded to Susan, "Kokumuo, I don't believe you have been formally introduced to Dr. Ryerson."

Kokumuo bowed low to Susan, showing great respect despite the fact she was a Young One. Ryan continued.

"Susan Ryerson," Ryan said with emphasis, "is my friend."

Kokumuo nodded his understanding. "I see," was all he said.

Susan was not certain exactly what had just transpired, but as Marilyn pulled Ryan away, two enormous, ebony-skinned men settled in behind her. When Susan turned to glance at the fearsome pair, they nodded to her respectfully, then returned to their vigil. Susan felt equal parts embarrassment and relief, but relief quickly won out as she took comfort in their presence.

The room had settled into silence as the scene unfolded, and now the murmuring slowly returned. The shock of seeing the recently-crowned ruler appear out of nowhere had been intense; watching the erotic power play between Marilyn and Ryan had been even more so. Many had heard about the sensual interplay between the leader and the members of the Grand Council. Few thought they would ever see it first hand.

Marilyn pulled Ryan to a couch in an alcove, which provided a degree of privacy since every eye in the room was following them. There were many such alcoves about the chamber, offering many opportunities for whatever purpose might suit them. Marilyn had not released her hold on the girl since she had arrived, knowing how formidable her temper could be. Ryan, for her part, was in a rare, reckless mood, perhaps brought on by the rage she had been forced to suppress. When Marilyn sat, Ryan sprawled next to her, placing her head on her lap so that she could look up at the dark-haired woman. Marilyn gazed down at her in amusement, the intimacy and casual vulnerability of the position arousing an instant predatory response.

"You should be careful, little one. King or not."

A smile played about Ryan's lips. "I wondered what would change if I became King. Apparently, nothing at all."

Marilyn brushed the girl's hair from her eyes, the sensuality and deep affection in the gesture apparent to the many attempting to watch the pair through the sheer curtains. It sent waves of longing throughout the room. Most were astonished that the sovereign would appear so casually dressed, although in truth she did not appear any less imposing in the simple garb than she had in the armor. They were more astonished that she would settle so comfortably into the arms of the temptress.

"You would be surprised at what has changed," Marilyn said. "You are very much like your father in certain ways, and in other ways very different."

"And how am I different?" Ryan asked curiously.

Marilyn continued to toy with her hair. "Victor never would have appeared in so relaxed a manner, and he certainly never would have lain here openly in my arms."

Ryan grew solemn. "And does that make me appear weak?"

"No," Marilyn said thoughtfully, "it does not. In fact," she continued, nodding to those still trying to furtively peer through the curtains, "they are astonished at how casually you wield enormous power." She was silent for a moment, still thoughtful when she continued. "Victor inspired immense loyalty and respect." She glanced down at the girl, "You, my dear, inspire adoration."

"Then it was probably a good thing I did not kill them all," Ryan said.

Marilyn laughed quietly. "Yes, that was a good thing. And if you are no longer in any danger of annihilating anyone, then I should introduce you about the room." Her tone was less than enthusiastic. She preferred the position she was in. "Abigail will not be pleased if you spend the evening lying with me as opposed to fulfilling your royal obligations."

Ryan reluctantly sat upright. "And since when do you concern yourself with Abigail's displeasure?"

Marilyn smiled knowingly. "It is not me she will take it out on, little one."

"Good point," Ryan said, standing. "Then let me at least act like I know what I'm doing."

In the following moments, Marilyn was impressed that the girl was able to do far more than act. Ryan was gracious and well-spoken, able to make each person she addressed feel they had the whole of her attention. Her warm manner and gentle touch elicited numerous blushes, but as usual, the girl was only fractionally aware of the effect she was having on everyone. Although far more informal than Victor, Ryan possessed the casual elegance of her father, and none would dare presume upon that informality. Ryan acted with utter self-confidence, a confidence that was irresistible. In her own inimical way, Marilyn realized, the girl was seducing everyone in the room.

Perhaps not everyone. Marilyn's eyes narrowed as she felt the weight of one man's stare. Ryan felt it as well, and turned to the handsome blond haired man who was watching her with a guarded expression. Without hesitation, she approached him. The tension in the room rose perceptibly.

"Devon," Ryan said cordially, "I am pleased you accepted my invitation."

Devon stared at the striking creature in front of him. She was taller and appeared younger than he had expected. She was also far more powerful than he ever could have imagined.

"I must confess I was surprised to receive it, my liege" he responded stiffly.

Ryan assessed him. "I thought Aeron's line required representation in his absence," she said quietly, no trace of sarcasm in her voice.

Devon was aware that they were the focal point of the room.

He carefully controlled his anger, but his words were just as stiff. "The representation will be temporary because I do not believe my lord is dead."

The room grew quiet. Now all eyes were on Ryan to see how she would react to this potential challenge. To everyone's surprise, most of all Devon's, Ryan merely smiled. There was a gleam in her eye as she responded.

"I happen to agree with you," Ryan said casually. Several gasps greeted her words. "And I trust you will have the courtesy to notify me when he returns. Although," Ryan continued, more to herself than anyone else, "I am quite certain I will be the first to know."

Devon was stunned by the response. Ryan appeared more amused by the thought than genuinely concerned. He suddenly understood why Aeron had been taken with this one. She was extraordinary.

Ryan turned to leave but had made it only two steps when Devon's words stopped her.

"My lord?"

She turned back to him expectantly.

"Yes?"

The room fell into silence.

"You have a son," Devon said. It was not a question.

There was a fiercely predatory gleam in Ryan's eye.

"Yes," she said mildly, "I do."

The silence in the room was now tomb-like.

"It is Aeron's," Devon said cautiously, and again it was not a question.

Ryan smiled, revealing dangerously perfect teeth. "No, he is my mine." This thought seemed to amuse Ryan, and she relented slightly. "Although Aeron was somewhat instrumental in the process."

A curious gratitude settled on Devon. Ryan could have easily reacted in fury, punishing him for his impertinence. Instead she seemed mildly entertained by the interaction, responding with complete frankness. He bowed low. "Thank you, my lord."

Ryan nodded and resumed her departure. She glanced around the room. Marilyn was nowhere to be found and Ryan realized she was probably already lining up suitors for the evening. She could feel the tell-tale pressure that indicated pairing would commence soon. It was time for her to take her leave. She paused before the door, addressing Susan and Raphael in a wry tone. "This will very soon descend into complete debauchery, you may want to make your exit."

Thankful for the warning, Susan was equally thankful that Ryan escorted them out. She could feel the weight of those ever-present stares, realizing that for a moment, everyone in the room wished they were her. The thought brought a strange warmth to her, but she scolded herself and pushed it away.

Ryan left Susan and Raphael to the safety of their quarters, then continued toward her own. She smiled to herself as she felt Kusunoki briefly touch her. He was with Ala, which made Ryan greatly happy. It was a strange but perfect pairing, the absolute essence of yin and yang.

Ryan felt other pairings begin and quickly shut them out. It was not out of embarrassment or even out of a respect for privacy. At this moment, she simply had no interest in the inevitable death dance of her Kind. She pushed through the doors to her chambers, finding Edward holding the only thing that did interest her. The manservant set the small boy down, and Drake ran to Ryan.

"You are up terribly late, little monster," she said, swinging him up toward the ceiling. He squealed with joy, then clung to her when she settled him into her arm. Ryan nodded to Edward.

"I will put him to bed shortly, I just wanted," Ryan paused for a moment, then cleared her throat, "I just wanted to take care of something."

Edward bowed. He knew exactly where Ryan was going.

Ryan pushed through another set of doors, walked a set of steps, then wandered down through the arched hallway. As she approached the large doors at the end of the hallway, the two guards took a knee, then quickly resumed their vigil. Ryan gave them a brief nod, then strode through the doors they held open. The doors, heavy as they were, whispered closed behind her.

Ryan stared at the man resting peacefully on the dais. She had been unwilling to leave her father, and at Abigail's suggestion, had made quiet arrangements to have him brought here. The execution of the plan had been flawless and few knew Victor was present.

Ryan settled into the chair at his side, resting her head against the backrest. Drake imitated Ryan's mannerisms, leaning back against her. He somberly watched the sleeping man. Ryan glanced down at the little mimic, thinking how entertained Victor would be by the boy. She held his tiny hand in her own.

"Your grandfather would be very proud of you, little crown prince," she said quietly.

Drake looked up at Ryan, digesting every word she said. "And that," she continued, "is now your job since it is no longer mine." Drake appeared very interested in what she was saying, so she added, "I was promoted."

This seemed to satisfy the boy and he leaned back against Ryan, returning to his solemn appraisal of Victor. Ryan, too, gazed at her father, her thoughts just as solemn. She wondered if he would have been pleased by her performance today, and was comforted by the thought it would have pleased him greatly.

Ryan rested for awhile at Victor's side, The events of the day had not been that stressful, but the strain of mentally shielding both her father and son was exhausting. Not to mention the fact that being around the Others was draining. She had always been incredibly sensitive to the thoughts, emotions, and sensations of their Kind. It was actually less difficult being around the Old Ones because their power, although immense, was so controlled.

Drake shifted on her lap and Ryan realized the boy was fast asleep. She stood, laying his head over her shoulder. She retraced her route, quietly thanking the guards as she left, and was soon back in her chambers. She laid the tiny boy down in his bed, covering him with his favorite blanket. He curled up into a ball, his sleep undisturbed.

She returned to her own room, removing most of her clothing until she was comfortably in a soft shirt and flannel pants. As she leaned over to fold her garments, she smiled at the voice behind her.

"Did you really think you would be spending your first night as

King alone?"

Ryan glanced over her shoulder. "I rather assumed the Queen Mother had other plans."

The title, although gently mocking, still pleased Abigail greatly. She moved in behind the girl, and to Ryan's surprise, slipped her hands about Ryan's waist. Ryan turned to face her, gazing at her intently. It was not unusual for Marilyn to physically display affection toward her, but it was nearly unheard of for Abigail to do so. It brought a new sensory dimension into play, one that left Ryan completely off-balance. Abigail tightened her embrace, and they were now standing so close their lips were nearly touching. Abigail leaned forward, pressing against Ryan fully. She brushed Ryan's cheek with her own as she whispered in her ear.

"How long," Abigail said softly, "do think it will take me to put you on your knees again?"

Desire flared from spark to inferno and it took so much effort for Ryan to restrain herself it made her teeth ache. Longing twisted upwards from the center of her body, and although she could not counter this woman's attack, she could make certain Abigail's weapon impaled them both.

Abigail stiffened with shock and pleasure as she felt the girl's lips on her throat. Ryan did not bite her but rather feathered the promise along the throbbing vein. The torturously light kiss created instantaneous arousal and it was Abigail's turn to struggle with restraint.

"You can put me on my knees," Ryan whispered back to her, "but I will take you to the ground with me."

Abigail smiled at Ryan's audacity, and the girl truly had pushed her too far. "We will see, little one."

Ryan arched forward at the bite on her neck, pressing fully into Abigail's embrace. It was good that the other woman was holding her so tightly, or without a doubt she would have gone to her knees so quickly did they give way. Abigail leaned back in satisfaction.

"That did not take long."

Ryan had a languorous look in her eye, but was not quite ready to concede defeat. She stared at her blood on Abigail's lips, and in a completely startling move, leaned forward and kissed her. The lingering kiss sent a shock through Abigail. In all their years of prolonged seduction and intense eroticism, she did not think she had ever kissed the girl.

It was Ryan's turn to lean back in satisfaction. Abigail had changed the rules of engagement with her initial embrace, and Ryan was certainly willing to do battle on a more physical level. Abigail gazed at the girl, impressed. It had been a long time since anyone had introduced anything new to her in the act of Sharing. She took a step forward, forcing Ryan to take a step backward. Ryan felt the edge of the bed against the back of her knees.

Abigail leaned forward to whisper in Ryan's ear once more.

"Even if you take me to the ground," Abigail said, pushing her down onto the bed, "I will still be on top."

The sensations coursing through Ryan were almost unbearable. Although Abigail had held her before, Ryan had never been in such full, bodily contact with her. It felt as if every vein in her body were throbbing for release.

"That," Ryan said through clenched teeth, "would be acceptable."

CHAPTER 17

MANY, MANY HOURS LATER, RYAN AWOKE to find herself alone. She smiled to herself. She had not been alone for very long, and for most of those hours, she had not been sleeping. She arose from the bed, took a quick shower, and changed clothes. These festivities could go on forever, and as most of her Kind did very little sleeping, one of the only ways to mark time was to change attire.

Ryan went to look for Drake and found him happily engaged in a board game with Jason. Ryan stood in the hall watching the two children. The older boy was extremely patient with the toddler which was good since Drake was having more fun throwing the pieces about the board. Edward sat in a chair nearby, ever vigilant.

"That is going to be dangerous in about twenty years," Marilyn said, beside her.

Ryan smiled. She had felt the other woman's presence. "I give it fifteen," Ryan replied.

Marilyn glanced over at her, surprised. "You will Change your son when he is that young?"

"No," Ryan said, shaking her head, "I hope to Change Drake when he is physically older than I was. Which will be somewhat strange," she admitted, "because my son will appear older than me."

Marilyn was curious as to her reasoning, and Ryan answered the unasked question. "My youthful appearance has been somewhat," she paused, clearing her throat, "inconvenient at times."

"I rather like it, ma Cherie," Marilyn said, the intimation evident.

Susan approached, noting the look of slight exasperation on Ryan's face. She was concerned for a moment that the boys were misbehaving, but one look at Marilyn's expression told her it wasn't the boys. Susan was still a little overwhelmed being around Marilyn, but felt like she was starting to get used to it.

Or so she thought.

"Do you know," Marilyn said, addressing Ryan, "that having Dr. Ryerson around has been most educational."

Ryan gave her a skeptical look. She could hear the undertone in Marilyn's voice. "In what way?"

"Did you know," Marilyn said conversationally, "that the femoral artery is one of the largest in the body?"

Susan blushed deeply while Ryan just looked at Marilyn. Poor Susan. Lord knows how that conversation went.

"Is that a fact?" Ryan said evenly.

Marilyn let her eyes drift downward and Ryan felt her own color rise. "Perhaps we could explore that medical phenomenon later?" Marilyn suggested.

"I don't imagine you're talking about reviewing some medical texts," Ryan said, struggling to keep her tone even.

Marilyn's gaze swept back upward, enjoying the flush in the girl's cheeks. "No, I prefer practical experience to theory, although you're welcome to read them to me while I'm otherwise occupied." She turned her heated gaze on Susan, who was, if possible, redder than Ryan. "Or we could let Dr. Ryerson read them to us while she acted as observer, a kind of internship, if you will."

"That is enough," Ryan said abruptly. She glanced at Susan, who quickly excused herself to check on the boys. "Is there a reason, other than torture, that you came to find me?"

"Hmm, yes," Marilyn said, reluctantly stopping her teasing, "your taskmaster has requested your presence at another social event."

"Does Abigail know you refer to her in such a way?" Ryan asked dryly.

"And how do you know I was referring to Abigail?" Marilyn replied.

Ryan merely sighed, knowing she was beaten.

Ryan entered one of the many gathering halls. Each one was decorated in a particular style with a particular theme. Some were thoroughly modern, and others, like this one, were a monument to the past. It seemed somewhat incongruous to see people dressed in modern clothing lounging about in what appeared to be a medieval chamber. She herself was dressed in a simple black turtleneck and jeans, giving up any further pretense at formality.

She approached Abigail, who was seated in one of the raised partitioned areas surrounded by her consorts and other admirers. Ryan stepped up onto the platform, extending her hand to the matriarch. Abigail took the proffered hand, assessing the girl's appearance. She decided Ryan could appear in sackcloth and still be stunning. Ryan bowed to kiss the hand in a chivalrous manner and did not release it when she stood upright.

Abigail was amused at the girl's flirtation, and shifted slightly, indicating Ryan should sit next to her. She was fully aware that all in the room were watching them, some attempting to do so casually, others openly gaping. Soon Ala joined them, and after a warm greeting from Ryan, she settled on the cushions adjacent to them. Kusunoki soon followed, and he settled comfortably opposite Ala. Finally, Marilyn strolled in, finding just enough room on the vacant cushion to Ryan's left to situate herself fully pressed against Ryan's side, her arm draped about the girl's shoulders.

The conversation between the newly crowned King and the Grand Council was relaxed, animated, and enjoyable. The interaction was spontaneous and utterly sincere. It had also been fully anticipated by Abigail. As she glanced about the room, she was pleased to see it was serving its purpose.

Outside of formal ceremony, few of their Kind would ever get to see a single Old One, let alone the leader of the hierarchy. To see such an aggregation of power in a single place was a millennial event. To see such a congregation under such casual circumstances was utterly unheard of.

The Others watched their upstart King with wonder and growing admiration. The members of the Grand Council treated Ryan with great respect, a respect she reverently returned. What was even more surprising was the contentment that seemed to surround the group. For a species that was inherently predatory, viciously possessive, and lethally competitive, the Old Ones seemed to have found some curious balance in regards to their new King. The affection they held for Ryan was a novelty; to see it openly displayed, especially by One known for her aloofness, was startling.

The thoughts flowing about the room pleased Abigail, even those regarding her, and she returned to the conversation at hand. Ala was finishing the very entertaining story of how she had first met Ryan in the Congo.

"And so," Marilyn asked, "you actually allowed yourself to be crucified?"

Ryan cast a mischievous look at Kokumuo, who was stationed behind Ala. He glanced away in some embarrassment. Ryan lowered her eyes to Ala, who was recalling the scene with some pleasure.

"I had to make an offering to the earth mother," Ryan said, her words playfully suggestive, "and that was all I had to give."

Ala took a deep breath at the fond memory. "It was quite a sufficient sacrifice."

Ryan glanced down at her hands. She was enjoying the physical sensation of Marilyn on one side, Abigail on the other, and the incredible heat and light of Ala and Kusunoki so close to her. The power, warmth and comfortable sensuality of the group was extraordinary. It was perhaps a perfect moment, utterly complete in and of itself.

A shadow drifted across her consciousness. Although Ryan had lived for centuries, the first nineteen years she spent living as a human still profoundly influenced her. And she had come from a people who refused to celebrate good fortune, superstitiously believing that such celebration would tempt disaster.

Abigail, ever attuned to the girl, glanced sideways. Ryan was not particularly mercurial in her moods but she had just had a very sudden, albeit subtle, shift. Ryan, aware of Abigail's scrutiny, turned to her, shaking the feeling off. She smiled, ridding herself of the feeling entirely.

"I think I am going to go check on my son," Ryan said rising. "I forget he needs to eat and sleep." She felt Marilyn's hand on her leg, and she glanced down. "I will be right back." She turned to Abigail. "I promise."

She stepped from the platform in a single, graceful step and began striding across the room. About halfway across, she slowed, then came to a stop. Conversation amongst the Old Ones had resumed, but Abigail's gaze remained on the girl. Kusunoki caught sight of Abigail's expression, and he, too, glanced over at Ryan.

Ryan stood paused in the center of the room, a puzzled look on her face. Her uncertainty was evident as she cocked her head to one side, as if trying to discern a single conversation from the myriad in the room. Now Ala and Marilyn were watching her as well, all curious as to what she was doing.

Ryan turned her head slightly, her uncertainty even more pronounced. She looked up at Abigail, as if seeking some sort of sign or confirmation, but Abigail was at a loss as to what the girl was searching for. Slowly, the puzzlement on Ryan's face changed to faint understanding, then to utter certainty. Ryan closed her eyes at the sensation, reveling in the feeling but also resigned to its implication. Everyone present was now studying her curious actions. When she opened her eyes, they were surprised that she smiled, although it wasn't entirely pleasant to see.

Ryan took a deep breath, aware of the humanness of the gesture, and turned to the shadows in the doorway, seeking the One she knew stood there.

"Hello, my love," came a clipped, aristocratic voice filled with sarcasm.

A devastatingly handsome man with light hair and ice blue eyes stepped into the room. Enormous power stepped into the room with him, generating violent currents that caused people to shudder for reasons both pleasant and not. The strength of this One inspired terror, even in those who did not know him. Sensuality and malevolence swirled about him, battling for dominance, and for the moment, malevolence was winning handily.

"You look remarkably well for a dead man," Ryan said casually. Although her tone was as dangerous as his, those around her were surprised that amusement was predominant in hers. She was obviously not afraid.

Aeron took another step forward, his pale blue eyes cold with fury. There was, however, a trace of amusement in his voice as well. "You didn't quite finish the job. I thought I taught you better than that as a child."

Ryan smiled a lethal smile. "There wasn't enough left to consume."

This provoked another icy smile, although one that was slightly less entertained. Ryan continued.

"I don't suppose you've come to congratulate me on my coronation."

"No," Aeron said with mock regret, "I have not. I come with a challenge."

This elicited several gasps from the room, which had grown completely silent. If the challenge itself was surprising, then Ryan's reaction to it was even more so.

"Very well, then," she said with complete nonchalance, "I accept your challenge. We will fight here, three days time, standard rotation of weapons. Although," she said, half to herself, "I doubt we will need more than three sets."

Aeron had the feeling he had been brushed off like some annoying insect. The girl right now possessed an air of complete self-confidence, an infuriating certainty he had felt only in one other, the whelp's father. Not only that, but she had named all of the terms of the engagement, although some by right were his. To add insult to injury, she had chosen exactly the terms he would have, making any argument appear foolish.

"Very well," he said, his jaw clenched.

"Excellent," Ryan said smoothly, "three days time." She began to turn, then paused.

"And Aeron?"

"Yes?" he said, fairly grinding his teeth.

"Do not disturb me before that time."

She turned on her heel and left, dismissing him. Incensed, he cast one furious look at the Old Ones, the turned on his own heel and left the gathering.

Abigail calmly smoothed her skirt, then slowly stood. "I suggest we convene ourselves in Council Chambers."

"How can this be?" Kusunoki demanded, not from anyone in particular. He slammed his fist down on the table, a lack of self-control extremely uncharacteristic of the samurai. "How can he still be alive?"

Abigail's mood was greatly restrained, and Ala watched her closely. She was intensely curious how Abigail would respond to this turn of events, or to see if the matriarch was even surprised. Abigail raised her eyes to Ala, sensing, then addressing, her concerns directly.

"I must say I am not surprised that Aeron survived."

Kusunoki's jaw clenched spasmodically.

"But," she continued, "I am extremely surprised to see him this soon. I assumed it would take decades, perhaps even centuries for him to return."

Ala sensed no deception in Abigail at the moment, nor any real attempt at disguise. She slowly nodded her agreement. "I am amazed that none of us could sense his presence."

"I knew he was here," Ryan said as she strolled through the doorway, "but I misinterpreted the sensation."

There was slight self-criticism in the comment. Ryan settled into the chair at the head of the table, directly across from Abigail. She gazed at the older woman a long moment, an enigmatic expression on her face. She turned her attention to Ala.

"Something has been troubling me lately, something I could not quite identify. I am almost relieved to find this is the source."

Ala nodded. She had sensed the girl's unease and Aeron's return would certainly explain it. Ryan settled into silence as the conversation about the table continued. The discussion was at times heated, other times frustrated and puzzled. Oddly, Marilyn simply sat. Normally, such a dramatic turn of events would have fully engaged her, but now she merely sat, watching Ryan with interest.

Aware of the scrutiny, Ryan raised her eyes to the dark-haired woman.

There was a lull in the conversation and Marilyn chose that moment to speak, addressing Ryan directly.

"You're not the least bit concerned, are you, ma Cherie?"

It was not so much a question as a statement, and Ryan did not so much answer as agree.

"No," she said calmly, "I am not."

Marilyn nodded, a smile playing about her lips. She knew whom she was betting on in this altercation.

Kusunoki picked up on Marilyn's assessment, turning to evaluate his pupil. He understood what Marilyn was discerning from Ryan.

"I sense no doubt in you at all," he said.

"That is because there is none," Ryan said in the same calm voice. There was no bravado in her tone, no arrogance, no pride. Her words were spoken matter-of-factly, and her manner was understated.

Kusunoki's eyes narrowed. There was a supreme self-confidence surrounding Ryan right now, a poise and self-assurance that reminded Kusunoki of Victor. It seemed to put everything immediately into perspective.

"Do you wish to train for the next few days?" Kusunoki asked her.

"No," Ryan replied. "I've been training for this for almost 700 years." She shifted in her seat. "I will spend my time in meditation."

Kusunoki nodded. "I will reflect with you."

Ryan turned to Marilyn, then to Ala. "Dr. Ryerson and Edward will care for Drake while I prepare. I would ask, in turn, that you care for them."

Ala understood exactly what Ryan was requesting, as did Marilyn. "Nothing will happen to your son, or to Dr. Ryerson," Ala promised firmly.

"Very well," Ryan said, nodding her thanks. She gave one last, long look at Abigail, then took her leave.

Aeron stalked about his chambers impatiently. His belongings were exactly as he had left them, something that was welcome but unexpected. He was surprised that Ryan had not completely demolished his suites, or at least given them to someone else. He found it peculiar that they were completely unchanged and in immaculate condition. It gave him pause.

The slight knock on his door also gave him pause, but not because it was unexpected. Abigail entered, her graceful elegance and beauty a stark contrast to the dark masculine furnishings.

"My ally," Aeron said, greeting her sarcastically.

"Aeron," Abigail said smoothly, unperturbed by his anger or sarcasm. If anything, she seemed slightly entertained by the position he was in.

"You ever were one to hedge your bets," Aeron said, his cynicism pronounced.

"How odd," Abigail said. "Victor accused me of exactly the same thing, using almost those exact words." She fingered a letter opener on a nearby shelf. "But you must admit," she said, glancing at him, "it is a strategy that has proved both prescient and successful."

Aeron crossed his arms over his chest. "So, have you come to plead for the sake of your precious Ryan?"

There was a pause as Abigail again fingered the letter opener. "I did not come here for Ryan's sake," she said, glancing at him once more, "but for yours."

Aeron's eyes narrowed and Abigail turned fully toward him. She was deadly serious. "You cannot defeat her, Aeron. Ryan has grown immensely powerful."

"No doubt helped by you," Aeron interjected sardonically.

"Yes," Abigail said, unruffled, "there is that. But I do not believe that Ryan can be defeated any longer, only contained."

Aeron was even more sarcastic. "A containment I understand you've been glad to provide."

"A containment you could assist in," Abigail proffered, her words and gaze suddenly intense. The offer caught Aeron off guard, as intended.

"What did you have in mind?" he asked, his distrust evident.

"Ryan did not dissolve the Grand Council as expected," Abigail replied. "she maintained it in an advisory capacity." She glanced about the unchanged room. "Your position on the Council remains unfilled, and you have the absolute right of return."

She turned to him, both persuasive and admonishing. "You could return to your previous position and assist in keeping our powerful little monarch in check."

"Or," Abigail said, turning her back on him, "you could continue with your challenge and suffer an ignominious defeat."

She gave one last glance over her shoulder before she disappeared.

"It is your decision."

Several hours later, another tap on his door interrupted Aeron's dark reverie.

"Enter," he bellowed.

Devon came in, bowing low before him. As pleased as he was

to see his master, he was very wary of Aeron's current mood. People tended to get decapitated when Aeron was in such a state. He stood before him patiently.

"You will act as my Second at the challenge," Aeron said.

"Of course, my lord. Thank you for such an honor," Devon replied.

Obviously in a foul mood, Aeron made a dismissive hand gesture. "That is all, you may go."

As much as Devon wanted to leave, he stood firm, knowing he had to speak his piece. Aeron raised glowering eyes to him.

"What?" he demanded, his tone scathing.

Devon gathered his courage and did his best to steady his voice.

"Perhaps you should reconsider your challenge," Devon said, resignation in his voice. Aeron would probably kill him.

The table between them took the initial brunt of Aeron's volatile temper as he leaped to his feet and smashed his fist downward. It was a testament to its construction that it merely split down the middle as opposed to exploding.

"And is her influence so great now that she turns my own line against me?" Aeron asked, both fury and frustration in his voice.

Devon kept his eyes to the floor. "Of course not, my lord. I live to serve you." He knew he was pushing his luck, but he had to continue, "It's just that…"

"What?" Aeron said through clenched teeth.

Devon took a deep breath, then blurted it out. "She has a son, my lord."

Aeron stopped dead in his tracks. "What did you say?"

Devon was now able to hold his master's gaze. He felt he might actually live through this conversation. "She has a son, my lord. Your son," he clarified, as if there was any need.

Aeron was frozen. Out of all the things that could have come from his manservant's mouth, this was truly the most startling. He could not even process what he was hearing.

"How do you know this?" he asked slowly.

Devon's confidence was returning. "I asked her, my lord, in front of the general assembly."

"And she told you?" Aeron said, incredulous.

"Yes," Devon said, "she did."

"What exactly did she say?" Aeron asked, his astonishment even greater.

Devon thought back to the conversation. "She said she had a son, and when I asked her if it was yours, she replied no, that it was her son. She then relented, saying something to the effect that you were," Devon paused delicately, "instrumental in the process."

That sounded exactly like something the girl would say, Aeron thought to himself, slowly settling into the chair in front of the now-demolished table. This was almost impossible to comprehend. If Victor was capable of reproducing outside of the Change, however, then his unruly progeny probably was, too.

"You may leave now," Aeron said without looking up. Devon bowed but his master paid him no mind, so deep in thought was he. Devon quickly departed.

Aeron stared at the destroyed table without really seeing it. If anyone else knocked at his door this evening, he was not answering. He leaned back in his chair, placing his feet on the half of the table still standing.

In all of his complex and convoluted musings, he did note that Abigail failed to mention this most momentous news.

CHAPTER 18

RYAN STOOD IN THE COURTYARD. Although this portion of the council chambers was also underground, it was one near the surface. Through clever construction it was actually well-lit with natural light from the sun. It was even possible to tell it was morning by the quality and brightness of the light.

A series of weapons were laid about on a nearby table, and Ryan inspected them without urgency. She was early and Aeron had not yet arrived, so she had ample time to examine the armaments. She picked up a katana and swung it experimentally. It was the sword Kusunoki had made her. Since Aeron had made the challenge, the first rotation of weapons was her choice. She would have chosen the katana even if it had not been one of her favorites, simply to irritate Aeron who despised the weapon.

She replaced the katana and lifted the much heavier broadsword. She anticipated that this would be Aeron's preference, the second rotation his choice. Its heavier weight and sturdy composition would favor his fighting style. Still, she swung the weapon effortlessly, enjoying its balance and feel. The weight would not matter; although it was not her preferred, she had been born to use the English broadsword.

She set the broadsword down and lifted the third set of weapons, Sais, a pair of forked blades designed for elaborate defensive moves and blinding offense. These had become Ryan's favorites, complementing her speed and lightning fast reflexes. If Aeron made it this far, he would be at a distinct disadvantage.

Ryan replaced the weapons. She did not think they would get to the third round. And if they got to the fourth, she did not have much of a plan. Perhaps they could throw rocks at one another.

This thought amused her, and Kusunoki, sensing the mirth, glanced over at his pupil. She appeared completely poised, not overconfident but rather pleasantly taut, a tension born of anticipation rather than fear. He grinned. That was another thing she had in common with her father: Ryan ever loved a good fight.

Several figures filed in, and Ryan glanced up to see Abigail, Marilyn, Ala, and Susan take their seats. Ryan had forbidden all others to attend, a move that had been unexpected and greeted with much speculation. Ryan kept her own counsel on the matter, saying only that the decision had been final.

Kusunoki glanced at his favored student once more. He wondered if she wanted to avoid humiliating Aeron in front of the Others. In her younger years, the thought never would have crossed her mind and she would have proceeded in such a way just to make a point. Now that she had accepted the responsibility of the hierarchy, she seemed to take a more measured course, acting with great maturity. It was one thing to be responsible for herself; it was another to be responsible for all of her Kind.

Ryan glanced over at her teacher, her affection obvious. She looked up into the stands, catching Ala's glance. She could feel the earth mother's warm encouragement settle upon her. She turned her attention to Marilyn, who was eying her lithe form with appreciation and very little subtlety. The inspection brought a different type of warmth to Ryan, one located slightly lower in her body. Susan was next in line, sandwiched uncomfortably between the primal forces of Marilyn and Abigail. Susan caught Ryan's eye, her anxiety evident. Ryan had asked her to attend on the off-chance either she or Aeron were injured, although Susan had protested she had little idea how to treat any injuries they might incur. Ryan had responded that Susan knew more about the anatomy of their Kind than anyone, and Susan had relented.

Lastly, Ryan turned her attention to Abigail, who was watching her with the same unreadable expression she had adopted the minute Aeron returned. Ryan glanced down, scuffing the ground with her boot. It did not matter, it would not change the events of this day. She felt herself glancing back up, not of her own volition as Abigail fully extended her power. Ryan felt the intensity of the matriarch's gaze burn into her as she heard Abigail's voice in her mind.

I have not betrayed you.

Ryan held her gaze, her intensity as great as Abigail's.

I know, Ryan replied simply, silently.

Abigail smiled.

Ryan turned her attention to the doorway and the ensuing commotion there. Aeron stalked in, followed by Devon and some other nondescript manservant. Aeron, although handsome as ever, appeared distinctly disheveled. He actually gave the appearance of having spent a few sleepless nights although in truth he could have gone months without sleeping with no repercussion.

Ryan gave a quick glance to Kusunoki, who was eyeing Aeron with some misgiving. She quickly hid her smile, returning to scuffing her boot along the ground as if it were an all-consuming task.

Kusunoki furrowed his brow, examining Aeron. The man looked like he was recovering from a drinking binge, although none of their Kind was significantly affected by alcohol. This fight would not last a single round. He looked to Ryan, who was watching the three at the other end of the courtyard, mildly expressionless.

There seemed to be some sort of quiet but passionate discussion between Aeron and his Second, which resulted in some pacing about from Aeron. Further discussion ensued, but no apparent action was produced, other than more pacing from Aeron. In an unusual role-reversal, Kusunoki was more impatient than Ryan, who seemed quite willing to let the scene play itself out.

"You're already late," Kusunoki said loudly, "is there some problem?"

"A minute, samurai!" Aeron replied heatedly. There was

additional, furtive discussion at the other end of the yard, which still did not produce any action.

The four women in the stand glanced at one another. Ala looked upon Aeron with obvious disapproval. Marilyn seemed very entertained by the drama while Susan was baffled as to what was happening. Abigail's gaze was on Ryan. The older woman had the growing suspicion that the girl had perhaps outfoxed them all. Ryan picked up one of the Sais, content to twirl it about her wrist in a practiced manner.

There was no more discussion occurring at the far end of the yard, just a lot of pacing from Aeron. Devon stood off to the side, staring at the ground in front of him. Ryan's eyes were on Aeron, and he became very aware of her intense and somewhat amused scrutiny. He stopped abruptly.

"You–" he began, then trailed off.

"We–" he began again, stopping once more. He finally just blurted it out.

"We have a son."

"No," Ryan said, casually twirling the short sword, "you were right the first time. I," she said with emphasis, "have a son. You get credit for–" she paused, searching her mind for the contemporary sports metaphor, "–an assist."

Aeron glowered at her. "How could this happen?" he demanded.

There was a wicked glint in Ryan's eye. "Well, if you're uncertain about exactly when it occurred, I believe it was right after you attempted to kill me and just before I attempted to kill you. Now," she continued, "if it is the actual mechanics of the act you are unclear on, I am certain Dr. Ryerson can explain that to you."

Ala muffled laughter and Marilyn sat forward in her chair. This was much better than sword fighting.

Aeron struggled to maintain his temper. The girl's infernal sense of humor always infuriated him, which she seemed well-aware of as she spun the Sai through her fingers.

"The boy–" Aeron trailed off again.

"His name is Drake," Ryan said dryly.

"Drake," Aeron continued, "he is human?"

Ryan was thoughtful, still effortlessly spinning the weapon. "Not entirely. I imagine he is much like I was at that age. Something more than human, but not yet Changed." Ryan punctuated her statement by tossing the Sai with a practiced flip and impaling it in the ground.

Aeron settled into silence and began pacing once more, appearing to be trapped in some walled enclosure that only he could see.

Kusunoki glanced over at Ryan, suddenly understanding the brilliance of his beloved pupil. Ryan had a secondary motive for forbidding an audience, which was to give Aeron the opportunity to withdraw his challenge without losing face before the Others. He stood only before the Grand Council, and there would be no shame in withdrawing from the contest.

Kusunoki decided to press the issue, "Do you wish to relinquish your challenge?"

Aeron, still distracted within his enclosure, did not reply. Devon leaned toward him.

"My lord…"

"A minute!" Aeron demanded heatedly.

Ryan still seemed content to let him thrash about in indecision. She scuffed the ground experimentally a few more times, then shifted her weight to a comfortable standing position. A thought occurred to her, a question that had been bothering her. She felt she might as well ask while they were waiting.

"I do have one question of you," Ryan began. Her tone was deliberately casual, but the undertone immediately caught the attention of all present. Aeron stopped his pacing and looked up at her.

Ryan's tone was still offhanded, and the undertone deadly serious. "It took my father almost two centuries to recover from my attack, and he has yet to recover from the virus which affected you as well."

The tension in the room rose dramatically.

"How exactly," Ryan asked, "did you recover so quickly?"

Ryan expected Aeron to respond with boasting, given such a perfect opportunity to declare his superiority to Victor. She expected him to attribute it to the inferiority of her attempt. She expected him to do any number of things that would be consistent and in character with his arrogance. Instead, he did something that sent a chill down her spine.

He lowered his head, unable to meet her eyes.

"I had assistance."

The chill down her spine increased, spreading out to her extremities. Her hands actually felt numb from the cold.

"From whom?" she asked quietly.

Aeron just stared at her across the expanse, a mixture of shame, resignation, and hopelessness on his features. Ryan felt that he was desperately trying to communicate something to her, something she was about to learn for herself.

A stabbing pain shot through her head, creating such a violent visual disturbance she thought for a moment she was going to pass out. Nausea swept upward through her system as her knees buckled. Kusunoki reached out to her, grasping her about the waist else she would have fallen to the ground. The room spun about, tilting madly, and the pain increased until Ryan thought for certain every blood vessel in her head was going to burst.

Kusunoki was at a loss. He could not see or sense anything that was harming Ryan, but she was obviously in great pain. She could barely stand, and in fact required his support. Just as suddenly as the attack began, it seemed to end. Ryan clung to him for a moment, uncertain if the pain would come again. As she slowly stood upright once more, her attention was not on Kusunoki, but rather on something she was reaching out to, something she was trying to grasp. And as she succeeded, the realization on her face mirrored that of Aeron's: utter hopelessness.

Slowly, Ryan stood upright to her full height. She squared her shoulders as one wholly resigned to fate. Without looking at Kusunoki, she slowly turned around. He turned to see what she was looking at.

There was a woman standing in the doorway. An extraordinary woman. A terrifying woman.

Extremely tall, she was perfectly proportioned, a goddess with long dark hair, flawless skin, and dark green eyes. In age she appeared somewhere physically between Marilyn and Abigail and was undeniably beautiful. But there was something not quite right about her. Perhaps it was the perfection of her walk as she began gliding towards them, seamless and lacking any of the character of a normal stride. Perhaps it was the high, sharp cheekbones, ideal in structure but threatening to cut through the flawless skin of that perfect face. Perhaps it was the faultless lips that seemed an unnatural shade of red, a color deviant from nature. Perhaps it was the reptilian coldness of her eyes, eyes that were locked onto Ryan as if no one else in the room was present.

Perhaps it was because, although Kusunoki could not sense her, he knew instinctively that the woman was an Old One, ancient, in fact, far older and more powerful than anyone else in the room.

In the stands, Abigail stood, her hands on the railing in front of her. She could not feel the woman either, but was filled with horror at her presence.

Ryan simply stood there as the woman approached. The woman was so tall Ryan had to look up when she stopped in front of her.

"Rhiannon Alexander," the woman said, her voice melodic but possessing a strange inflection, one that Ryan could not identify even with all her travels. There seemed to be a minor sibilance as she pronounced the "x" in "Alexander," the slightest hiss as the consonant was imperceptibly lengthened.

"I have longed to meet you," the woman said, her eyes still locked on Ryan.

The enunciation was again strange, as if this language were an uncomfortable fit, although Ryan could not place or even identify an accent. It really did not matter, and Ryan did not respond other than to maintain the woman's gaze.

"You know who I am," the woman stated.

"No," Ryan said, then reluctantly, "and yes." The woman seemed satisfied with the answer. "Then you know enough."

She turned to the men who had accompanied her into the courtyard, men everyone seemed to have missed entirely, so mesmerized by the woman were they.

"Then you will come with me now."

Ryan glanced at the men. They were strange as well, but she did not have time to ponder that at the moment.

"Yes," she said, "I will."

Kusunoki took a step toward her and Ryan turned to him. Her voice was forceful in his head.

Do not follow me, she commanded silently.

Without another word, silent or spoken, Ryan turned and fell into step beside the woman who guided her across the courtyard and through the doorway. The woman did not touch her, but the exit was as forced as if Ryan had been bound, gagged, and dragged out by a rope about her throat.

CHAPTER 19

KUSUNOKI SHOVED AERON BACKWARD against the wall so hard that his body was momentarily embedded in the rock. Kusunoki was on him immediately, his arm across Aeron's throat, pinning him in his own imprint.

"What have you done!" Kusunoki demanded, his fury spilling out in his words.

Aeron, under normal circumstances, was stronger than Kusunoki but the samurai was so angry right now his strength was tremendous. Aeron was able to wedge his hand between Kusunoki's forearm and his own throat just enough to allow speech.

"I did not do this," Aeron insisted angrily.

Abigail entered the inner council chambers, and her wrath was even greater than Kusunoki's.

"And what is it," she said with icy fury, "that you have not done?"

Aeron pried Kusunoki's forearm away a little more. His words were strained from the force on his larynx. "I did not know she would come for Ryan."

Ala came up behind Kusunoki, gently placing her hand on his shoulder. She was angry, too, but this would not help.

Kusunoki sensed the wisdom of her silent words and released Aeron. He took several steps back because the urge to attack Aeron again was almost uncontrollable. Aeron rubbed his throat as Abigail eyed him, her own fury unabated.

"And who, exactly, is 'she'?"

Aeron closed his eyes for a moment, rubbing his forehead. "Her name is Madelyn," he said finally, "and I know almost nothing about her."

"Well," Abigail said coldly, settling into the chair at the head of the table, "why don't you begin with what you do know?"

Aeron slumped heavily into his own chair, and the others took their seats about the table. The two adjacent to Aeron remained empty because no one wanted to be near him right now.

"Ryan was right," Aeron began, "my recovery was significantly aided. Madelyn was there when I woke up."

"And where were you when you awakened?" Abigail pressed.

Frustration was evident in Aeron's voice. "I don't know." He shook his head. "I awakened in some type of fortress, and when I left. I was restrained so I could not see or hear anything."

This brought a chill to Kusunoki. If they were capable of so completely restricting Aeron…

"Did you take her blood?" Ala asked.

"No," Aeron said, "I mean, I must have before I awakened, it's the only thing I can think of that would have allowed me to recover so quickly. But I did not Share with her." He looked at Abigail. "I don't believe she wanted my blood."

Aeron's remorse was apparent, for under normal circumstances he would never have admitted such an inadequacy. Abigail, however, was unyielding.

"It's pretty obvious who she wanted," she replied, her tone scathing.

Abigail turned to Marilyn. "I have never heard of this woman, nor do I have any Memories of her. How is it possible that an Old One exists that none of us know?"

Marilyn simply shook her head. She could not get Ryan's hopeless expression out of her mind.

Ala leaned forward. "I have heard rumors of Ones before us,

dating back to the time of the Egyptians, but there has never been any proof."

Kusunoki's temper finally cooled enough for him to rejoin the conversation. "I, too, have heard stories." He replayed the previous scene in his mind. "Strange that I could not get any reading from her, no sense of her presence. I could not with any accuracy guess her age." He looked to Ala, his expression grim. "But I think you have to go back farther than the Egyptians."

Ala nodded her agreement. She turned back to Aeron. "The men with her, our Kind as well?"

Aeron nodded. "Yes."

"How many are there?" Kusunoki asked quietly.

"Dozens," Aeron said, his expression also grim, "and each one stronger than me."

Kusunoki felt despondency settling upon him.

"How long were you with them?" Abigail asked Aeron.

"A day, maybe two. But that was all. They did not seem to have any purpose in keeping me, and communication was almost non-existent."

"You say 'almost'," Abigail noted.

Aeron closed his eyes.

"Aeron," Abigail prompted, not gently.

Aeron reopened his eyes. "Madelyn came to me when I awakened. She said she had felt a tremendous force pass through her, and she wanted to know if I knew what it was."

"And what did you tell her?" Abigail asked, knowing the answer.

"From what she described," Aeron said resigned to his culpability, "I knew it had to be Ryan."

Kusunoki slammed his fist down on the table, and Ala reached over to place her hand on his arm.

"When was this?" Ala asked.

"A few days ago," Aeron replied.

Ala and Abigail exchanged glances. The coronation, when the girl had revealed her full power.

"I did not know Madelyn would come for the girl," Aeron insisted, "she seemed completely uninterested in us."

"Apparently she was uninterested in you," Kusunoki said derisively.

Aeron ignored the taunt. "I did not know she would come until Ryan asked me the question in the courtyard. Then I realized that was exactly what Madelyn was going to do, but by then it was too late."

Abigail was still furious at Aeron, but she did not sense any trickery in him or any attempt to mislead. He seemed as shocked as the rest of them, if not more so because he had a better grasp of what Ryan was now up against.

The group settled into somber silence, broken finally by Ala's solemn words.

"I could not get a good impression of what Ryan was feeling, so quickly did she shut down," Ala said, "but I do know this, the girl was terrified."

Kusunoki's reply was brusque. He did not want to believe it. "I have never known Ryan to even be afraid."

"That very well may be," Ala replied slowly, "but she was not afraid for herself."

All eyes turned toward the ebony-skinned woman.

"Ryan's fear," Ala said pointedly, "was for us."

CHAPTER 20

RYAN FELT AS IF SHE WERE LAYING on a slab of rock. Her eyes covered, she could not verify this fact, but that was certainly what it felt like.

As soon as she and her captors had reached the surface above the Grand Council chambers, she had been bound and blind-folded. She had tested the strength of her restraints as surreptitiously as possible, but they did not yield. They seemed to be made of some strange metal that was both flexible and incredibly strong. The manacles almost seemed to shape themselves to her wrists so closely did they fit.

She had been placed into some type of motor vehicle, a limousine perhaps, and she carefully marked the time that they were underway, alertly recording sounds and smells to orient herself. They stopped on what was obviously an airfield or runway of some type, and she was pulled from the vehicle, pushed forward to walk on her own although she was still blind-folded. Perhaps her captors wished to make her look foolish or helpless, but Ryan utilized a technique she had learned from Kusunoki. She changed her gait slightly, shifting her weight so that her heel struck the ground sharply. She listened carefully to the sound, using a subtle form of echo-location as she moved forward. When she reached the stairs, she mounted them effortlessly, even dipping her head as she entered the doorway of the aircraft. She was led, not gently, to a seat, where her feet were further restrained.

Ryan sat silently, noting the movements and sounds around her. She could not identify the type of plane, although it was some sort of extremely advanced jet. That classification was important because it would give her the ability to calculate the distance she traveled based upon the sound of the engine, her sense of the altitude, and the potential air speed of the plane.

Or at least it would have had someone not placed a needle beneath her skin, injecting her with a drug that astonishingly had an immediate affect. Ryan felt herself begin to slide toward blackness and had a sudden despairing thought. Although she could not feel the woman's presence, she knew Madelyn had been right next to her, watching her futile efforts with some amusement the entire time.

And now Ryan was laying on some sort of rock. Her wrists were still restrained, but her feet were free. She lie very still, listening intently. The room she was in was not large and seemed to made of rock. She was not alone. There was slight movement, and she identified three others present. She was certain the woman was not one of them. She used the subtle movement of those present to identify the remaining features of the room. There were no windows and a single door, perhaps made of some type of heavy wood. There did not seem to be any furniture in the room except the bed she was lying in, which seemed less of a bed because of its narrowness and height from the floor, more something along the lines of an altar.

Great, Ryan thought to herself. An altar. Things got sacrificed on altars.

Ryan remained motionless as one of the figures approached her and removed her blindfold. The guard seemed startled that she was already awake. Ryan stared back at him, taking the opportunity to examine him thoroughly.

He appeared a normal man, although an exceptional specimen, as they all did. Tall and muscular, there was a cruelty about his stony face. There was also an odd, very faint cast to his skin, a bluish color, something a little darker than the pallor of death. But it was very faint and seemed to shift with the light, making Ryan wonder if she was imagining it. He was dressed in a uniform of sorts, sleeveless, revealing massive arms and bulging biceps. His expression was one of arrogance and utter contempt.

Ryan turned her attention to the other two, noting she had been correct in the number present. They were very similar to the first, their features only slightly different. The resemblance, in fact, was enough to suggest that they were related, even if distantly. They too were dismissive and contemptuous of their captive, a fact clearly evident as one moved to remove Ryan's wrist manacles. He grabbed her by the shirt, yanked her into a seated position, and roughly removed the restraints.

Ryan watched the technique carefully, but they were unlatched so quickly she could not see how it was done.

"Lie back down," the guard commanded harshly.

Ryan just looked at him as if she suddenly did not speak English. It infuriated the guard, and he stepped forward, grabbed her shoulders, and forced her downward.

It was a mistake. Ryan knew he was far stronger than she was, so she did not resist at all, causing him to pitch forward, off-balance. She immediately snapped her knee upward to the back of his head, sending him crashing to the floor. She continued the movement, rolling the somersault backward until she was on her knees on the platform.

The other two were on her immediately, and within seconds she was back onto her back from sheer force. Ryan was shocked at how strong the men were, all easily surpassing her strength. Still, even as the third rejoined the fray, they had difficulty restraining the thrashing girl. It took each man both arms to restrain a limb, leaving one limb free, which happened to be Ryan's right foot. With blinding speed, she snapped a kick upward, striking one man full across the face and sending him flying. The man on her left arm moved to restrain the deadly lower limbs, leaving that appendage free. Ryan took that opportunity to leverage herself into a half-seated position, then took aim to deliver a left cross to the guard pinning the right half of her body. It would have been a stinging blow since his face was fully exposed.

Except that Ryan's left arm was now encased in steel. The forward motion had been stopped so abruptly her shoulder dislocated as the force redistributed when the arm failed to move.

Ryan stopped struggling.

She turned to look at Madelyn, who held her trapped wrist with one hand without effort. The woman gazed at her with a mixture of amusement and vexation. Ryan let her eyes rest on the captive, motionless wrist, incredulous at the force that had stopped it. She raised her eyes again to those of Madelyn's. Since the wrist was not going anywhere, Ryan reversed the pressure on the arm, now using the leverage to put her shoulder back into place. It relocated with an audible pop.

A smile played about Madelyn's lips at the defiant gesture, but it did not diminish the predatory look in her eye. Nor did it lessen the hostility in her tone as she addressed her men.

"Leave us," she commanded in disgust. She released the wrist.

The men knew the disgust was fully directed at them and hung their heads in fear and shame. They quickly departed. Ryan sat upright, rubbing her wrist. It felt as if it had been fractured. Madelyn was behind her, and the sensation was very uncomfortable, as if she were being stalked. It was even more disturbing because she could not sense the woman and was not certain where she was. The voice in her ear startled her, immediately pinpointing the women's location and proximity to her. Ryan swallowed hard, struggling to calm herself.

"So, Ryan Alexander," Madelyn whispered mockingly, "will you fight me?"

Ryan sat silently for a moment, the muscle in her jaw clenching and unclenching. "No," she said finally.

"And why not?" Madelyn asked in a tone reserved for a recalcitrant student, one forced to verbal repetition because she could not learn the lessons.

"Because it is futile," Ryan said.

Madelyn was pleased with her student. "Good," she said.

Ryan swallowed again, bracing herself for what she knew was to come. But even that did not prepare her for the tremendous pain of the woman's bite, and although she had said she would not, she instinctively struggled. It was as ineffectual as the attempted left cross. Madelyn simply wrapped her arms about Ryan and now Ryan's entire body felt as if it were encased in steel.

The pain was intense, blocking out all sight and sound, and there was no accompanying pleasure. Worse, Ryan felt her lower extremities begin to go numb, almost as if there was some paralysis to the bite. The paralysis seeped upward and Ryan began to lose feeling in her arms and torso. Madelyn's embrace no longer immobilized her but rather was supporting her as she went completely limp. Madelyn adjusted the girl's position, her pleasure at the immobilization pronounced. She continued to drink from the carotid artery, leisurely taking her fill. Unfortunately for Ryan, the paralysis did not diminish the pain in any way. It seemed to actually increase it, for now Ryan could do nothing to relieve or escape it. She closed her eyes in misery and despair, praying she would spin off into unconsciousness, but that welcome blackness was denied as well. Ryan was fully aware the entire time, unable to slide into oblivion.

Finally, after what seemed like hours, the woman was finished. Madelyn stood, releasing Ryan and allowing her to fall to the floor. Ryan lie in a crumpled heap, still unable to do more than flex her fingers.

"So you are the best they have to offer," Madelyn said mockingly. She examined the crumpled heap with a predatory smile, then departed, leaving Ryan to her agony and despair.

Harrian stood outside the captive's door. As Madelyn's chief familiar, he was responsible for the security of the prisoner. News of his men's failings had shot through the compound, and he now stood ready to face his mistress's wrath.

Madelyn, however, seemed serene as she entered the hallway, an uncharacteristic disposition that, in a way, was more unsettling than her wrath. He bowed low before her.

"Shall I have the girl killed, or simply allow her to succumb to her injuries?" he asked with what he hoped was the right amount of subservience.

"You will do neither," Madelyn said, her thoughts on the previous moments. "You will tend to her wounds and see that she fully recovers."

"What?" Harrian asked, astonished. He immediately regretted his tone because those who questioned Madelyn suffered the consequences. Fortunately for him, Madelyn seemed engrossed in her own thoughts and did not notice his insubordination.

Or so he thought. She turned upon him, and although her tone was mild, her words left little doubt as to her threat.

"If the girl 'succumbs to her wounds,' then so will you," she said, brutally clear.

"Yes, your highness," Harrian said, bowing low. He did not raise his head until Madelyn's flowing garments had disappeared down the corridor. Once upright once more, he stared a long moment after his mistress. This was most unexpected.

Half a world away, two very dark and very furious eyes opened.

CHAPTER 21

ABIGAIL PUSHED THROUGH THE DOUBLE DOORS, hope and disbelief on her features at what she thought she would find.

A wickedly handsome man, broad through the shoulders and slender at the waist stood with his hands on his hips, facing away from her. His black, silky hair brushed his collar, and as he turned, his dark eyes flashed.

"Where is my child?" Victor demanded, "Where is Ryan?"

There were so many things Abigail wanted to say to him, but knew that right now there was only one thing he wanted to hear.

"She has been taken, my lord," she said simply.

"By whom?" Victor asked, a very dangerous undertone in his voice.

"A woman," Abigail replied, "an Old One by the name of Madelyn."

"I do not know a Madelyn," Victor said, his fury barely controlled.

"Nor do I," Abigail replied, "nor any of us for that matter." She was something at a loss, there was so much to explain, and Victor clearly did not have the patience for a long-winded account.

Victor interrupted her reverie, clearly reading her thoughts. "There is one way in which you can bring me up to the moment very quickly."

Abigail knew to what he referred, because if Victor Shared her blood he would also share her Memories. But she was mildly affronted by his presumptuous manner.

"Is that a request, my lord? Or a command? For you should know you are no longer King."

Victor's anger softened for a moment. "Ryan is King?" he asked.

Abigail nodded. "Her coronation was but a few days ago."

Victor realized his anger was misdirected, at least until he knew otherwise. His tone was formal, but there was a trace of apology in it as well. "Then it is a request, my lady."

"Then I live to serve you," Abigail replied.

Victor moved to her and without prelude took her into his arms. They had been in such an embrace numerous times throughout the centuries, but today it was more a business transaction than a coupling. Abigail stiffened slightly at his bite, seeking to repress any pleasure she might feel in order to control the ebb and flow of her thoughts.

But Victor would have none of it. He took everything that he could see, attempting to absorb the events of the last few years. He saw Ryan's success at the purge, culling their Kind in an extraordinary manner. He saw the complicity between Aeron and Abigail as Ryan sought to battle his nemesis. He saw Abigail ultimately come to the girl's aid, as well as his own. With pride, he saw Ryan's relationships with the Old Ones, and her final assumption of leadership of the hierarchy. And he saw the woman Madelyn, at the very end, taking his child prisoner, leading her away like a lamb to slaughter.

Victor raised his head, Abigail's blood still on his lips. He took a step back, removed a tissue from a nearby table, and wiped his mouth. His eyes were on the matriarch.

"You played a very dangerous game with my daughter's life."

Abigail gazed at him, unruffled. "At your request my lord. If you remember correctly, you asked two things of me. And until a few days ago, I had accomplished both."

Victor nodded slowly, unable to generate any anger at her. He had taken a dangerous gamble and it had paid off. He had given Abigail only goals, not methods, and how she chose to carry out her objective was entirely up to her.

"I can see it has cost me greatly."

Victor was referring to the intimacy that had flourished between Abigail and Ryan. He sensed Abigail's hold on the girl was great.

"You did promise her to me," Abigail reminded him.

"Yes," Victor said, "I did." He glanced at the already-fading bruise on Abigail's neck. "Perhaps when I am no longer seeking information I can find a way to distract you from that pursuit."

Abigail felt desire flare in her, but carefully suppressed it. Victor Alexander was a formidable player in the game of seduction. "Perhaps," was all she said.

Victor turned abruptly, business-like once more. "I want the Council convened," he paused, and his eyes grew dark with fury once more, "and I want to see Aeron."

"Victor," Abigail interrupted him, "there is one more thing you should know."

She had withheld one bit of information from him, if for no other reason than she was not certain how he would respond. And there certainly had to be a better way to tell him.

"What?" Victor asked impatiently. He turned to the opening doors as Marilyn and Kusunoki entered, followed by Ala. Although he had not seen them in years and they were joyful at his recovery, there seemed to be a hesitancy about them that Victor did not quite understand. Did not understand, that is, until Marilyn stepped to the side, revealing what Ala held in her arms.

Victor stared.

After what seemed an interminable moment, Abigail quietly noted, "He has his grandfather's hair."

Victor continued to stare at the boy. "And Aeron's eyes," he said finally.

It was difficult to assess Victor's reaction, perhaps because it was taking him a moment to have one.

"But beyond that," he said at last, "he looks exactly like Ryan."

If there was any remaining doubt as to his feelings, he added, "he is beautiful."

Ala walked to Victor, who could not take his eyes from the boy. She held him out. Victor took him and held him for a moment as if he was so fragile he might break. He then clutched him to his chest, overcome with emotion. The boy sat contentedly sucking his thumb.

"He could be Ryan at that age," Victor said.

Abigail had suspected as much, although none of the Others had known Ryan as a child. "His name is Drake," she said gently.

Victor held him out once more, examining his perfection. "Drake Alexander," he said.

For the first time since his mother had disappeared, the boy smiled. It seemed as if he knew exactly who Victor was, and took great comfort in his presence. And for the first time since Victor had awakened, he, too, smiled.

CHAPTER 22

RYAN LAY ON HER ROCK SLAB. They had given her one concession to comfort, a cushion-like pillow that she could prop herself up on. The guards seemed very concerned for her welfare, checking on her on a regular basis. She ignored them, sprawled out on her altar bed, mainly because she did not think she could yet move. The woman's feeding had taken a tremendous toll on her and she spent much of her time in an exhausted sleep.

The door opened and Ryan ignored whomever entered, but only for a moment. Some instinct told her she should immediately open her eyes. Madelyn towered over her.

"What has happened?" Madelyn demanded.

Ryan just stared at her. She had felt the change as well, as if a breeze had arisen from nowhere on a still summer day. She did not respond.

Madelyn bent down over her and it took all of Ryan's self-discipline not to flinch away.

"I will not ask you again."

The threat in her voice was unmistakable and Ryan delayed her response only enough to incur irritation, not wrath.

"My father has awakened," Ryan replied quietly, concealing any joy it might have given her.

In contrast, Madelyn disguised nothing. "Victor Alexander,"

she said with pleasure, the same strange enunciation of the last name, "another I have longed to meet." She turned her attention back to Ryan. "Perhaps I should arrange a reunion between you and your father."

Ryan felt fear and rage at the proposition and desperately struggled to hide her emotions. Something, however, suddenly occurred to her.

Madelyn had not known about Victor.

"You cannot read my thoughts," Ryan said slowly. Madelyn simply looked at her, the simmering anger in her eyes the only validation Ryan needed. Ryan glanced at Madelyn's familiar who stood in the doorway.

"None of you can," Ryan said in wonder. This was an ability that the older of her Kind took completely for granted.

In an instant, Madelyn snatched her upward by her shirt collar, jerking her so that they were face-to-face. It was immediately obvious that Ryan had been prone not out of disrespect but out of pain as she muffled a groan at the wrenching movement.

The pain Madelyn inflicted seemed to regulate her anger, but her words were still coldly furious.

"I cannot read your thoughts, but I can sense when you are communicating with them," she said, "which is why I forbid you to do so."

Ryan stared at her defiantly. She would not reach out to the Others, but that limitation was of far less consequence than the fact that these Ones could not read her mind.

It did not seem an entirely necessary ability at the moment. Madelyn pulled her even closer until they were almost cheek-to-cheek. Her gaze lowered, then lingered on the prominent bruise on Ryan's neck.

"If I feed on you again," Madelyn said softly, "before you are fully recovered, you will not survive."

Ryan's gaze was steady. "Why would you want to?" she replied, just as softly, "when I was such a disappointment the first time?"

Madelyn gazed at the girl, and Ryan was quite certain she was going to be killed. But the woman surprised her by smiling.

"You are entertaining, Ryan Alexander." Madelyn stood upright, abruptly dropping her back onto the rock slab. Ryan suppressed another moan and curled into a ball.

"Pray that you stay that way," she said as she departed.

CHAPTER 23

AERON STOOD BEFORE VICTOR, far more patient than Abigail had ever seen him. She sat off to the side and took turns examining the two men. Victor sat behind his desk, one long leg crossed over the other, his arms crossed over his broad chest. He gazed at the man standing before him, his face nearly expressionless except for the slightest trace of disdain. Aeron stood ramrod straight, his hands clasped in front of him, his gaze on the great expanse of desk in front of him.

Abigail was rather shocked. Under normal circumstances, these two would be at each other's throats, and under the current circumstances, Abigail was quite surprised Aeron was not in a fight for his life. Instead, there seemed to some strange undercurrent that was keeping both in check, and Abigail was desperately trying to understand the nuance. She glanced from one to the other, and it suddenly struck her.

Aeron now had the air of the less-than-desirable prom date standing before the disapproving father. The thought filled Abigail with such mirth she had to muffle her laughter. Both men were aware of at least the essence of her thoughts and cast baleful glances her direction.

Victor uncrossed his arms, rested one arm on the desk, and began tapping his index finger on the wood. After what seemed an eternity of this torture, he ceased tapping and at last spoke.

"I will settle with you later on all that has occurred, including your attempt on both my life and Ryan's," Victor said coldly, "but now is not the time."

Aeron said nothing.

"My only concern right now is the safe return of my child," Victor said, "and as you are the only one who has had contact with this woman who has taken her, I require your assistance."

Still, Aeron said nothing. When Victor gave him a menacing look, he nodded stiffly.

"I will assist in any way I can."

"Good," Victor said, dismissing him.

Aeron was not ready to leave. "I have one request," he said, the humiliation of having to ask straining him.

Victor merely stared at him. He did not wait for the request but responded to it instead. "I will consider it," he said brusquely. He knew Aeron wanted to see his son.

Aeron realized it was the only answer he would receive at the moment, and at least it wasn't "no." He nodded, and quickly disappeared. Abigail watched his departure with interest. At last, she voiced her observation.

"He is completely in love with the girl," she said.

Victor returned to the paperwork at his desk. "Yes," he said, unconcerned, "he is."

Abigail turned to him, a shrewd look on her face. "But then again, you knew that would happen."

Victor did not look up. "Yes," he said simply, "I did."

Abigail smiled. She could concoct the most prolonged, elaborate, and convoluted scheme over centuries, and Victor Alexander would still be one step ahead of her. It was why she so adored him.

Victor glanced up from his paperwork, quite serious. "Ryan has accomplished more for our Kind in a few years than I have managed to do in centuries." His tone was not self-incriminating, but rather matter-of-fact. "She is able to bring our Kind together in a way I am unable to because she is able to fill so many roles." He thought of Aeron and Marilyn. "Whether that role is as a lover," his thoughts shifted to

Ala and Kusunoki, "or as a child," he glanced over at Abigail with a meaningful expression, "or both—"

Abigail smoothed her skirt unapologetically.

"—she binds us all together," Victor finished.

"Do you think that is why she was taken from us?" Abigail asked.

Victor began tapping his finger on the desk once more, the gesture unconscious. Abigail watched as dark thoughts flitted across his beautiful features.

"I don't know," he said finally, "I just don't know."

CHAPTER 24

RYAN FELT THE PAIN IN HER ARM race up to her shoulder then spread throughout her chest. It jerked her back into consciousness, wrapping ice-cold fingers around her heart and squeezing. She gasped as one drug reversed the effects of the one given to her previously.

She instinctively jerked her arm away from the man sitting next to her, and looked up to find Madelyn watching her. Ryan rubbed the injection site on the arm, glancing around.

She was in the back of a limousine seated next to one of Madelyn's familiars. She had been blindfolded and bound when she had left her cell, but now her hands and legs were free, and she could obviously see. She had no idea how long she had been unconscious, which was apparently the point since she now had no concept of where she was. She could have been a hundred miles from her prison, she could be thousands.

Ryan eyed the needle the familiar replaced in an odd-looking medical case. The needle interested her because no normal needle could penetrate her skin, and this one appeared to do so easily. She wondered what material it was made from. The drug itself was a mystery because Ryan had never known any drug to affect her so, not even when she was human. The medical case also attracted her attention because it appeared ancient but simultaneously modern in its construction.

She filed each piece of information away, a small part of a puzzle that for the moment had no boundary and no apparent image to aid in arranging the pieces. She became aware of the unblinking scrutiny of the woman across from her. Although Madelyn could not read her thoughts, Ryan felt transparent to her most of the time. Even now, she felt Madelyn was entertained by her amateur sleuthing, as if Ryan were engaged in some sort of harmless child's game.

Attempting to hide her despondency, Ryan looked out the window and instead felt it grow exponentially. She knew exactly where they were.

"I thought you would like to see your father," Madelyn said with her uncanny precision. "I am certain he would like to see you."

Without thinking, Ryan reached out to Victor. He was close, and she could feel his presence in a way she had not been able to in years.

"Ryan," Madelyn said, threat in her voice, "you are forbidden to communicate in that manner. I will not tell you again."

Ryan immediately shut down, but not before she could feel the Others reach out to her. They were all here, Abigail, Marilyn, Ala, Kusunoki, Edward, Susan, even Aeron. In a last, desperate message, she pleaded with Susan to hide her son. She then shut her mind completely.

Madelyn watched the girl, aware of the last-minute desperate communiqué, but not its contents. The girl would bear watching.

Victor stood on the steps of the estate, watching the limousines pull to a stop at the bottom of the stairs. They had moved from the Grand Council chambers, but their movements clearly were known.

Several men exited the forward and rear vehicles. These must be the familiars Aeron spoke of. He, too, sensed how strong they were, and noted their strange appearance and marked resemblance to one another. They moved with the lithe grace of their Kind, but in a brutally athletic way. Victor turned his attention to the center limousine.

A tall, dark haired woman stepped from the opened door, and Victor knew this was Madelyn even had he not seen her in Abigail's memories. Her presence was staggering, but in a clouded way, as if he could not grasp her full extent. She was strikingly beautiful, but Victor noted the peculiarities, the strange coldness at her center, as if she could reach out and touch him, freeze him immobile, then shatter him with a second touch. He noted the unnatural flow of her gait as she stepped to the side, but then his attention was completely redirected to the one stepping from the open door.

Ryan stood upright and Victor clenched his jaw as she winced with pain. She looked up at him and her expression was guarded, giving him all the warning he needed. She did not look well, appearing both tired and pale. She squared her shoulders, however, and started up the steps toward him, moving quickly enough that her captors had to hurry to catch up with her. Victor smiled grimly. His child was waging a very subtle rebellion.

When she reached the top of the stairs, Ryan stopped in front of her father. For a moment, all she did was stare at him, drinking in the beauty of the man she had so desperately missed. All she wanted to do was fall into the arms of her father. It was all Victor wanted as well, but he sensed Ryan's taut reservation and honored her judgment. His gaze turned to Madelyn, who stood at Ryan's side.

"And to what do I owe the pleasure of this visit?" Victor asked, his anger barely contained.

Madelyn gazed at him mockingly. "Are you telling me you do not wish to see your daughter?"

"Are you telling me you are returning her to me?" Victor fired back.

"No," Madelyn responded coldly, "I am not." She glanced about, noting he had not invited them inside. "And is this the extent of your hospitality?"

"This is my home," Ryan interjected into the conversation, her own anger seething, "any hospitality extended or not is my discretion." She turned fully to Madelyn, her sarcasm distinct. "Won't you please come inside?"

Without waiting for a response, Ryan started through the doors, again requiring Madelyn's familiars to scramble to keep up with her. Victor eyed Madelyn a moment longer, then gave a short, mocking bow. "After you," he said.

Ryan strode through the foyer and into her den, followed by her complement of guards. Both Edward and Abigail got to their feet at her entrance, reaching out to her, but she quickly mentally warned them not to correspond with thought. She gave Abigail a long look, trying to communicate so many things, uncertain if she was at all successful.

She turned back to Victor, and the anguish evident in his eyes caused a lump to form in her own throat. Never had she felt so constrained or helpless. She glanced at Madelyn, who seemed very aware of her pain, and Ryan wondered if that had been the purpose of this staged reunion all along.

Victor approached her and they stood face-to-face, both aware that they were being closely watched by Ryan's captors. Victor felt his frustration mount, uncertain of what he should say or should not say, knowing he did not have much time.

"You are well?" Victor asked, knowing she was not.

"I will survive," Ryan said, her voice as calm and emotionless as his. "And you?"

"Some great disturbance seems to have awakened me," Victor said.

Ryan smiled. It was his way of expressing absolute fury. "I see," Ryan said, "then there is some good that has come from this situation."

Ryan raised her hand in a casual gesture, appearing almost to wipe her mouth. She continued the gesture upward, as if she were reaching to tenderly touch Victor's face. He did not move, knowing full well what she was doing. It seemed Madelyn had a sudden understanding of her intention as well, but she was half a second behind the act.

"No!" she commanded.

But it was too late. Ryan had already touched the blood on her fingertips, drawn by brushing her skin across her own razor-sharp teeth, to Victor's lips. In an instant, he had all of Ryan's Memories from the moment she was taken. And although Ryan's captors were springing towards both of them, they could not take that knowledge from him. They wrestled Ryan backward from Victor, but she was not struggling. Victor did not resist, either, when they pulled him away. His eyes were locked with Ryan's, the bond between them at that moment absolute. When she was certain he had everything he needed, she looked away, closing herself off from the world once more.

The dramatic events had taken but a few seconds, but Victor had seen all. He wanted to attack the woman across the room, but knew that supreme restraint was required at this moment, both for his life and Ryan's. He gazed at his daughter, proud of her strength and fearlessness, as well as her ingenuity.

Madelyn, although angry, did not seem particularly surprised at the girl's actions. "Ryan," she said, both calm and threatening, "time to go."

Ryan did not resist as she was led roughly from the room, and although Victor clenched his jaw so tightly the grinding of his teeth was audible, he did not do anymore than follow them out. He stood at the top of the stairs as Ryan was practically dragged down the steps. Madelyn stopped briefly before beginning her descent.

"Thank you for your hospitality," she said, her smile utterly devoid of warmth. She turned and Victor watched as she flowed down the stairs.

Ryan winced from the rough treatment she was receiving. She knew she was probably going to receive far worse, perhaps even death. But she had at least given the Others all of the information she had in hopes they could save themselves.

Although Ryan was not resisting, her captors were still treating her brutally, perhaps because they themselves were going to pay for her disobedience. Ryan did not mind the pain so much, it matched her internal state. But when one guard put his hand on the back of her head, attempting to force it downward in a manner both humiliating and degrading, she snapped. She threw an elbow rearward, catching the man off guard and landing a blow squarely on his chin. He went comically backward, knocking one of his comrades down as well.

Immediately, Ryan was lifted off her feet, but this freed her legs. She snapped a kick outward at the nearest guard, catching him fully in the chest and sending him sailing. She twisted in the grip of the one holding her, trying to land another kick at a nearby assailant.

Madelyn stood in the opened door of the limousine, watching the scene with a mixture of exasperation and disgust. Her exasperation was for the girl, the disgust for the incompetents trying to restrain her.

"Bind her," she commanded, her patience having reached its limits.

Four men set upon Ryan, and she found herself encased in what felt like a straightjacket. Her legs were still free, but only for a second, then they, too, were bound at the ankles. Within seconds she was completely restrained, almost cocooned. She was unceremoniously thrown through the open car door, landing face down on the floorboards.

Madelyn glanced upward. Victor watched the scene, his fury nearly overwhelming his self-control. She smiled her cold smile, and Victor had the sudden impression the entire scene had been orchestrated. She gracefully settled into the limousine, and the door closed behind her.

Once in the car, Madelyn reached down, grasping Ryan by the back of the collar and pulling her upward without effort. She held her so that Ryan was across her lap and they were face-to-face. Ryan again had to calm herself to keep from flinching away. She held Madelyn's gaze steadily.

Oddly, it did not appear Madelyn was particularly angry with her. If anything, she seemed to view Ryan's antics as those of an unruly child, and her words reinforced this perception.

"You," she said with emphasis, "need to behave."

Ryan arched her back as Madelyn's teeth pierced her skin. The pain was so intense, Ryan involuntarily kicked outward, her feet striking the window glass. And although the glass was weapons grade and several inches thick, a crack spider-webbed outward from the blow.

Outside the limousine, the guards who had been humiliated by

Ryan saw the crack and smiled sadistically. At least the girl would pay for her actions. They climbed into their own vehicles.

Inside the limousine, Ryan felt the paralysis begin to spread throughout her body. She desperately wished to pass out, but again, unconsciousness would not come. Madelyn drank a little longer, but did not drain her. When she finished, at least for the moment, Madelyn gave her immobile figure a slight push, and Ryan tumbled back onto the floor. Ryan lie there, grateful at least that she was not in contact with the hated creature.

Some time passed, but Ryan was not in a position to judge time or distance. The limousine stopped, and Ryan felt Madelyn exit. She was then pulled roughly from the floor and dragged out the open door. Her head struck the doorframe, causing her even more pain. She was suddenly jerked from the arms of the one who was handling her so roughly, and she struggled to open her eyes to see what was happening.

Ryan was now being held by Madelyn's Chief familiar, who was cradling her far more gently. This was probably because Madelyn was holding the rough-handling familiar by his throat as his feet dangled in the air. She was furious, but did not raise her voice as she addressed him.

"I am allowed to cause her pain," Madelyn said, "not you."

Madelyn tightened her grip and a crunching noise could be heard as she crushed the man's larynx. His feet kicked futilely, but only for a few seconds, and then he went limp. Madelyn tossed the man to the side like a rag doll. She whirled about and stalked up the stairs of the waiting jet.

Ryan could not keep her eyes open and all went black for her once more. Although she could not read the thoughts of the Chief familiar who was holding her, she sensed his consternation at these events. She was carried up the steps, then placed onto what felt like a bed. She again made an effort to open her eyes and saw that the jet apparently had a sleeping berth, a fairly luxurious one. Her restraints were removed and she was rolled onto her side facing away from the door. She heard the door close and knew that she was alone.

Madelyn settled into her chair across from the sleeping berth. Her servants tiptoed gingerly about the plane, making hurried preparations for departure. Within minutes, the jet began moving and was in the air. Harrian settled into a seat close to Madelyn.

"That could have gone better," Harrian commented.

"I don't see how," Madelyn said, "the girl is utterly predictable."

Harrian gave Madelyn a sharp glance. "You knew she would attempt to communicate with her father?"

"I knew," Madelyn corrected, "she would succeed. And now, Victor Alexander knows exactly what I want him to. Just enough to demoralize him."

Harrian lowered his gaze. He would not presume to know his Queen's plans. Madelyn stood up. She glanced at him, then to the surrounding men. "I am not to be disturbed."

She pushed through the door to the sleeping berth, and it whispered closed behind her. Two of the men smirked at one another. The girl was going to continue to pay for her crimes.

Harrian, on the other hand, watched his master's departure with the beginnings of concern.

Ryan could not see who had entered the room but knew it was Madelyn. This determination was proved correct when she felt the woman settle into the bed behind her.

"As I said before, Ryan Alexander, if nothing else, you are entertaining."

Ryan flinched as the sharp teeth again sliced her skin, and felt her heart struggle sluggishly in her chest as Madelyn began to take her remaining blood. She did so leisurely, but even so, the strain on Ryan was immense. Once more, there was no pleasure, no mental connection, no lethargy, and no welcome oblivion.

Ryan felt she was very close to death, and Madelyn seemed to sense it as well. She pulled away just far enough to whisper in Ryan's ear.

"And so, shall I let you die, little one?"

Ryan recoiled, more from the sarcastic endearment than the question. Very few were allowed to call her that.

"Please do," Ryan articulated through clenched teeth, her defiance unbowed.

Madelyn settled comfortably behind Ryan, slipping her arm about the girl's waist.

"I don't think so," she replied.

Ryan lie stiffly in the woman's embrace. She was not certain, but it almost felt like Madelyn was sleeping. Ryan herself felt sleep approach, and she welcomed the impending darkness.

As she began to at last slide into an exhausted sleep, Madelyn's arm was heavy about her body. In truth, the intimacy of their position was far more disturbing to Ryan than any amount of physical pain the woman could cause her.

CHAPTER 25

VICTOR SAT AT THE HEAD OF THE TABLE, his gaze distant. The Others sat about the table around him, waiting patiently. They knew he was sorting through the Memories Ryan had given him, attempting to put them in some coherent order.

"Ryan does not know where she is being held," Victor began slowly. "She has been taken by plane, but both times has been drugged."

"They have a drug that can affect Ryan?"

All heads turned in surprise to Susan. Victor had requested she sit with the Old Ones in case she had anything to add, but all were surprised she had spoken up so quickly. Susan herself was surprised she had blurted out the question.

"I am sorry," she stammered, feeling the need to explain, "it's just that I have studied Ryan's system so extensively, I can't think of anything that would affect her that way." Susan thought back to her research. "I couldn't even get a needle beneath her skin."

This statement triggered something else in Victor. He sorted through the Memories once more, a strange sensation akin to remembering something he himself had never personally experienced. "You're right," he said slowly, "Ryan was surprised both by the drug and the way it was administered. It seems to be some sort of material she has never seen before. Her restraints were made of the same material, and she could not budge them."

"What does the place look like where she is being held?" Kusunoki asked.

"She has seen only her cell, which is solid rock," Victor said, visualizing the room in which Ryan was being held. "She believes the surrounding structure is rock as well, but she has no idea how large it is."

"What does she know of Madelyn?" Abigail asked, voicing the question all wanted answered but none wanted to ask.

Victor's expression grew dark. "Madelyn is immeasurably powerful, so much so that Ryan believes the woman could kill her at any time. It is Ryan's belief that Madelyn nearly did so when she fed upon her, and it was only Madelyn's restraint that kept her alive."

"Then Madelyn does want her alive," Abigail noted.

"At least for now," Victor said. "Ryan is uncertain how long that will continue." As painful as it was for him, he relived Ryan's Memories of Madelyn's first attack. Those at the table lowered their eyes, the anguish reflected in his eyes too much to bear.

"Ryan feels no mental or physical bond with Madelyn when she takes her blood, nor is there any pleasure. There is only pain." Victor grew puzzled. "There is also some sort of paralysis that accompanies the act."

"Perhaps Madelyn transmits some type of neurotoxin with her bite."

All eyes again turned toward the voice at the end of the table, and Susan inwardly cursed her newly-acquired Tourette's syndrome. The conversation was, however, in her area of expertise.

"I have not studied your–" Susan stopped, correcting herself, "–our Kind exhaustively, and I've not seen it in anyone I've studied. But certain species like snakes and spiders are capable of transmitting a neurotoxin that paralyzes their prey." She looked up at Victor. "It sounds almost like what you're describing."

Victor nodded slowly. "Yes, it does." The train of thought brought something extremely significant into focus. "Ryan does not think Madelyn, nor any of her men, can read her thoughts."

179

"What?" Ala asked, stunned. "Is she certain?"

Victor shook his head. "Not entirely. It could be a trick. But Ryan is fairly certain they are not adept at reading her mind. And it is why she was forbidden to communicate with us in that manner. Apparently Madelyn can sense the flow of communication, but cannot sense the content."

"How can this be?" Ala asked, her disbelief evident. "How can they be so powerful yet lack such a fundamental skill?"

Victor was uncertain. "Well, not all of our Kind possess such a gift, but still…" His voice trailed off, and it was apparent he was dissatisfied with his own explanation. He again turned his attention to the far end of the table.

Susan was deep in thought, and suddenly realized everyone at the table was looking at her expectantly. Reluctantly, she gave voice to her musings.

"I once had a conversation with Ryan, describing her as a form of accelerated evolution. But evolution is not merely a forward progression of never-ending improvement. There is a reason why Darwin used the term 'descent of man,' not ascent, and it is often misunderstood."

"Go on," Victor said.

"Evolution," Susan explained, "involves adaptations that are advantageous for a particular set of circumstances. If those circumstances change, then the adaptations may no longer be advantageous. It has very little to do with progress or advancement, but rather suitability."

"So how does that fit in with Madelyn's abilities or inabilities?" Victor asked.

Susan was reflective. "If Madelyn, as you are suggesting, is significantly older than any of you, and has lived separately under different conditions, she may have developed different skills."

"Or perhaps she is so old that she has actually lost skills that are unnecessary to her," Marilyn commented.

It was such a prescient comment and so out-of-character coming from Marilyn's mouth it momentarily silenced everyone at the table. They simply stared at her.

"I do occasionally read a book or two," Marilyn commented

dryly.

As sober as the conversation was, Susan hid a smile. She mentally returned to her analogy, carefully searching for flaws. "Traits that are advantageous are generally passed along by reproduction and mutations may take millions of years to take hold. However, I watched Ryan's body adapt to certain stresses in ways that I can only describe as mutagenic. And since your Kind, at least traditionally, creates offspring by Sharing blood, the entire process may be accelerated to," Susan shook her head, "to almost real-time."

"So what you are saying," Victor said slowly, "is that Madelyn may have taken a different evolutionary path."

Susan nodded, "Or merely may be further along the same path. It's hard to say without knowing her background."

"And I think that is what concerns me the most," Victor said, "that I know nothing of her past. I find it impossible that none of us have ever heard of One this powerful."

Everyone nodded agreement.

"Does Ryan know why she has been taken?" Abigail asked.

Victor again sorted through the confused maze of thoughts, perceptions, feelings, and sensations, none of which belonged to him. He saw through Ryan's eyes, saw the disdain and condescension with which Madelyn treated her.

But Victor saw something else, something Ryan could not see. It was one of the unique features of perception through Memory. Although he saw the world through Ryan's eyes, as if he were actually her, he also retained the ability to process the information with his own mind.

"Ryan believes Madelyn is just toying with her," he said slowly, "keeping her alive until she is done playing with her."

Abigail picked up on Victor's hesitation. "But you do not believe that."

"No," Victor said, searching his thoughts for the subtle cues Ryan had missed, "I don't believe that at all." He pieced together the few images of Madelyn that troubled him, as well as the fleeting impressions of Ryan's captors and Madelyn's chief familiar. He carefully chose his words.

"Ryan is an infant to Madelyn, young, weak, and powerless."

Those around the table had difficulty grasping the concept that Ryan could ever be considered in such a way. Victor seemed to fall into a dark reverie.

"So…?" Abigail finally prompted.

"So Madelyn cannot figure out why Ryan satisfies her."

Victor glanced up, his certainty growing. "And although it is more of a guess than any impression from Ryan's Memories, I believe it has been a very long time since anyone has satisfied Madelyn."

CHAPTER 26

RYAN WAS ONCE MORE ON HER BACK, staring up at the rock ceiling. It was how she spent most of her time, the hours that she did not spend sleeping or in meditation. She had no real concept of the passage of time. There was no natural light and therefore no cues. It was difficult to even tell where the artificial light was coming from in her cell.

It was one of the pieces of information Ryan filed away. Although her prison cell appeared ancient, almost like the medieval castles of her childhood, its construction was far more modern and precise. Ryan examined the rock wall. It was meticulously smooth, with no signs of tool markings, almost as if it had been removed as a single whole from a mountainside. The wall to her right was different, constructed of large bricks made of the same rock material. But again, the bricks were unreasonably precise, meticulously sized and placed in an unusual geometric pattern.

Ryan stood upright and moved to the solid rock wall. She placed her hands on the smooth surface. Perhaps it had not been removed from the mountainside but was still a part of the mountain. That would mean she was in some sort of mountain range.

Ryan sighed and turned away. It could just as easily mean she was ten stories underground, and the rock cut from earth much like the chambers of the Grand Council. She sat back down on her slab.

And the compound she was in could easily be older than a medieval castle because, although the construction was extremely advanced, it did not seem new.

The heavy door to her cell whispered open, another oddity of construction. By appearance it should have creaked open, pressed inward only with great effort. Instead, it opened smoothly by some silent mechanical means.

A young guard entered and Ryan eyed him with contempt. All of the guards were brutal and dismissive, but this one in particular grated on her. He was arrogant and cruel with a thinly-concealed streak of sadism. He looked at her in a way that suggested he would like to do many evil things to her if the opportunity ever arose.

She ignored him, if for no other reason than she knew it would irritate him. He seemed in a particularly foul mood today. He thoroughly examined Ryan's cell, which never ceased to amuse her since she had no idea what they thought she could accomplish in her solid rock jail.

"Stand up," he ordered harshly.

Apparently Ryan was a little too leisurely in her response, and he grabbed her upper arm and jerked her to her feet. He spun her around and began to roughly search her, his hands lingering in certain sensitive areas. Ryan glanced down. She found the display irritating but only mildly so because she possessed no shame regarding her body. One could not humiliate someone who refused to be humiliated.

The guard spun her around again so she was facing him, and as he did so, Ryan felt something bump her leg. As the guard continued his search, Ryan casually glanced down, trying to identify the object. When she did so, her heart leaped.

It was a sword.

Ryan surreptitiously examined the blade hanging from the guard's side. The entire time she had been captive, she had not seen a single weapon in anyone's possession, nor anything that could even be used as a weapon. But this man was wearing a wicked-looking blade that appeared to be made of the same material as the needle that had slipped so effortlessly beneath her skin. It was close to the color of steel, but with a bluish gray cast to it, and shaped somewhat like a katana, but with a broader blade.

Desperately trying to contain her excitement, Ryan calmed herself and focused. In all of her skirmishes with the guards, the only ability she had that was somewhat equal was her speed. They were all much stronger than her, but her preternatural reflexes had caused much damage.

Ryan inspected the sword as the guard continued his rough search. It appeared to be contained in a somewhat untraditional sheath, but drawn in much the same way as the ones she was familiar with. She focused all of her concentration, visualizing her next act.

"You know," the guard said, "when the mistress tires of you, she will give you to us." He stood upright, and the leer on his face was there only for a fraction of a second.

"I don't think so," Ryan said.

The sword was in her hand, seemingly having materialized there through thought alone. She swung a slicing blow across his neck, decapitating him instantly. His head fell to the ground and rolled to the side, but his body still stood there as if not quite certain what had happened. Ryan felt all of her helplessness coalesce into rage, and she swung the sword again, this time slicing the torso lengthwise in two. It fell neatly into two halves.

Ryan stared at the sword in wonder. It was a magnificent blade, having cut through the man as if he were a statue made from butter. But the lethality of the weapon was a little disconcerting as well. Ryan knew that if it could kill the guard that easily, it could kill her as well. She had no doubt that such a sword could slice through her skin and bone effortlessly.

Ryan smiled grimly. That was a trade she was willing to make.

She turned at the commotion at the door. Two more guards rushed in, stunned at the sight that greeted them. Unfortunately for them, they were not armed. With two more swings of the deadly sword, they went down in a spray of blood.

Ryan stepped over the bodies and pushed through the door. She was in a long hallway with numerous doorways and corridors branching off to each side. The walls were of the same rock construction as her cell. Ryan felt powerful misgivings. If this hallway was any indication of the size of this place, it was enormous.

Shouts and the sound of running feet approached from one direction, so Ryan went the other way. She sprinted down the corridor, then dodged right into a passageway. It was reasonable to suspect the entire compound was under surveillance, so Ryan did not believe she could hide. She could only run and fight, hoping she could get some sense of orientation to escape.

She sprinted around another corner and came face-to-face with a group of sentries looking for her. She was clearly outnumbered, but the guards were frozen in place, their eyes on the sword in her hand.

Ryan smiled, hearing Kusunoki's words in her head.

When too weak to defend, attack.

Ryan charged the group of men, the blade spinning and arcing through flesh and bone. She felt a strong grip on her shoulder and quickly dropped to her knee, taking the man's legs off at the thighs. She knew if they got a hold of her and were able to wrest the sword from her grasp, she would be lost.

The toll she was taking on them was too great, however, and the remainder of the group turned and fled. Ryan quickly dodged down another passageway, fully aware she had no idea where she was going. She saw a great arch ahead of her, opening onto something that looked like a terrace. And she could see daylight. She sprinted toward the opening.

Ryan broke into the daylight, and stopped in her tracks. She walked very slowly to the banister of what was indeed a great open terrace. She leaned over the banister, looking down, then stared around her in wonder and despair.

She was definitely in the mountains, and the terrace she was standing was cut from the face of the rock. What inspired both the awe and despair, however, was the fact that the terrace she was standing on was just one of hundreds. She looked across the ravine, and saw men rushing about on the cliffs, moving from terrace to terrace via the elaborate series of stairways connecting the decks.

She looked down again. The ground was a thousand feet below, and the great courtyard in the canyon was filled with activity, no doubt inspired by her escape. Ryan shook her head. The fortress was a marvel of construction, surpassing even the great pyramids in its size and engineering. She looked upward. The edifices cut into the cliffs continued into the clouds.

She turned on her heel, starting back into the citadel. She had been wrong about many things, most importantly, the number of men Madelyn had at her disposal. She had guessed a few dozen, but now knew there were hundreds, if not thousands.

Ryan stopped for a few moments, staring at the blood-stained sword in her hand. She would probably be dead very soon. But she would take as many of them with her as possible.

Harrian stepped over the bodies strewn about the corridor, his jaw clenched. One of his officers approached to report, snapping to attention.

"Where is she now?" Harrian demanded.

"Sixteenth level, outer perimeter. There is a cohort moving to intercept her."

Harrian glanced at the dismembered corpses. "Tell them to back off for the moment, until weapons can be retrieved from the armory."

The officer was stunned. "But our orders were—"

Harrian whirled on him. "I know what the orders were. But the prisoner is obviously capable of far more than we expected, and she will continue this slaughter unless we meet her with sufficient force."

The officer glanced down at the dead around him. "This does not seem possible."

"No," Harrian said in disgust, "it does not. And I will pay for that underestimation. Speaking of which," he said, unable to disguise the dread in his voice, "where is Madelyn?"

"She is in her inner sanctuary," the officer replied.

This brought slight relief to Harrian. "Then she may not be aware of what has happened."

"No," the officer agreed, "she may not."

This brought new urgency to Harrian. "Then distribute the weapons and let's find the girl."

Ryan moved stealthily down the hallway. It seemed as if the initial pursuit had cooled somewhat and the forces were regrouping. She had managed to make it down two levels of the vast fortress, uncertain if that put her significantly closer to the ground or to an exit. She was also not certain what surveillance devices she might be tripping or if she was simply being monitored the entire time. It did not matter.

She heard voices around the next corner and peered around the rock wall. Two of the uniformed guards were blocking the hallway. Ryan debated an all-out charge, but then saw something that gave her pause.

Both men were now armed with the same type of sword she carried. She glanced down at the weapon in her hand. Well, the odds had been good for awhile.

The two guards were engaged in animated conversation which stopped abruptly when Ryan walked around the corner and approached them. They were stunned at her boldness, and for a moment, neither did anything.

"Stop where you are!" one finally commanded, raising his sword. The other raised his as well.

Ryan obligingly came to a halt, her sword hanging loosely from her hand.

"Drop the weapon!" the guard ordered.

Ryan obediently set the sword down, its hilt near the heel of her right foot.

Both guards were surprised at the servility of the prisoner, especially given reports of the preceding rampage. Apparently the reports had been exaggerated, and this prisoner was not nearly so brave when faced with armed opponents. Nonetheless, they approached her cautiously.

Not cautiously enough, however. As soon as one guard was in range, Ryan stomped her heel on the hilt of the sword, flipping the blade upward. She snatched it from the air and swung it one smooth motion, decapitating the first guard before he could raise his sword in defense. The second blow landed blade-to-blade, however, as the second guard was able to react.

The guard attacked, and Ryan was again astonished at the strength of these men. She knew that if he was able to fully engage her blade, she would lose this fight and in all probability lose her life. As she parried the blows, the imbalance in strength reminded her of when she fought with Victor as child. The only difference was that this was not a training exercise, and this man certainly was not curbing his blows.

Still, Ryan was able to contend through speed and skill alone, greatly surprising the guard. Although he was able to slash through her defenses, she never seemed to be there when he was actually landing a blow. Several came dangerously close to Ryan, and she felt something she had not felt since being human.

It was the first time in centuries she was in a battle where she knew that she could die. And she found it exhilarating.

The guard was growing angry that he could not subdue the girl, and even more so at her seemingly reckless attitude. She actually seemed to be enjoying herself. He moved to end the conflict, preparing for the killing blow, but instead found himself impaled on the end of Ryan's sword. He stared down at the blade protruding from his chest in disbelief. Ryan yanked the sword from him and his body crumpled to the ground.

She glanced up, surprised to see that there were witnesses to their battle. A group of guards stood in the hallway, incredulity on their faces. They were so certain their captain would have defeated the girl, none had moved to help him. Now they raised their swords to attack.

Ryan slipped her blade beneath the fallen guard's weapon,

flipping it upward into her left hand. With a great heave, she sent it end-over-end down the hallway into the group of guards, satisfied to hear a thunk and a scream as one went down. She turned the other way and sprinted down the corridor.

She made it down another staircase, still uncertain what level she was on. As most of the guards she saw now were armed, she avoided them, relying on her speed and the shadows. She crouched behind a short wall as a cohort ran by her, trying to decide what to do next. She pressed against the rock wall behind her, sliding a short distance to the corner so she could peer around into the next passageway.

It was quiet and it appeared to be empty. There also appeared to be another terrace at the end of it, and she might be close enough to the ground to jump without serious injury. If she could get out of this maze of corridors and to the courtyard below, she might be able to disappear into the surrounding mountains.

Ryan had settled on this course of action and was preparing to slip around the corner when she felt a presence behind her. With lightning speed, she spun around to strike a killing blow at whatever stalked her.

Instead, her sword was stopped abruptly in mid-swing. She was lifted bodily from the ground and slammed backward into the wall so hard it felt as if her spine was crushed.

Madelyn stared at her with amusement, easily holding her off the ground. Ryan turned to the sword that Madelyn had caught in the palm of her hand. The deadly blade had not even broken her skin. Ryan felt utter despair as Madelyn grasped the blade and yanked it from Ryan's hand, tossing it aside as if it were a toy. Ryan stared at the weapon on the ground, knowing that all hope was lost.

Madelyn seemed to sense the hopelessness and it pleased her. She leaned closer to Ryan, pressing her fully against the wall.

"And where exactly did you think you were going?" Madelyn asked.

Ryan braced for the bite but even so could not anticipate the intense pain. She struggled impotently in Madelyn's iron embrace, but only for a few seconds as the paralysis began to seep into her system.

Everything in her body below the bite went limp, and she struggled to hold her head upright. Even that was difficult, and she was forced to lay her head against Madelyn's shoulder, a humiliatingly affectionate gesture.

"That's better," Madelyn said. She lifted Ryan into her arms, holding her as one would hold a small child, and again the mocking affectionate undertone was demoralizing for Ryan.

Two doors materialized in the rock wall next to them, and the doors slid open, revealing a hidden lift. Madelyn stepped into the elevator as Harrian and a cohort of guards rushed around the corner.

Harrian and the guards stopped hurriedly. Harrian was surprised, relieved, and terrified at the sight of Madelyn holding the girl. He bowed low.

"My lady, I beg your forgiveness."

"I," Madelyn said coldly, "am not to be disturbed."

Harrian and the guards went to their knees, and he did not raise his head until the doors whispered closed.

Ryan could not feel the lift move, so smoothly did it operate, but she had the sensation they were moving upward for a long time. She opened her eyes, then regretted doing so since Madelyn was staring down at her.

"You seem to have difficulty grasping this concept of being a prisoner," Madelyn said.

Ryan maintained an insubordinate silence.

"I shall have to try harder to educate you," Madelyn said.

The doors whispered open and Ryan turned her head slightly to get a glance at the room. They certainly were not in her prison cell.

The chamber was vast, with high arched ceilings and various sunken areas and half-walls that delineated space without enclosing it. There was furniture spread about the areas, some of it recognizable as couches, chairs, or beds, others less recognizable as anything functional, at least to Ryan. Perhaps it was artwork, although it certainly was not to her taste. The room had a slight reddish cast to it, and Ryan noted it was because the walls themselves were made with rock that had the same reddish hue.

Ryan realized these must be Madelyn's personal chambers, a realization that was greatly disturbing to her. She preferred her prison cell, and certainly preferred her rock slab to the soft divan Madelyn laid her down upon. She tried to move away from the woman when Madelyn laid down beside her, but the paralysis was near-complete. Ryan could barely flex her wrist.

Madelyn's feeding generally began quickly, without prelude, but apparently today she wished to torture Ryan more than just physically.

"So did you enjoy your little jaunt about the citadel?" Madelyn asked, toying with Ryan's hair.

"Yes," Ryan said, wondering how many she had managed to kill, "I did."

"Hmm," Madelyn said, leaning down to examine the bruise on Ryan's neck. Ryan braced herself as Madelyn again bit her, taking a long drink from the wound she reopened. It was painful, but not unbearably so as the first one had been.

Madelyn leaned back. "I must say, I am impressed with your persistence. Most would have given up hope long ago."

Ryan gazed up at her. "I do not need hope to keep fighting."

Madelyn leaned down to take some more blood, and it was more uncomfortable this time than painful. Ryan wondered if Madelyn was capable of moderating the amount of pain she inflicted, and decided to experiment to find out.

"I will kill you when I get the chance," Ryan added.

The bite was painful this time, and Ryan muffled a groan. She decided to stop testing theories. Madelyn, although she could not read Ryan's thoughts, seemed to know precisely what Ryan's intentions were at any given time.

"Do you wish me to cause you pain, little one?" Madelyn asked sardonically.

Ryan held her gaze. "It doesn't matter what I wish, does it? You will do as you want."

Madelyn smiled her cold smile. "Then you do understand me. Good," she said, as she bit sharply into the other side of Ryan's neck and began drinking deeply.

The pain was again intense, and Ryan thought for sure she would slip into unconsciousness. But again the darkness was elusive, and as Madelyn fed from her, she had the sudden prescience that it was Madelyn herself keeping Ryan from passing into that welcome oblivion.

"As I said," Madelyn whispered into her ear, "you do understand me."

Harrian entered Madelyn's outer chamber with great trepidation. He glanced over at the girl lying on the couch, pale and unconscious. At least the brat had paid for some of her misdeeds. Harrian could see the bruises on both sides of Ryan's neck, and revised his opinion. She had paid for all of them.

Madelyn came out of the double doors leading to her inner chamber, her gown flowing about her as she walked down the steps toward him. He went to one knee before her.

"Your Highness," he began.

Madelyn interrupted him, her tone deliberately casual. "At one point in time were my orders regarding weapons disobeyed?"

Harrian stood upright. "I gave the order to pull weapons from the armory once the girl–"

Madelyn whirled toward him, seething. "I mean before that, idiot."

Harrian readjusted his thinking. "Titus apparently entered her cell wearing a sword." Harrian did not particularly care for Titus, but felt the need to defend his men. "I don't think he meant any harm to the prisoner—"

Madelyn was furious. "Those rules were not for the protection of the girl, you fool." She glanced down at the prone figure, then turned back to Harrian. "Those rules were for your protection. I forbid weapons around her to keep her from taking them and doing exactly what she did."

Madelyn turned her back on him, but he could clearly hear her. "You have underestimated her twice now." She whirled back toward him, "Do so again, and you will lose your life."

Harrian went to one knee. "I understand, your Highness." He stood, but his head was still bowed. "Do you wish me to return her to her cell now?"

"No," Madelyn said, casting a glance at Ryan, "she will stay here."

Harrian's head jerked upward in surprise. Madelyn gazed at him malevolently, and he knew better than to say a word.

"It seems," Madelyn said, "that I am the only one capable of restraining her."

Harrian bowed his head, and quickly exited before he angered her further.

CHAPTER 27

RYAN JERKED AWAKE AT THE SLIGHT NOISE. She attempted to raise herself upright, but the pain from the movement was too great and she collapsed backward. She closed her eyes for a moment. At least now what she was lying on was somewhat comfortable.

She reopened her eyes to find Harrian hovering about her. He did not treat her as contemptuously as the other guards, but it was apparent he was not pleased with her presence. He gave her a quick, clinical examination, assessing the bruises on her neck. He pressed her fingernails, assessing the perfusion of blood in her extremities. He seemed satisfied and somewhat surprised at her rate of recovery. Ryan was not satisfied; her pain was still considerable. She wondered if it was associated with the paralysis.

While Harrian finished his exam, bending her legs one at a time, Ryan glanced about the room. Surprisingly, she was still in Madelyn's chambers, a fact that was unsettling. Madelyn was not present, however, so Ryan inspected the room. It was laid out in a semi-circular pattern, and in what would have been the center the circle was a set of steps leading to two large doors. The doors were elaborately decorated with geometric patterns, reminding Ryan somewhat of Egyptian hieroglyphics.

Harrian followed Ryan's gaze, disapproval on his features.

"What is behind those doors?" Ryan asked.

She did not really expect a response, but apparently she struck some sort of nerve with Harrian.

"Entrance into the inner chambers is forbidden," Harrian said harshly. He then muttered under his breath, "You should not even be here."

Ryan examined him thoughtfully. "Are you in the habit of second-guessing your master?"

This comment struck an even more sensitive nerve, and Ryan could see the flash of fear in Harrian's eyes. He stood upright, as if reluctant to even touch her at the moment.

"No," he replied, his voice quiet but his tone still harsh, "I do not question Madelyn's judgment." He took a step backward. "But if it were up to me," he continued, "you would already be dead."

"Well," Ryan said, "it's not up to you, now is it?"

At that moment, the doors from the lift whispered open and Madelyn entered. She assessed the scene, noting Harrian's angry expression and the girl's mocking one. She inwardly smiled. Harrian would not get the best of this one.

"You may leave," Madelyn said, addressing Harrian, and he quickly did so. Madelyn gave Ryan a brief glance, noting the way in which Ryan held herself. The girl might pretend to be fine, but she was still in pain. Madelyn smiled a cold smile, then started up the steps to the inner chambers.

Ryan watched Madelyn depart through the double doors, relieved to see her go. That did not stop her, however, from leaning slightly, trying to get a glimpse at what might be through the doors. She could see nothing and the movement caused her pain, so she fell back onto her makeshift bed.

Although the fact that Madelyn was so near was greatly disturbing, Ryan quickly slid back into blackness, returning to her exhausted sleep and fitful dreams.

Ryan relaxed in the saddle, enjoying the rhythmic motion of her horse. She and Victor had been traveling for weeks, some by sea, but mostly by land. Their progress at sea was limited by the speed of the ship and the weather, whereas their progress on land was limited by the stamina of their horses. They could have traveled much faster on foot, but would not have been able to bring the supplies the pack horses carried.

She glanced back at the pack horses. They carried no food other than what the horses required, because she and Victor did not need to eat. The horses did, however, carry two full sets of armor, a fact Ryan found curious. She herself disdained the heavy plated protection, but Victor had insisted. Since the advent of gunpowder there were many new weapons that could not kill them, but the projectiles definitely hurt.

This thought brought a deeper sense of scorn to Ryan. The projectiles, although faster than an arrow, still moved slowly enough for her to avoid. And a man could get off one shot, maybe, before he was cut down. The reloading process was ridiculous. She could fire fifty arrows in the time it took to reload a gun. Still, Ryan was thoughtful. Victor was certain the craft would only improve, because mankind was ever-diligent in finding new ways to kill themselves. The projectiles would get faster, the reloading quicker, and then new, more exotic ways of destruction would be invented.

Ryan smiled. She was becoming as cynical as her mentor. She gently kneed her horse to catch up with the dark-haired man in front of her.

Victor glanced down at his young protégé as she came alongside him. Dressed as usual as a young man, she possessed a startling androgyny that allowed her to easily pass as a male, albeit one who could only be described as beautiful. He mentally calculated her age, arriving at a figure somewhere in the realm of a century and a quarter. Although capable of greater precision in his calculation, it was meaningless and therefore he did not attempt it. It was also irrelevant as her power greatly exceeded her young age.

"So where exactly are we going?"

Victor smiled at the question. They had traveled a thousand miles and it was the first time she had bothered to ask.

"Constantinople," Victor replied.

This intrigued Ryan. It was a part of the world she had yet to see, but one Victor was greatly familiar with. She had spent many hours sitting before the fire listening to him tell stories of this mysterious land, and he spoke with a great admiration of its people and culture. He did not, however, like to speak of his original reasons for going there.

"Off to fight another crusade, are we?"

This brought a frown to his handsome face. "I don't know," he replied. "I certainly hope not."

Ryan settled into silence. Victor loved battle, but there were few reasons he deemed worthy to take up arms. Self-protection, defense of the homeland, injustice, and even the latter was an ideal so vague it was rarely worth the fight. This was something Ryan increasingly understood the longer she lived. When one lived only a few decades, all foes seemed new, all struggles seemed epic, and history provided only a dead and dry context for limited understanding.

When one began to live over centuries, however, the never-ending strife took on a very alive context. Barbarians invaded, conquered, then settled and became the status quo. They in turn would be invaded, sometimes conquered by force, sometimes by culture, sometimes by disease or even apathy. Rival nations would fight endless wars over boundaries, only to become great allies, protecting one another's interests. Some lessons were learned, but most were forgotten and had to be learned anew by each generation.

After awhile, an eternal observer such as Victor simply had to take a step back, engaging only when necessary. Ryan had once asked him why he did not involve himself more in the affairs of man, why he did not become a King or even an Emperor. His reply had been as succinct as it had been stunning.

"Now why would I want to do that?"

And Ryan intuitively understood. The suffering, the constant conflict would never end. And although she herself still had a shred of idealism, a desire to right wrongs, she was beginning to understand that "wrong" was a very complicated issue. Victor had a fine collection of Eastern scrolls, and she had pored over them with great interest. The concept of karma had deeply reverberated with her because it was something she could actually observe over life spans.

Ryan glanced back over at Victor, who was lost in his own thoughts. They received few visitors in their hidden and heavily guarded lands, so she was very aware that the papal messenger had come. Victor had no love of the church, but occasionally responded to requests he considered of great consequence.

"Are there any of our Kind in the land we are going to?"

"No," Victor said, "not that I know of."

This was something of a relief to Ryan. It had been several decades since she had first met the Others, and the experience had been overwhelming. It had been quite a revelation to her that there was anyone else like her and Victor. Having never met them, she assumed that she and Victor were the only ones.

How wrong she had been, Ryan thought, inwardly frowning. The one called Marilyn seemed to have some sort of love/hate relationship with her, apparently wanting to kill her out of jealousy over Victor. And Abigail, that One she could not figure out at all.

Victor was aware of his protégé's thoughts and smiled. As intelligent and intuitive as the girl was, there were certain things she was completely oblivious to, which was probably a very good thing. It was also part of the reason why he chose to keep her away from the Others as much as possible. There was only so much he could do to protect her from that group of predators.

He glanced down at her again. Although at times he wondered if she needed protecting, or if in fact it was the Others who were benefiting from her absence. He somehow had the feeling she could handle herself.

Ryan was increasingly able to sense Victor's thoughts, and she glanced over at him.

"What?" she asked.

He smiled. "Nothing."

Ryan settled into silence once more, musing on their destination. One thing was bothering her, however, and it was perhaps her greater access to Victor's mind that was causing it. She had sensed hesitation in him when she asked if there were any of their Kind ahead of them, and she had a vague sense that he was not being entirely truthful.

Ryan opened her eyes, awakening from the dream disoriented. Susan's eyes seemed a deeper shade of green since her Change, and her hair a more luminous shade of red. Ryan did not remember, however, such a great look of concern on her face before.

Ryan sat upright, groaning from the pain the effort caused her. She glanced around the room and her heart fell. She was still in Madelyn's chambers, which meant that Susan was there as well. She turned back to the younger woman. Fear, concern, and remorse flitted across Susan's features, and it was the remorse that caused Ryan the greatest concern.

"You are here," Ryan said, her distress at the fact obvious.

Susan lowered her eyes, close to tears. "It is worse than that."

Ryan shifted on the couch, moving into an upright position. She swung her legs to the floor and reached out to Susan. The movement caused her to grimace in pain, and Susan took the hand that faltered in its reach. Susan looked at her and Ryan did not want to hear the words she knew were coming.

She did not have to because Madelyn entered, removing all doubt as to the cause of Susan's anguish. Ryan turned to the dark-haired woman, who gracefully stepped down into the room holding her son. Ryan's gaze settled on the blue-eyed boy, and she could not help but reach out to mentally touch him.

"Ryan," Madelyn said with warning.

Ryan stood upright, ignoring the pain racing through her system. "He is a child, and he cannot speak. It is the only way I have of comforting him." Ryan knew she was almost pleading, "I hardly see the harm in it."

Madelyn approached Ryan, holding the toddler in her arms. Drake watched his mother somberly, knowing something was terribly wrong. Ryan desperately tried to calm her own emotions to keep from upsetting him.

Madelyn glanced down at the boy, brushing his dark hair. Ryan wanted to reach out and wrench him from her grasp. Madelyn turned her attention back to Ryan, holding her gaze for a long moment, then allowing her eyes to drift to the bruises on her throat. Very slowly and very deliberately, she handed the boy to Ryan.

Ryan clutched her son to her chest. She understood fully the lesson she had just been given. But lest there be any confusion, Madelyn placed a finger beneath Ryan's chin, forcing her to look up at her. They were very close to one another, with Madelyn's lips nearly brushing her cheek.

"I do not expect any more trouble from you," Madelyn said. She did not bother to acknowledge Susan's presence but turned on her heel and left, disappearing into her inner chamber.

Ryan could no longer stand upright, and Susan grasped her elbow, helping her back to the divan. Ryan held Drake tightly to her chest, who for his part was so happy to see his mother that for the moment, nothing else mattered.

"I am so sorry, Ryan," Susan began.

"It is not your fault," Ryan said tiredly. "How did this happen?"

Susan shook her head. "I am not certain. I was at the estate protected by all of the Old Ones. And yet Madelyn's men appeared, almost as if they materialized out of nowhere. Suddenly," she paused, at a loss, "they were just there."

Ryan cradled her son. "And then how did you get here?"

Susan was again uncertain. "I think I must have blacked out, because I don't remember anything. All of a sudden, I was in a large, rock room. Madelyn took Drake from me, and then I was escorted here." Susan looked at her. "I am so sorry, Ryan," she repeated.

"Don't be," Ryan replied. "this is my fault." She held up Drake, examining him to make certain he had come to no harm. He bore the inspection patiently, as if sensing his mother's distress. He laid his head back down on her chest when she was finished. "You were brought here to keep me in check," Ryan said, sighing. "I went on a little rampage the other day, and ended up killing several men before Madelyn stopped me."

"You were able to kill them?" Susan asked in surprise. This gave her great hope. Ryan had not succeeded in killing either her father or Aeron, yet from what she had just said, was able to kill her much stronger captors.

Ryan nodded. "I am as surprised as you. They have weapons, swords, the like of which I have never seen before. They are deadly and I am certain they could kill me as well." Ryan shrugged. "That is of no matter, Madelyn could kill me at any time."

It was strange to hear Ryan speak so, because Susan knew her only as an immortal. She had watched Ryan recover from extraordinary injuries, and had watched both Victor and Aeron literally come back from the dead. Yet now Ryan was talking casually of her own death.

"I have not seen any firearms," Ryan said, still musing on the arsenal, "which surprises me. It would seem they could construct an equally deadly gun with bullets of this material." Her expression darkened. "Wouldn't I like to get my hands on that."

"Maybe that's why they don't carry them," Susan said, "maybe they are more afraid of you getting your hands on an equalizer."

"I don't think they are afraid of me at all," Ryan said, laying her head back into the cushions. Her eyelids grew heavy. "Forgive me if I fall asleep on you."

Ryan quickly fell back into her exhausted sleep and Drake followed her example. Susan watched the two beautiful creatures sleeping and a great sadness settled over her. Ryan hardly looked old enough to have a child, but her youthful appearance made the similarity between her and her son even more striking. She leaned forward to brush Drake's hair from his eyes, then slowly, hesitantly, did the same for Ryan.

Susan became aware that her affectionate gesture was under intense scrutiny. She glanced up. Madelyn was standing just outside the doors to her inner chamber, a malevolent look on her face. Susan very slowly withdrew her hand and sat back. Madelyn watched her a minute longer, then moved down the steps, leaving the chamber.

Susan stared at the recently vacated doorway, then at the double doors at the top of the steps in the center of the room. She turned her attention back to Ryan, who was soundly sleeping.

Susan was going to side with Victor on this matter. There was much beneath the surface here between Madelyn and Ryan that Ryan did not see.

CHAPTER 28

MARILYN WATCHED VICTOR CLOSELY. Normally she would just be content to examine his perfect features, the sensual mouth, the long dark eyelashes, the strong jaw and sharp cheekbones. Today, she was waiting for him to explode.

"How is it," he asked, "that my grandson and Dr. Ryerson simply disappeared?"

Marilyn turned toward the door where the youngster stood. Jason was bravely trying to control himself. Not only were his mother and his friend gone, he was the only witness to their disappearance. And he was terribly afraid of the furious dark-haired man.

Victor realized he was terrifying the child. He forcibly calmed himself and gestured for the boy to approach him. Abigail, seated at Victor's right, mentally reached out to the boy and soothed him. Victor became aware he was towering over the boy, and sat down so he was closer to eye level.

"Can you tell me what you saw, Jason?" Victor asked.

Jason nodded, trying to still the trembling of his lip. He clasped his hands together so they would stop shaking.

"My mom was holding Drake in the courtyard. I was standing a few feet away. There wasn't really anyone else around." Jason replayed the scene in his mind, trying to make sense of it. "It was just the three of us, and then, out of nowhere, there were a lot of those strange men."

Victor glanced over at Abigail. It was possible that Madelyn's men could move so quickly that Jason would be unable to see them. "Please go on."

Jason struggled to hold back his tears, but one slipped out and ran down his cheek. "My mom started to run toward me, but they grabbed her. She screamed at me to run, and then the next thing I knew, they all were gone."

"And she was still holding Drake?" Abigail asked.

"Yes," Jason said, completely breaking down. Great, wrenching sobs shook his small frame. "Drake is gone, too."

Victor realized the boy not only missed his mother, but was traumatized by the loss of Drake as well. He nodded to Edward, who stepped forward to comfort the young man. Edward took Jason by the hand and led him from the room.

Victor sat down, pushing back in his chair. His expression was grim. "Once again I was unable to feel their presence, neither coming nor going."

"I did not feel anything, either," Abigail admitted. "Merely Drake's presence, and then his sudden absence."

Victor nodded his agreement, eyeing Marilyn for confirmation. She also nodded, confirming the experience.

"I was surprised," Abigail added, "at the suddenness of that absence. As if in one instant he was here, and the next he was gone." She glanced down at the envelope Edward had handed her on his way out. "Edward left this for you."

Victor took the envelope from the matriarch. It was not unusual for their Kind to eschew the modern conveniences of cellular telephones, email, and fax machines in favor of more ancient and meaningful forms of communication. He turned the envelope over in his hands. The envelope was heavy and the paper smooth, possessing a quality not found in even the most expensive manufactured papers. He glanced at the seal in surprise, and opened the envelope. He removed the letter, which was no more than a few lines. It was innocuous, really nothing more than a greeting and a wish for continued health. It was the fact that Victor had received the letter at all that stunned him.

"Something significant?" Abigail asked.

"Just greetings," Victor replied, his gaze suddenly distant, "from a very old friend."

The massive cannon discharged with a great explosion and the cannonball went hurtling toward the outer walls of Constantinople. It struck solidly, the collision causing brick and stone to fly in all directions. A large section of the wall crumbled inward.

Ryan's horse shifted nervously on the hill overlooking the great city. She stared at the great war machine with some misgivings.

"I don't think my armor will protect me against that."

"No," Victor agreed, "best to stay out of the way of something like that."

Ryan eyed the great gaping hole left in the wall. There were already workers scrambling to repair the damage.

"It must take some time to reload if they are confident enough to rebuild," she commented.

Victor, too, eyed the immediate repair crew. "That, and they probably don't have a choice."

There was resignation in his tone and a sense of sadness as well. Months of siege had left the beautiful city in ruins. A marvel of architecture and technology, parts of it were now little more than rubble. The stench of death and sewage hung heavy in the air, obscured only slightly by the smoke from the burning fires.

Ryan kneed her horse away from the battlefield. She knew Victor would remain on the hill awhile, assessing his course of action. "I will go make camp," she said over her shoulder.

Ryan found a small oasis some distance from the battlefield and watched the horses. It seemed as good a place as any to camp, and she expertly set up the tent in minutes. Since there was little else to do, she settled down by the campfire to wait for Victor. She closed her eyes, enjoying the heat from the flames. Although the days were temperate, she had the feeling the night would be very cold.

She reopened her eyes, having the disquieting sensation she was being watched. It was not yet dark, and she could clearly see in even the dimmest light with her preternatural vision.

There was a man standing on the ledge above her. He was dressed in the flowing robes and headdress of the Ottoman empire, but Ryan did not sense any danger from him. He was swarthy and handsome, and he was examining her as openly as she was examining him. She stood and took a step toward him, and he took exactly one step back.

Ryan cocked her head to one side, curious, and the man smiled, revealing beautiful white teeth that contrasted with his dark skin. Ryan took another, experimental step, and the man again took one step backward.

And then the chase was on. Ryan scrambled up the hillside with incredible speed, only to find the man had traveled the exact same distance and now waited for her on another hill. She broke into a sprint, but somehow the flowing robes always maintained the separation, tantalizingly close, yet out-of-reach. Ryan stopped, and the man stopped. Ryan walked, and the man walked. Ryan ran, and impossibly, the man kept pace with her. She could swear laughter drifted back to her, not mocking, but full of delight, as if simply enjoying the game.

Finally, the man disappeared, and Ryan slowly approached the place she had last seen him. It was a great hillside, at the bottom of which was a stone entryway. She eyed the hillside, noting that it looked somewhat like an ancient tomb, then looked back the way she came. She had traveled a great distance from the camp and she had left without a weapon. Somehow she did not think she would need one.

Ryan quietly made her way through the stone entrance, pausing only long enough for her eyes to adjust. She traversed a long, narrow corridor that seemed to slope slightly downward. She sensed she was not alone, but beyond that could not sense much of anything. The corridor gradually widened, then opened dramatically into a huge room. She stared around her in wonder.

The room was lit by candles and lamps, the scented oil pleasantly burning. Various couches were strewn about, draped with fine, sheer, linens. Beautiful women lounged about the chamber, their exotic features indicating they were from many lands. All eyed the newcomer with interest, a few giggling shyly.

Ryan was quite astonished to realize they were her Kind, although quite different from the European version she had met. The overt sensuality of these creatures was almost irresistible, without the complicated, underlying power struggles that seemed so prevalent among the Others. A man in flowing, military garb approached her, and Ryan recognized the uniform of a Janissary.

"Please come with me," the man said in heavily accented English. Ryan was surprised he spoke her language, and admired the melody of his speech. She followed him down another long corridor which exited into another large room. She was left alone in what looked like a study, filled with scrolls and elaborate gadgets. One such piece of machinery had all sorts of intricate gears and small parts, fascinating Ryan. She delicately touched the device, trying to fathom its purpose.

So fascinated was she by the strange objects, Ryan was not aware she was being watched.

The dark-skinned man watched the creature in his study with delight and amazement. Strikingly beautiful, her light hair was a stark contrast to the almost universally dark-haired occupants of this land. But it was not her physical beauty that stunned him, nor was it the power that flowed through her veins, power he had sensed miles away. Rather it was her fearlessness in approach, her casual inspection of his prized possessions, the utter concentration of a distracted child.

Ryan finally tore herself away from the intriguing device, standing upright. It was only then that she became aware of the presence behind her and turned toward the man watching her. She became very still.

The man was gorgeous, physically older than Victor with the handsome, swarthy features of the men of this land. He wore a beard and mustache as custom, but unlike convention both were neatly trimmed. His eyes were intense, black as night but filled with both wisdom and humor. He was definitely her Kind, and most definitely an Old One. And although she had never met him before, in this instant she recognized him.

"Salah al-Dīn," she said slowly, using his formal name.

Saladin was now even more stunned. "You know me?" he asked.

"I have my mentor's Memories," Ryan said slowly, "and it is he who knows you."

"That is not possible," Saladin said, "there is only one outside my troupe who knows of my existence, and he is too powerful to initiate Change."

Ryan did not speak, merely standing beneath Saladin's intense scrutiny. It was he, who at last spoke.

"And yet you bear Victor's mark, this is certainty."

Ryan was trying to remember through Victor's mind. It was very difficult because she was still young and not supposed to have such an ability. Although she possessed many of his Memories, some sat inert in her blood, triggered only by some familiar smell or taste. Then the Memory would rise to the forefront, creating the strangest sensation of clearly remembering something she had never experienced. She had such a sensation now, of clearly recognizing someone who, before this instant, had not existed for her. She realized Victor had lied to her about the presence of her Kind because he had been keeping a promise to Saladin.

"Victor met you during the Crusades," Ryan said slowly, "he greatly admired and respected you."

"The respect was mutual," Saladin replied, "your mentor was, and probably still is, a great warrior and an honorable lord."

Ryan was thinking through the implications of two of her Kind fighting such a battle. She assessed Saladin, thinking him very close to being Victor's equal. "How did it come to pass that either side could win such a war?"

"You truly are Victor's offspring," Saladin said, smiling. "The truth of the matter is that neither side could win, that what was gained would soon be lost, that what was lost would eventually be regained, and that as time stretched on, none of it made any difference." Saladin glanced up at an intricate map. "Jerusalem will continue to change hands, perhaps for centuries." He turned back to Ryan. "It was Victor who convinced me to withdraw, as did he, after the Treaty of Ramla."

Ryan was curious. "But history tells a different story of you. It is recorded that you were born in the 12th century, but you are clearly older than that."

Saladin nodded.

"It is also recorded," Ryan continued, "that you had children, and that you died. None of our Kind can reproduce other than by Sharing, and obviously you are not dead."

"History is written by the victors," Saladin said, pausing slightly, "and I won."

"Ah," Ryan said, understanding. Victor had on many occasions encouraged confusion regarding their existence, including once staging his own death. It was the only way they could survive through centuries without attracting unwanted attention. But Saladin had chosen an extreme path.

"So you have withdrawn completely," Ryan said, "even from the Others."

Saladin nodded. "I have everything I want and need, and I can think of nothing that would make me break my solitude."

Ryan found the man very curious, fascinating in fact. She understood Victor's admiration of him.

For Saladin, the fascination was mutual. This Young One, if she could even be called that, was mesmerizing. It was not unusual for their Kind to possess power and sensuality, although possessing it to such a degree at such a young age was remarkable. What attracted Saladin, however, was the air of mischief about her, as if she could at will and with great merriment create complete chaos.

"If Victor and I were not such close friends," Saladin said, watching the girl, "I think I would have to keep you here with me."

"Then it is a good thing we are close friends," Victor said, coming through the door. He glanced at his wayward offspring. "I see you have met Ryan."

Saladin stood. "Assalamu alaikum," he said, grasping Victor's forearm.

"And to you be peace with God's mercy," Victor replied.

Although Ryan had seen Victor's respect for Saladin through his Memories, she was still surprised to see the affection between the two men. She had rarely seen Victor display that type of warmth toward any of their Kind. Victor turned to Ryan.

"Why don't you," Victor suggested, "go wander about while I visit with my old friend?"

Ryan knew she had been dismissed but did not mind. There was much about the compound she wished to see, starting with the Janissary weapons. She thought she could find some helpful young soldier to show her the swords and firearms. She started toward the door with some enthusiasm, but was unable to keep herself from touching the intricate mechanism one last time before she left.

"That is quite something," Saladin commented, watching the girl leave.

"You have no idea," Victor said wryly. He shifted, perhaps with slight discomfort, as Saladin turned his unblinking gaze to him.

"And how exactly did you accomplish that?" Saladin asked.

"It is–" Victor paused, wanting to tell his friend the truth, but unable to do so. "It is complicated."

"Hmm," was Saladin's reply.

Victor hesitated. He had never told anyone the truth, and Ryan herself did not know.

Saladin watched his friend shrewdly, then turned to look at the recently vacated doorway. His expression slowly turned to one of amazement.

"She is your daughter."

Victor did not respond, but he did not need to.

"And she does not know," Saladin finished.

"No one does," Victor said.

Saladin was now more than amazed. "How is this possible?"

Victor simply shook his head. "As I said, it is complicated. Quite frankly, I am not certain myself."

Saladin sat back in his chair. This was truly stunning. He had never heard of any of their Kind reproducing other than through Sharing. Some, mostly Young Ones, still engaged in the act of sexual congress, but none had ever had a child.

"That is why you were able to Change her," Saladin mused, "because she was born transformed, or at least partially so."

"That would be my assumption," Victor said. He, too, gazed at the empty doorway. "There is much about that one I am not certain of." Victor glanced about him, taking in much more than the room itself.

"I have always admired your way of life," Victor began. "You have largely divorced yourself from the politics of our Kind. You have chosen your offspring wisely, not merely for their physical beauty or for their ability to satisfy you, but because of attributes such as wisdom and equanimity."

"It has allowed us to live much more peacefully than most of our Kind," Saladin said. "I am not so sure we could remain so isolated without that balance. But you," Saladin said, eyeing his friend, "do not have that choice."

"No," Victor agreed, "someone must take responsibility for the hierarchy."

The two men settled into silence, their thoughts very similar. As powerful and predatory as their Kind could be, considerable checks and balances were required. One of the most important functions was to make certain that Young Ones who were not worthy of immortality did not survive. That problem generally took care of itself, but every once in awhile there was someone who seemed about to slip into the ranks of the middle ground, and required elimination. There was nothing more dangerous than one of their Kind who was mentally unbalanced or too desirous of attention. All were allowed to do their time on the world's stage, but then were required to slip quietly back into oblivion. Any time legends of the undead began circulating a certain part of the world, it generally meant someone was guilty of indiscretion.

"So you have taken the opposite approach," Saladin said,

breaking the silence.

"Hmm?" Victor asked.

Saladin made an expansive gesture. "I have spent my time creating well-balanced, stable offspring, who in turn create more favorable offspring. You, on the other hand, have chosen to create only a single progeny."

Saladin gazed at his friend. "One, perfect, offspring."

Victor held Saladin's gaze, sensing the other man's misgivings.

"Perhaps it is because I am far more religious than you, my friend," Saladin said, "but historically, a perfect only-child is generally sacrificed."

CHAPTER 29

RYAN SLEPT FOR A VERY LONG TIME. Susan herself slept for awhile, and spent the rest of the time caring for Drake. Her captors obviously understood the boy needed nourishment because they brought him appropriate food on a regular basis.

When Ryan finally awoke, she glanced around quickly to ensure that her son and Susan were still present and unharmed. Ryan relaxed when she saw them sleeping on adjacent couches, noting that no one else was present. She stretched, gingerly at first, then encouraged by her lack of pain, more vigorously. She stood, still stretching, pleased that she seemed to be recovering. She again wondered if the pain was associated with the paralysis rather than the actual feeding.

Ryan glanced around the room. It was the first time she had been able to move enough to explore her surroundings. She walked to the far wall, certain she was seeing natural light, and was rewarded by finding a small window. She peered outward, unable to see much but clouds. At least now she would be able to mark the passage of time.

Ryan turned back to the room. The architecture, furniture, even the decorations seemed to have some arithmetical basis to them. The same, geometric patterns repeated themselves, the only difference being in scale. The walls themselves were either carved with the patterns, or if brick, set in the patterns. Ryan returned to examining the outer wall. The bricks were set perfectly, and did not appear to have much in terms of grout between them. Ryan ran her fingers along the spacing between the bricks. It was a pleasant sensation, the pattern very rhythmic as she moved her hands. Again, she had the sensation that the construction was much like the pyramids, but on a grander and more advanced scale.

The stairs leading up to the center of the room caught Ryan's attention. Although she wanted to examine some of the furniture in greater detail, the large doors at the top of the stairway were a greater curiosity. Ryan stepped down into the main floor, crossed the chamber, then started up the steps. She had reservations, picturing Madelyn bursting through the doors and toppling her backwards down the stairs. The picture was humorous to Ryan and in no way daunting. Besides, she was not even certain if Madelyn was within the citadel, let alone within her chambers.

The doors were engraved with the same geometric pattern, although their size suggested they were more hieroglyphic in nature than mere ornamentation. Ryan ran her fingers along the pattern, again noting that it was a strangely pleasurable sensation. She leaned closer, peering at the carvings. It was odd, the markings had a definite meaning, and Ryan had the curious sense she should know what that meaning was.

"So what do they say?" came the mocking voice in her ear.

Ryan jumped, which unfortunately pressed her fully against Madelyn who was standing behind her. She would have turned to face her, but that would have put her back against the doors. So Ryan did not move from the somewhat humiliating position.

"Obviously," Ryan said sarcastically, "I do not know."

Madelyn smiled. "That is unfortunate. Perhaps it would have kept you off my stairs."

Madelyn reached over Ryan's shoulder and touched the door. It immediately responded to her touch, silently swinging inward. Madelyn began to step forward, and Ryan had no choice but to begin moving forward herself or be trampled, although trampling was only slightly the lesser of two evils.

Madelyn pushed them both into the inner chamber, and the

doors whispered closed behind them. Ryan quickly stepped away from her, breaking the contact between them. Madelyn did not appear to care, moving toward a nearby table. She picked up a goblet and poured some dark red liquid from a glass carafe. She swirled the contents of the crystal cup, then took a long drink. The wine, or whatever it was, pleased her, and she settled into a nearby chair.

Ryan examined the room. It was large, but not as large as the outer chamber. It seemed to be a sleeping suite, as Ryan uncomfortably noted the large bed in the corner. It had the same, spare, geometric décor as the outer room, but with a few more luxurious touches. It, too, was arranged in a semi-circular pattern and Ryan noted there was another set of double doors above a few stairs, again in the center of the half circle.

"Would you like a drink?" Madelyn asked.

The question seemed almost a challenge to Ryan. Without responding, Ryan walked to the table, lifted the remaining glass, and poured a drink from the decanter. She swirled the contents in the glass for a moment, steeling herself for whatever it might be, then tilted the glass to her lips.

It was something less than a full drink, but more than a sip, but either way it burned fire down her throat. Ryan could feel the liquid enter her stomach, so distinct was its fiery progress. She felt heat travel up the back of her spine, spread out through her shoulder blades, then engulf her skull, settling firmly on her cheeks. Incredibly, Ryan felt dizzy for a moment, and quickly sat down in the chair opposite Madelyn.

Madelyn watched the reaction with some pleasure. The girl continued to surprise her, and the fact that she had not died on the spot was somewhat of a revelation as well. Ryan carefully set the glass back down on the table.

"I think that's enough," Ryan said unsteadily.

"You continue to surprise me, Ryan Alexander," Madelyn said, voicing her previous thoughts aloud.

There seemed to be two of Madelyn sitting across from her, and Ryan was not certain which one to address, so she maintained her silence. For a moment, Madelyn's image seemed to shift, then shimmer slightly, as if Ryan were seeing something that was not quite there. She stared at the image, a strange expression on her face, then glanced about the room. It seemed to have the same shimmering quality, as if she were glimpsing some sort of underlying reality that otherwise could not be seen.

Great, Ryan thought to herself, returning her attention to the dark-haired woman, I'm intoxicated.

Madelyn watched the girl closely. Impossibly, she felt her hunger for the infant stir once more.

"Come here," Madelyn commanded.

Uncertain if she could even stand, Ryan rationalized that she was passively resisting It did not matter, because in an instant she was seated in the chair with Madelyn. In her somewhat inebriated condition, she wondered when she had learned to fly.

"You are much more pliable in this state," Madelyn noted, "perhaps you should dine with me more often."

"No," Ryan said, trying to clear her head, "I don't think that's such a good idea."

"Hmm," Madelyn said, adjusting Ryan's head, "we shall see."

Ryan winced at the bite, but it was not nearly as painful as it was normally. Either Madelyn was moderating the pain, or whatever intoxicant she had consumed was dulling it. In fact, Ryan felt herself begin to relax.

Although her head was still groggy, Ryan began to struggle wildly. Madelyn easily caught her flailing limbs, restraining her completely. She bit into Ryan's neck again, and this time the pain was intense, clearing Ryan's head almost completely. The familiar paralysis began to seep into Ryan's body, and she went limp in Madelyn's arms.

"It is your choice to struggle," Madelyn said, adjusting Ryan's position so that she could feed better, "the end result will be the same."

Madelyn resumed her feeding, and for once, Ryan welcomed the pain and the paralysis. She also welcomed the fact that Madelyn could not read her mind, or else the woman would have known the end result most definitely would not have been the same.

Susan watched the double doors with some trepidation. She had awakened when Madelyn trapped Ryan on the stairs, but had pretended sleep. There was nothing she could have done, and Ryan was far more vulnerable with Susan than without her. Still, Susan felt a sense of shame that she could do nothing to help Ryan.

Harrian entered the room from the lift. He glanced around the room, his expression darkening.

"Where is she?" he demanded.

Susan knew he was not talking about his master in that tone of voice. She nodded toward the double doors at the top of the stairs.

"She is in there, with Madelyn."

Harrian's annoyance transitioned to disbelief and outrage. He did, however, lower his voice to a furious whisper.

"The prisoner is in the inner chambers?" he demanded.

"Yes," Susan said impatiently, "she is."

Harrian's face turned apoplectic. He turned on his heel and stalked from the outer chambers, knowing his anger would get him killed.

Susan watched his departure thoughtfully, grateful that he was gone, but again troubled by all of the undercurrents she did not understand.

Several hours later, the double doors finally whispered open. Madelyn exited, carrying Ryan's limp body. She approached Susan, who could not hide her concern. Madelyn dropped Ryan's limp form onto a nearby couch, neither gently nor roughly, then turned and left without a word.

Susan rushed to Ryan's side, thankful at least that Ryan had found unconsciousness. She settled beside her, knowing her long vigil was just beginning.

CHAPTER 30

RYAN AWOKE TO FIND DRAKE SLEEPING on her chest. Her entire world seemed distilled down into exhausted sleep intermittently broken by periods of wakefulness in which she was forced to rest to recover.

She sat up, gently laying her son on his side on the couch. She turned to find Susan watching her with some concern.

"How do you feel?" Susan asked.

Ryan stretched experimentally. Much of her pain was gone, having diminished to an overall soreness. She stood, careful not to jostle Drake, and again stretched.

"I feel better," Ryan replied. She glanced up at the double doors. "For the moment."

Susan followed her gaze. "I don't think Madelyn is here right now. She left some time ago, and I have not seen her return."

"Hmm," Ryan said. She walked over to the solid rock wall and leaned against it, pressing her palms into its surface.

"What are you doing?" Susan asked curiously.

"I am not certain," Ryan said, "but it seems to make me feel better."

Susan walked over to the wall to stand next to her. "Lift your hand," she ordered.

Ryan glanced at her mildly. "Yes ma'am."

Susan blushed, aware that she had fallen into her role as doctor. Still, she leaned closer to where Ryan's hand had rested. There was the faintest outline of her palm.

"Are you applying enough pressure to create that indentation?"

Ryan, too, leaned closer, surprised at the outline. "No," she said, "I'm not applying any pressure at all." She glanced upward at the reddish rock. "I believe some of this rock is hematite, which would not be that difficult to scratch. But I don't think I'm applying enough pressure to do so."

Susan was always surprised at Ryan's breadth of knowledge, and Ryan seemed to know her thoughts.

"I have learned a few things in 700 years," Ryan said with a wicked grin. She turned back to the rock. "But I remember this particular fact from my human upbringing. My first father was a blacksmith, and hematite is nothing more than iron ore."

The final piece clicked into place in Susan's brain, Ryan noticed her expression.

"What?" Ryan asked.

Susan tried to control her excitement. As dreadful as their current situation was, nothing could decrease her enthusiasm for her research.

"When I was studying your anatomy, I kept trying to figure out how you could survive without eating."

"I remember the conversation," Ryan said.

"Right," Susan said, "one of my working theories was that you absorb what you need from the environment around you."

"Okay," Ryan said slowly, staring at the imprint on the wall.

"Have you taken any blood from Madelyn?" Susan asked.

"No," Ryan said vehemently.

"And yet you continue to replace your blood supply at an extraordinary rate." Susan glanced around the room. "The climate here is very humid. I imagine you can pull moisture from the air." Susan nodded to the imprint in the wall. "And hematite and hemoglobin sound similar for a reason."

"Iron," Ryan said, comprehending.

"Yes," Susan agreed, "I think you are pulling the iron your body needs from the rock itself."

"So I am like some great frog," Ryan said mischievously.

"Right," Susan said, caught up in her enthusiasm. "Wait, what? No." She frowned at Ryan, knowing what she was implying. "True, certain amphibians absorb nutrients through their skin, but I hardly think this is a comparison."

Ryan was already walking back toward the couch, seeing that Drake was awake. He was watching them intently, and Ryan scooped him up and tossed him in the air.

"Did you hear that, little one?" Ryan asked him. "Now I am the frog king."

Drake seemed delighted by this news, and Susan sighed in exasperation. Ryan was never impressed by the miracle of her own anatomy.

"And now you," Ryan said, tossing him upward once more, "are the frog prince."

This news sent the toddler into fits of laughter, and the two fell to the couch together. Ryan shifted the boy's weight, settling him comfortably on her lap. Susan realized the brief exertion had tired her. She sat back down near Ryan.

Ryan was quiet for a moment, lost in thought. The subject of her thoughts became apparent when she addressed Susan.

"Have you noticed a strangeness about Madelyn?"

"You mean other than the obvious?" Susan asked.

"Yes," Ryan said, "other than the obvious. I mean, I know she is very ancient for our Kind, but every once in awhile…" Ryan thought about the shimmer she had seen, the shifting of the image. The thoughts troubled her, so she merely shook her head. "I don't know."

Susan tried to be helpful, but was uncertain what Ryan was getting at. "I have noticed that her speech is very strange, but I assume it is because her native language is very old, perhaps not even spoken anymore."

Ryan nodded. "I was thinking Sumerian, one of the few language isolates."

Susan was shocked. "You think Madelyn is 6000 years old?"

Ryan shrugged. "It would not surprise me. Her power is immense. I have no way of even comprehending its extent."

Susan felt hopelessness return. That would mean Madelyn was well over three times Victor's age. Something occurred to her.

"Then it is no wonder she has captured you," Susan said.

"What?" Ryan asked.

"She has to stop you."

Ryan shook her head. "I'm not following you. I hardly see how I could be considered a threat."

Susan was insistent. "I may not know a great deal about our Kind, being the 'neophyte' that I am, but I have figured out one thing, you are a complete anomaly."

"Flattery will get you nowhere, Dr. Ryerson."

Susan frowned at her. "I'm not kidding, Ryan. You are as powerful as the Old Ones, even though you are half their age. It might take a millennium, or even more, but you are the only one capable of catching Madelyn."

Ryan saw one huge flaw in her reasoning. "That would mean I would have to Share with her."

Susan just looked at her. "I am not suggesting that you do so."

Ryan reached down to brush Drake's hair from his eyes. "First off, Madelyn does not seem inclined to want to Share. She seems quite happy taking me by force. Secondly, I am quite certain Madelyn's blood would kill me instantly. Finally, I think I would rather die than," Ryan paused, seeking a sufficiently pejorative term, "suck that woman's blood."

Susan muffled a giggle, and Ryan glanced over at her. "What?"

Susan covered her mouth with her hand. "It's just—"

"What?" Ryan asked in exasperation.

"It's just that you sounded like a Dracula movie for a moment."

Ryan grinned. Yes, it had kind of sounded that way. Her eyes grew distant as long-ago memories bubbled to the surface.

"You know, I met Dracula once, or at least the man the character was based on."

"You met Vlad Tepes?" Susan asked in astonishment.

"Hmm," Ryan mused, "yes." She shook her head. "It ended badly." She turned away, not wishing to relive the memory at the moment. "That is a story for another day."

Susan awakened to find Ryan standing across the room next to the small window. Ryan was doing something strange. She was running her fingers along the grooves between the bricks, tracing the geometric outlines with her fingertips. She did this with great concentration, and Susan had now seen her do it on several occasions. The behavior was a bit worrisome to Susan. It reminded her of laboratory mice that had been mistreated and began exhibiting random, repetitive behavior.

Ryan turned to glance at her, a wry expression on her face, and Susan blushed. Ryan could read her face even if she was forbidden to read her thoughts.

Ryan strolled across the room and sprawled into the chair next to Susan. It seemed by her lithe gait she was feeling much better, but it was apparent she was still fatigued. Drake stirred on the couch next to her, and she placed her hand on his back, calming him in his sleep. She leaned back and put her hands behind her head, closing her eyes.

"Ryan," Susan began hesitantly.

"Hmm?" Ryan asked, her eyes still closed.

"Would it help you…" Susan's voice trailed off.

Ryan opened one eye and glanced over at her. "Would what help me?"

Susan gathered her nerve. "Would it help you if you drank my blood?"

Ryan opened the other eye. "Are you trying to seduce me, Dr. Ryerson?"

Susan was indignant. "Of course not," she said, both outraged and defensive. "I was just trying to—"

Susan's words drifted off as she became aware of Ryan's teasing expression. Susan punched her in the arm. "You are horrible."

Ryan pretended the blow hurt, rubbing her arm, so Susan hit her again. Or at least tried to, as Ryan fended her off easily. Ryan snatched her wrist and pulled her forward off-balance, and Susan went spilling into her lap. Ryan was clearly amused at Susan's predicament, and Susan was clearly embarrassed.

"Well," Ryan said, "I don't know, Dr. Ryerson, I've never Shared with a Young One before."

Susan had always been amazed at Ryan's strength, but having it demonstrated in such close quarters was overwhelming. However, she was not about to fall prey to Ryan's considerable charm.

"I probably wouldn't satisfy you, anyway," Susan said through gritted teeth, trying to pull away. Ryan would not let her go.

"Oh, I don't know about that," Ryan said, playfully struggling with her, "I have learned there is much more to Sharing than power."

Susan became acutely aware of Ryan's nearness. Since the day she had met these creatures, she had struggled to deal with the strange, sensual world they lived in, a world in which the concepts of sex, gender, and familial kinship were meaningless. Heterosexuality, homosexuality, monogamy, incest, all were concepts without significance or consequence because true sex was almost unknown to them. They Shared blood, but it was rarely an act of reproduction. Susan's world, the world of science and rationalism, had methods to examine these creatures, but no ways of understanding them.

Ryan gazed down at her intently. "You have to remember, Dr. Ryerson, I came from a very different world than you. A world of magic and witchcraft, of superstition and ignorance, of faith and conviction. It is far less of a leap for me."

Ryan put her hand on Susan's chin, guiding her head gently so that her throat was open to her. Susan was terrified, but her fear was of her own loss of control rather than anything Ryan was about to do to her.

"Sometimes," Ryan said, brushing her teeth along Susan's throat, "you just have to let go."

The sensation was electrifying, and Susan swooned as Ryan began taking her blood. Although she had Shared with Raphael and others of his group, she had never experienced anything like this. She could not even compare it to sex, for sex had a build-up and a climax, and this was a constant climax. Each second held an unbearable tension, as if the pressure must release, but instead, the pleasure just increased. She could feel her heart rapidly beating in her chest, desperately trying to keep pace with the blood that was leaving her system.

A pleasant heaviness began to settle upon her limbs and a languor stole over her thoughts. Susan understood now why so many Young Ones of their Kind were killed. It was such an extraordinarily pleasurable experience, one lost the will to even fight. And if the more dominant of the pair gave into the gratification of the kill...

Susan abruptly was on the edge of a cliff in a blood-red world, teetering towards an abyss. She had no desire to even stop her forward progress, and felt herself pitching head-first into the blackness. She felt powerful hands grasp her shoulders, pulling her back from the brink.

"I don't think so," Ryan said with some amusement.

Susan pressed backward into Ryan, aware she had almost just died. The fact that she was willing to give up her life in the act of pleasure, without a thought to Jason, was greatly frightening to her.

"Do not be so hard on yourself," Ryan said, "it is our way. And it is why," she said with a trace of mischief, "you choose your partners wisely."

Susan turned and buried her face against Ryan. They were still in the blood-red world. Ryan brushed Susan's hair from her face, a trace of concern on her features.

"It will be painful for you, but you must take a little of my blood to survive."

Susan nodded her understanding. It was moments like these that she truly grasped the fact that Ryan was almost 700 years old. She took the wrist Ryan offered. Susan was able to take only a single drink because it was like consuming liquid lightning, burning through every artery, vein, and capillary in her system. It initially weakened her, and her knees buckled, but then she felt strength surge through her system.

Ryan glanced at the abyss with unease, and took a large step back from the brink, pulling Susan with her. She generally had no fear in this world, but she had also never been here with someone so vulnerable before.

The few ounces of blood Susan consumed continued to strengthen her, and she began looking around her in astonishment.

"What is this place?" she asked.

Ryan glanced about at the infinite red sky, the blood red mountains stretching behind an endless reddish plain. She glanced at the edge of the cliffs, the black abyss that stretched out into infinite darkness.

"I am not certain if this is a physical place or a mental construct," Ryan replied, "but I do know this is the edge of death."

All of Susan's years of education and research on genetics, immortality, life extension, all seemed to pale in the face of what she was seeing. This place had a truth and reality to it that went far beyond mere scientific fact.

Ryan was staring into the abyss with some concern. She stretched out her senses, uneasy at what she feeling.

"What is that?" Susan asked.

Ryan glanced at her sharply. "You can feel it, too?"

They both turned back to the blackness, and Ryan again stretched her senses into the abyss. She recoiled in alarm.

The malevolent presence was stronger, closer, than it had ever felt before. It was ancient, cold, reptilian, even arachnid in an abstract way. It was immensely and terrifyingly powerful, possessing a single-minded intent of assimilating, subjugating, or destroying everything in its path. Ryan could feel great claws reaching out from the depths, seeking to drag her back into them. The voice came, that horrifying, sibilant voice, the sibilant, hissing voice of a dragon.

"I—"

Ryan took a step backward, pulling Susan with her.

"—AM COMING—"

The horrible voice rolled across the plain, then echoed through the mountains.

"—FOR YOU."

Perhaps it was Ryan's frustration with her captivity. Perhaps it was the fact that her son and Susan were in constant danger. Perhaps it was the fact that she was separated from her father after his long illness. Or perhaps it was merely the fact Ryan was so very, physically tired. But regardless of the motivation, Ryan was at breaking point. And after many years, it was enough.

"Then get on with it," Ryan said quietly, unafraid. "I am tired of waiting."

Strangely, this seemed to please whatever malevolent creature was in the darkness, and Ryan swore she could hear laughter whisper on the hot winds that stirred.

Ryan glanced down, clutching Susan's shoulders. "We should go."

Ryan awoke, holding Susan in her arms. Susan was pale, but Ryan was relieved to see she was not near death. And although Susan was still a Young One, Ryan felt the act had in fact strengthened her.

Ryan gently disentangled herself from Susan and laid her down beside Drake. She gazed at the two of them, feeling a tremendous sadness that she had placed them in such danger. Then, because she had little else to do, she returned to the outer wall and began her rhythmic tracing of the geometric patterns.

It was only a short time later that the doors from the lift whispered open, and she could hear Madelyn make her way toward the stairs. Ryan studiously ignored the woman's presence, choosing instead to stop her activities and stare out the window. She heard Madelyn's footsteps slow to a stop, and Ryan decided she should probably turn around.

Madelyn was standing at the base of the stairs, her eyes on the bruises on Susan's throat. Ryan began moving toward the sleeping pair, trying to appear unhurried. She was, however, greatly concerned at Madelyn's sudden change in demeanor, and at the fact Madelyn was now moving toward the pair as well. Fortunately, Ryan won their measured race and reached Susan and Drake a second before Madelyn, inserting herself directly in front of the woman.

Madelyn was seething. She glanced down at Susan with disdain. "I am surprised you would lower yourself to such fare."

Ryan was now angry as well, but she understood how dangerous the current situation was. Madelyn could easily kill Susan and still hold her in check with her son's presence.

"I was not aware it mattered. You did not forbid it," Ryan replied.

"It is forbidden now," Madelyn said curtly. She gave Ryan a quick once-over, as if assessing her for some type of contamination. "I require your presence."

Madelyn turned and started towards the stairs, and if there was any misunderstanding or hesitation on Ryan's part, it was instantaneously corrected.

"Now!" Madelyn emphasized.

Ryan gave one last look at the sleeping pair, then hurried to catch up with Madelyn. Ryan followed her through the double doors, and had no sooner crossed the threshold than Madelyn picked her up and slammed her backward against the wall.

"You grow more trying and less entertaining each day, Ryan Alexander," Madelyn hissed between clenched teeth.

Ryan was on the verge of spewing a sarcastic retort when she became aware of something different about Madelyn. Or perhaps in her previously weakened condition, she had simply not noticed it.

Madelyn normally wore clothing that covered nearly every square inch of her body. And although her customary flowing garments hinted at the well-formed body that might lie beneath, Ryan had only the firmness of their usual forced contact to assess that probability.

That was, until today.

Ryan felt the color and heat seep into her own cheeks. She looked to the right, trying to feign interest in the blank wall, then to the left, apparently mesmerized by a nondescript table. Her eyes swept the room, searching for anything to alight on, until finally, reluctantly, she met Madelyn's gaze once more.

As Ryan's flustered inspection of the room took place, Madelyn's expression changed from anger to curiosity, then to dawning understanding and amusement. Her anger dissipated entirely as she noted the girl's high color and chagrined look.

"I stand corrected," Madelyn said, "you are still very entertaining."

Ryan could no longer meet her eye and returned to her desperate perusal of the room, seeking anywhere for her errant glance to settle. She could feel the relationship between her and Madelyn subtly shift once more, moving in a very dangerous direction. Madelyn seemed to finally become aware of the shift, as well. She leaned very close to Ryan.

"I asked you in the beginning if you would fight me," Madelyn whispered, "and you said you would not because it was futile." Ryan's heightened senses made the whisper torturous in her ear. Madelyn shifted, bringing the torment her other side. "Very soon you will not fight because you do not wish to."

Ryan began struggling, and Madelyn laughingly bit her. Ryan welcomed the pain, and felt the paralysis begin to seep into her body. She tried to push Madelyn away, but the woman easily caught her wrist, imprisoning it despite her efforts.

Madelyn stopped for a moment, staring at the wrist she held in her hand. There was a look of amazement on her face, and a bit of wonder in her tone.

"You grow resistant to my bite," Madelyn said, oddly pleased.

Ryan stopped as well, staring at the imprisoned wrist. Generally by this time she was completely paralyzed, and although she could feel the paralysis progressing, she was still able to generate significant movement. She stared at Madelyn.

"One day it will not affect me at all," Ryan promised defiantly, "even if it takes a thousand years."

Madelyn gazed down at her with gentle mocking. "Do you really think you could satisfy me for a thousand years?"

Although the paralysis was progressing, Ryan's gaze and voice were steady. "Yes," she said simply, "I do."

Madelyn leaned forward and bit her again, taking a long drink that made Ryan's knees give way. "I almost believe you could," Madelyn murmured, settling down to drain her.

Ryan awoke to find Drake curled up on her chest. She was relieved to see she was back in the outer chambers, alone with her son and Susan.

"How are you feeling?" Ryan and Susan asked at the same time.

Ryan nodded for Susan to go first.

"I am fine," Susan said, self-consciously brushing her hair. "I awoke when you were gone, and assumed Madelyn had returned."

Ryan's expression darkened, thinking of Madelyn's last feeding. "I am that woman's dog."

"What?" Susan asked, astonished at the characterization.

"I am like some favored pet," Ryan elaborated.

Susan did not bother to hide her skepticism. "Ryan, I think there is far more to it than that, and if it means anything, so does your father."

Ryan was doubtful, although she respected Susan's opinion and most certainly Victor's. Susan continued.

"For instance, when Drake and I were first brought here, Madelyn's assistant was shocked that we were placed here in her outer chambers. If I am correct, it is a huge honor just to see this room. It is certainly not anywhere prisoners would ever be kept."

Ryan listened to Susan's reasoning.

"And," Susan said, "from what I understand, no one goes into the inner chambers."

Ryan was quiet for a moment, but did not relent, possibly because she did not want to think otherwise.

"Even a dog sleeps at the foot of his master's bed."

The two settled into silence, a silence that was finally broken by Ryan's verbalization of her musings.

"Did you know there are another set of doors in Madelyn's inner chambers?" Ryan said, her curiosity evident. "I wonder what is behind those?"

Susan felt a distinct sense of foreboding. She was quite certain Ryan was going to find out what was behind those doors.

CHAPTER 31

VICTOR SET THE SWORD DOWN, and Kusunoki followed suit. As Victor's strength returned, he spent hours sparring with Kusunoki, partially to hone his skill and partially to burn off energy. Kusunoki greatly enjoyed the contests because although Victor's style of fighting was distinctly different than Ryan's, he was a master swordsman and as difficult to defeat as she was. Ala and her men sat and watched the two while Jason and Edward sat nearby. After Susan disappeared, Ala had made a point of looking after the boy, as had Edward.

"Thank you, Kusunoki," Victor said.

Kusunoki bowed. "The pleasure is mine, my lord. I am glad to see you are fully recovered."

"Almost, my friend," Victor said, "almost." A servant approached and Victor took the damp cloth he proffered. He set to wiping his hands clean, absorbed in the action. But as he continued to clean his hands, his motions slowed, then stopped. He stood unmoving.

Kusunoki watched Victor, aware of his pause. The dark-haired man had a far-away look in his eye, as if he were seeing something from a great distance.

"What is it, my lord?" Kusunoki asked.

Victor's gaze refocused on his surroundings. "It is the oddest thing," he replied, "I feel almost as if someone is trying to communicate with me, sending me images although no words."

Kusunoki felt a twinge of hope and cast a glance in Ala's direction. Although he and Victor were speaking quietly, he knew she could easily hear their conversation.

"Is it Ryan?" Kusunoki asked, giving voice to his hope.

"No," Victor said, a strange look on his face "at least not directly."

"I am afraid I do not understand, my lord," Kusunoki said.

Victor glanced at the samurai, then over at Ala. His gaze settled on Jason for a long moment before he turned back to the Kusunoki.

"It seems impossible, but I think the images are coming from my grandson."

Ryan leaned back in a chair, Drake resting against her chest and napping. Susan sat across from her, reading one of the books that had been provided her. For the moment, Ryan was almost content. It was gift Kusunoki had spent decades trying to give her, the ability to stay in the moment. With her restless spirit and wandering mind, it had been nearly impossible at times, but for this small interval, she was at peace.

That peace was disrupted when Madelyn strode through the door, her gown flowing about her. She took in the familial scene, her face expressionless. Ryan tightened as she approached and Drake awakened, but Madelyn did not pause and continued up the stairs to her inner chambers, disappearing within.

Ryan relaxed, and Drake settled back down. She ran her fingers through his silky black hair. It reminded her so much of Victor it made her heart ache.

Although Susan was not nearly as attuned to the emotions of their Kind as Ryan was, Susan was particularly adept at sensing Ryan's. There was a pensiveness about Ryan, a restlessness that appeared when Madelyn did. Susan examined her friend, noting the high cheek bones, the perfect mouth, the eyes that constantly shifted in hue. Susan noted that Ryan's hair was now so light it was almost white. When she stood up, Susan noticed the same, lithe athleticism and grace that had astonished Susan the first time she saw her.

Ryan ran her fingers through Drake's hair once more, and for a long moment stared into his blue eyes. She then walked over to Susan and handed the child to her.

"If you wouldn't mind watching Drake for a moment, there is something I must do."

The resignation in Ryan's voice sent a shudder through Susan. "Ryan—" Susan began.

Ryan gently cut her off. "I will be fine," she said. She glanced up a the double doors. "I will be back in a little while."

Drake somberly watched his mother as she mounted the stairs.

Once Ryan was at the top of the steps, she paused in front of the double doors, but only for a brief instant. She reached out and touched the engraved surface, and was not surprised when it whispered open before her. She turned and gave Drake and Susan one last glance, then stepped inside. The doors whispered closed behind her.

The inner chamber was empty. Ryan paused in the entryway, glancing about the room. She walked over to the table and picked up the glass decanter, examining the red liquid within. She swirled it for a moment, then set the carafe back down. She walked over to the bed, then ran her hand along the sheet. It was a strange fabric, like many things in this place, familiar, but not quite identifiable to her.

Ryan turned to the center of the room, to the few steps that led up to the other set of double doors. She hesitated, but only a moment, then approached the stairs. She took them two at a time, her steps echoing in the empty chamber, then stood before the entryway. These doors were even more elaborately engraved than the outer ones, the same geometric patterns representing something equally unfathomable but doing so with more urgency. Although incomprehensible to Ryan, she somehow knew them to be a warning. Very slowly, she extended her hand to the door and pressed her fingers to the surface. And very slowly, with a barely audible click, the lock released and the door whispered open.

Ryan stepped into something that was not a room.

The walls seemed to shift, shimmering with tantalizing glimpses of things that were not there. Hideous objects took shape in her peripheral vision, solidifying, then disappearing when she turned to look at them fully. She looked at the floor in front of her, blurred her gaze, and tried not to focus on any one thing.

The walls were alive. They twisted and turned like the inside of some great beast. Tentacles slithered outward then snapped back. Claw-like appendages encrusted with scales clacked sharply together, creating an accompaniment to the wet sliding sounds. It was dark and warm, and the air was heavy and moist.

Ryan tried not to look directly at the walls, but rather see them out of the edge of her vision. She could see what looked to be fangs, and slime-covered carcasses of creatures she had never seen before. Ryan jumped at the hand on her shoulder.

"Entrance into the inner sanctuary is punishable by death," Madelyn whispered into her ear.

Ryan did not sense any anger at her presence, but rather pleasure, as if her arrival had been expected. "Then kill me," Ryan replied shortly.

Madelyn laughed as she pulled the girl down onto some type of ledge.

"There are worse things than death, Ryan Alexander," she said.

Ryan desperately tried to control her fear. The ledge itself seemed to be alive, the same tentacles snaking up the sides then across towards her. It was difficult to tell if the appendages were plant or animal, or even what they were attached to. They wrapped about her arms, slithered across her torso, then snaked up her calve. The hellish limb moved to caress her inner thigh, then moved obscenely to caress a more sensitive area.

"No!" Ryan cried out, struggling wildly. She tried to free herself from the tentacles, but the harder she struggled, the tighter they held. One snaked its way about her throat, pinning her down so that she could not even see, and another snaked up her shirt and began tracing the lean muscles of her torso. The clacking and slithering in the room seemed to reach a crescendo, drowning out even the pounding of Ryan's heart.

And then all was silent.

Madelyn was propped on an elbow, staring down at her with amusement. Other than her hand, which rested on Ryan's stomach, there was nothing in the bed with them. Ryan glanced around the room in disbelief.

There was nothing there. The walls were completely white. There was nothing out of the ordinary, and in fact, there was nothing in the room at all other than the bed, Madelyn, and her. The inner sanctuary was empty and pristine.

"Did you see something?" Madelyn asked mockingly.

Ryan gazed up at her, but said nothing. She was completely losing her mind.

Madelyn's hand began to retrace the pattern on Ryan's midsection. Ryan, still befuddled, became aware of the sensation and looked down at the hand as if it were a foreign object. Although her right side was pinned beneath Madelyn, her left arm was free. She reached down and grabbed Madelyn's wrist, halting the movement.

"Stop it," Ryan said, none too certainly.

"Stop what?" Madelyn replied, still mocking. She easily shook her wrist from Ryan's grasp, and continued to do as she wished.

Ryan tried to shift away from her, but her movement seemed only to please Madelyn more. Ryan made a genuine effort to free herself, only to find her free wrist pinned as tightly as the rest of her body.

"Stop it," Ryan repeated, gazing up at her nemesis.

Madelyn, finally aware of what was transpiring, simply stared down at her, fully entertained.

"Who knew, Ryan Alexander," Madelyn asked, gently sarcastic, "that pleasure would be far more dangerous to you than pain?"

Ryan closed her eyes, knowing she was lost. The razor-sharp teeth whispered across her throat, but it was not pain that caused her to arch upward. Madelyn was not causing her pain, nor was she paralyzing her. Ryan tried one last time to push Madelyn away, but the effort was as weak as it was futile. And Madelyn enjoyed the girl twist beneath her so much, she wondered why she had ever paralyzed her at all.

"Stop," Ryan said between clenched teeth, "it."

"You already said that, little one," Madelyn said, still gently mocking. She paused in her feeding only long enough to get the words out.

And Ryan was lost. The sensation of having Madelyn take her blood, sans the pain and the paralysis, was as extraordinary as Ryan had known it would be. The waves of pleasure that washed through her were almost unbearable. And when the languor began to steal over her, Ryan knew she would welcome death.

For Madelyn, the experience was just as extraordinary. Taking the girl by force was one thing; having her yield to pleasure was another entirely. It seemed to intensify the experience a hundredfold. Having the girl cling to her as opposed to push her away inflamed her desire. She knew she was having one of the consummate experiences of her life, and just as surely knew that she would not kill the girl, no matter how much she wanted to.

When at last sated, Madelyn lay atop the girl, uncertain she could even move. She was finally able to roll to the side, where she lay staring up at the ceiling for quite some time. At last, she felt she had somewhat regained her senses, and propped herself up onto her side, gazing down at her unconscious prisoner.

The girl was far more dangerous than she had imagined.

CHAPTER 32

RYAN SAT IN THE OUTER CHAMBERS in a perfect meditative state. She was aware of Susan and Drake's presence, especially the latter as he sat in her lap as she sat cross-legged on the floor. He himself seemed to possess a focused mindfulness at the moment. Susan watched the two, once again marveling at the similarity of their features. It was growing more pronounced as Drake lost some of his chubbiness and began to grow leaner. The fact that Drake was beginning to acquire some of Ryan's mannerisms made the resemblance all the more striking.

Susan glanced up but Ryan did not as Madelyn exited from her inner chambers. Madelyn glanced at Susan dismissively, then paused when she saw Ryan. She examined her for a moment, then turned to the lift. As the elevator doors opened, Susan could see Harrian standing inside. The doors closed behind them.

As the elevator began to move downward, Madelyn turned to her chief of staff.

"I want you to double the guards on duty."

Harrian turned to the Queen, surprised. "As you wish, Your Majesty. Is there something in particular you wish them to be aware of?"

Madelyn shook her head. She had nothing to go on other than a nebulous feeling.

"No, I just want them to be extra vigilant this evening."

Harrian bowed low. "As you wish, my Queen."

Victor stood in the shadows of the mountain fortress, gazing upward at the magnificent structure. Although he had seen the citadel vaguely in his visions, seeing its actual construction was both awe-inspiring and dispiriting. The architecture itself was incredible, but he had grossly underestimated the size of the fortress.

Kusunoki stood silently at his side, also assessing the vast size of the stronghold. He was mentally calculating how many men were probably stationed within the fort, based upon what he could see. The number was devastating.

"My lord," Kusunoki said quietly, "I will follow you into any battle, but we are too few."

Victor clenched his jaw, knowing the truth in Kusunoki's words.

When he had sent out the general call for assembly, he had been gratified at the overwhelming response. Most of those who volunteered for the mission, however, had to be turned away. Knowing the strength of their adversaries, only the most powerful of their Kind were accepted. The rest would have been little more than cannon fodder, and as Victor was not certain of success as an outcome, he preferred the others go into hiding if the mission failed.

Victor turned back to look at the troops waiting in the shadows. Nearly three hundred of their Kind, none less than seven centuries old. All hand-picked by their lieges for their power and fighting ability. Aeron's line was well-represented, and he stood at the head of the men and women who were his offspring. Kusunoki's line, all dressed in black and carrying their traditional weaponry, stood calm and ready. Both Abigail and Marilyn had come, and although both preferred other methods of conquest, Victor knew them to be outstanding fighters. Their carefully chosen warriors stood by, tense but prepared.

Perhaps the most striking present were of Ala's line, the ebony warriors choosing to fight almost naked, their dark skin covered with ancient, fearsome markings. Ala herself wore the garments of the warrior queen of her people. There were others present, representing a vast, cross-section of their Kind.

Victor turned back to gaze at the citadel, his frustration palpable. Just the logistics of preparing such an assault were overwhelming. He had to deal with the surveillance he knew he was under, which fortunately had lessened as time had passed. Apparently Madelyn had so little respect for them as foes, the observation had been cursory at best. Then the matter of getting everyone to such a remote location, again, under secrecy without generating alarm, had been nearly impossible.

And now they stood before the gates, within striking distance, and Victor could taste defeat. He himself would gladly storm the citadel, but he could hardly lead his Kind to what surely would be total annihilation. And if Madelyn destroyed the greatest of their Kind here, it would be a simple matter for her to track down the Others and destroy them.

Kusunoki could feel Victor's absolute frustration. "Are you getting any sign or signal from Ryan through Drake?"

Victor calmed himself, careful to maintain his mental shield. All of them were controlling their mental presence. Although Ryan was certain these men could not sense their thoughts, she was not entirely certain they could not sense their presence. Madelyn's men did seem to possess some sort of the psychic gifts of their Kind, just in a cruder way.

Victor's expression changed slightly, and Kusunoki noted a look of surprise on his features.

"What is it?" Kusunoki asked.

"Ryan," Victor said, looking upward at the citadel, "is telling us to wait."

Ryan carefully set Drake to the side, then unfolded herself lithely upward. She lifted her son, smiled into his blue eyes, then handed him to Susan. Susan glanced up at her friend, a look of concern in her eyes. Ryan was acting strangely, very methodically but with an air of melancholy. She had a curious mixture of resignation and relief, like a death row inmate who has just finished his last meal.

Ryan's next actions did not allay Susan's concerns. Ryan walked to the outer wall and placed her fingers in the grout lines. As she had done so many times before, she began rhythmically tracing their outlines. She did so as a study of concentration, tracing and retracing the geometric patterns.

Susan watched her friend, wondering if perhaps she had finally gone mad.

Kusunoki watched Victor closely. He had not stopped pacing for the last few hours. He approached his liege.

"Do you know how long we are supposed to wait?" Kusunoki asked.

Victor shook his head. "No," he said. Both men glanced up as Abigail approached, a strange look on her face.

"Someone is coming," she said.

Victor glanced into the blackness behind them. He had avoided extending his senses, but this was a strength of Abigail's, so he had no reason to doubt her.

"Is it a rear attack?" he asked.

"No," she said, the strangeness of her expression increasing, "it is not Madelyn's men."

Victor again peered into the darkness, willing his preternatural sight to reveal who advanced.

Abigail's expression changed to one of wonder. "They are our Kind, but I do not recognize any of them." She continued to assess the sensation. "And they are many."

Victor and Kusunoki looked at one another, then began making their way to the rear of the assembly. This began to attract attention, and soon everyone was peering into the blackness behind them to see who approached.

One by one they began to slip from the shadows. Dark-haired and dark-eyed with olive skin, they wore flowing black robes and carried fearsome weaponry. Their headgear was black, and many of their faces were covered. Those few with uncovered faces revealed intricate paintings across their cheeks, just above their beards.

Kusunoki stared at the army in amazement. They were all Old Ones, more than he had thought existed.

"Who are they?" he asked.

Victor smiled. "They are Janissaries," he replied.

The lead Janissary stopped in front of Victor. He gave a short bow. "I am captain of the guard," he stated, "and we are at your service."

Victor stared at the assembly in wonder. "How many of you are there?"

The captain gave another short bow. "We are five hundred in number."

Victor took a deep breath, unusual for him, because unlike Ryan, he did not maintain his human gestures. But this time he did.

"You will have to thank your master for me," Victor said.

The captain shook his head vigorously. "I cannot do that, my lord."

Victor looked at him curiously. "And why is that?"

"Because you must thank him yourself."

It was not the captain who spoke, but a voice from the crowd of men that was now parting. The speaker stepped forward.

"Although thanks is really unnecessary," Saladin said.

Victor stepped forward, embracing his friend with great emotion. "Assalamu alaikum," he said, grasping Saladin's forearm.

"And to you be peace with God's mercy," Saladin replied, his fondness for the other man obvious.

The Others present, especially the very oldest among them, stood in stunned silence. Abigail leaned slightly toward Marilyn.

"I hate it that Victor is able to keep such secrets from me," she said to Marilyn under her breath.

Marilyn was examining the newcomers with great appreciation. "And Mon Dieu, what a secret."

Victor stepped back from his friend. "You have broken your solitude, my brother."

Saladin shrugged. "I did not think I would ever find another battle worth fighting." He glanced up at the citadel. "Apparently I was wrong."

After quick introductions, the leaders began to hurriedly alter their strategy, preparing their next move.

Ryan was a study of concentration, carefully tracing the geometric patterns with a single-mindedness that was almost frightening to Susan. Ryan had increased the pace of her tracing, continuing with that inexorable rhythm. It was gripping to watch, but in a deeply disturbing way. Susan was about to say something to her when Ryan stopped abruptly. Ryan put her hands flat on the surface of the wall, then rested her forehead against the smooth stone for a moment.

"Um, Ryan?" Susan asked.

Ryan did not answer. Instead, she gathered all of her strength, braced herself, and began to push outward.

Victor and his group of warriors were creeping across the huge courtyard. Other groups were fanning out, pressed against walls and disappearing into shadows. Victor could see several begin to climb upward. No alarm had been sounded yet. He felt Kusunoki's hand on his arm.

"How are we going to find her?" Kusunoki whispered to him.

Victor was slightly embarrassed. This part of the plan had been somewhat vague in his mind.

"I rather thought she would make herself known," he whispered back.

A tremendous creaking sound coming from above attracted all attention, including the watch guard. Both Kusunoki and Victor looked upward. A huge section of rock wall, strangely shaped in a geometric pattern, appeared to be peeling outward from the citadel.

Victor looked back at Kusunoki. "Something like that," he said in a furious whisper.

Kusunoki grinned as the alarm was sounded.

Susan stared at Ryan in amazement, at last understanding. For weeks, if not months, Ryan had been carefully carving out the grout lines of the wall, weakening the structural integrity of a huge section. As Ryan pushed outward with her incredible strength, the entire wall began to give way in one great piece, falling outward. Susan felt a blast of cold air as an enormous portion of the room fell away.

Ryan stood in front of the gaping hole, a look of satisfaction on her face. She brushed her hands together, then turned back toward Susan and her son.

"I think we should probably be leaving now."

Susan jumped as the alarm sounded. It echoed loudly in the room because the chamber was now open to the outdoors. Ryan gestured toward her impatiently. Susan grabbed Drake, and joined Ryan at the opening. Ryan took Drake from her as Susan gazed into what appeared to be an endless abyss.

"How exactly are we going to get down from here?" Susan asked uneasily.

Ryan looked straight down. There was a terrace beneath them, perhaps a hundred foot drop, easy for her to manage even with extra weight. She shifted Drake into one arm and lifted Susan bodily from the ground with the other.

"Keep your feet up," Ryan instructed, then jumped.

Susan screamed the entire time they fell, which seemed to be several days. Ryan landed solidly on both feet. Cracks in the marble spread outward from the force of her landing.

"You know," Ryan said mildly, standing upright, "it's going to difficult to escape with you screaming the whole time."

Ryan set her back on her feet and Susan hit her in the arm. Drake just kicked his feet in delight.

"You want to do that again?" Ryan asked him, laughing, and he wriggled in joy.

"We are not," Susan said with emphasis, straightening her clothing, "doing that again."

Ryan shrugged. "Very well," she replied, glancing around in an attempt to get some type of bearing.

"Would you mind telling me what is going on?" Susan asked. It seemed there was a lot of commotion, even for the stunt Ryan had just pulled.

Ryan started down the hallway, gesturing for Susan to follow her. "My father is here," Ryan said.

Susan stopped. "Victor is here?"

Ryan again gestured to her impatiently to keep up, and Susan complied.

"They are all here," Ryan said, extending her senses outward for the first time. She could not afford to do so continuously, because it would alert her enemy to her location, but she did so now with great joy. She smiled to herself, sensing Saladin and his men. "All of them."

Susan's head was spinning as she tried to keep up both physically and metaphorically. "So, do you have a plan?"

Ryan nodded. "I have to find the armory. It is our only hope of equalizing this battle."

Victor was already engaged in pitched battle in the courtyard. He was not certain if it was fortunate or unfortunate, but the combat was primarily hand-to-hand. Once the alarm had sounded, guards swarmed the central square, and Victor and the Others had quickly discovered their weapons were useless against Madelyn's men. Strangely, the guards carried no weapons themselves, so the fighting was brutal, face-to-face brawling.

Their adversaries were viciously strong, and Victor did not know how long they could last under these conditions. They currently had their foe outnumbered because they had caught the fortress completely by surprise, but Victor knew it was only a matter of time before the entire force was assembled. Once that happened, he knew they would begin to fall.

He sensed that Ryan was fleeing through the stronghold, and that she had some sort of destination in mind. Wherever she was headed, it gave Ryan some sort of hope. He gestured to Kusunoki to follow him, and he began fighting in that direction.

Ryan went skidding around a corner, then leaped back the way she had come just in time to collide with Susan, sending her to the ground. Ryan put her finger to her lips, silencing Susan's protest, then helped her to her feet. She handed Drake to Susan, then cautiously peered around the corner.

There were several guards milling about down the hallway, but they had not seen her. Ryan turned back to Susan, wordlessly indicating they should go back the way they came. They began inching down the hallway, but this route of escape was quickly blocked as well as several guards gathered. Ryan's only other choice was another open terrace, and Susan followed her uneasily. She was not looking forward to another jump.

Ryan started onto the vast terrace, but stopped abruptly. A single guard stood with his back to them. Ryan gestured for Susan to wait, then stealthily approached the guard from behind. Uncertain exactly what to do and definitely certain she could not defeat the guard by strength alone, she noticed he was wearing a necklace made of the same strange material the weapons and needle had been made of. Without hesitation, she grasped the necklace with both hands and garroted the guard. So strong was the material and so desperate was her attack that his head was nearly severed by the strike. He slumped to the ground.

Ryan gestured for Susan to join her. She glanced down into the melee below, searching for her father with both preternatural vision and extrasensory concentration. She sensed him before she saw him, and quickly tried to communicate. She turned to Susan, articulating the message aloud in case it had not been received.

"There must be an armory here," Ryan said urgently, "if something happens to me or we are separated, the Others must find the weapons. That is our only hope."

Susan nodded fearfully. If something happened to Ryan, she was not certain there was any hope.

Ryan glanced around, searching for a way down. But before she could identify an escape from the terrace, a group of guards crowded through the doorway. They raised a great cry, and Ryan could hear additional guards begin to respond to their location. Ryan, in frustration, pushed Susan behind her for protection. Susan cradled Drake in her arms, realizing they were trapped.

The guards stared at them contemptuously and Ryan's frustration increased. She glanced around her, searching for anything that could be used as a weapon, then looked down at the dead guard at her feet.

She looked back up, and very slowly smiled.

The guards shifted uncomfortably, glancing down to see what had given her such great pleasure. Their expressions fell.

The guard Ryan had killed was holding a sword in his hand, one he had drawn but been unable to use so swiftly had she killed him. The soldiers standing in the entryway again shifted uneasily. They had seen what this one could do with a sword. They drew their weapons, but without the confidence such a superior force should possess.

The sun pierced the thick cloud cover, bathing the terrace in filtered light. Ryan charged the group. The sunlight glinted off her blue-steel sword as she sprinted toward them. The glint caught the attention of several below, who looked upward, and began fighting in her direction.

Ryan clashed with the first wave violently, and should have been dead at first contact, but surprisingly, the fearsome soldiers began to fall before the flashing blade. Blood spattered her arm and she glanced down in surprise. The blood burned her skin like a mild acid, and although she began to heal almost immediately, the effect was distracting because it was so unexpected. She pushed the phenomenon from her mind, and renewed her battle, amputating a nearby arm, then taking a leg off at the knee.

The soldiers backed off, their numbers depleted but still able to surround her. Others appeared and fell in behind them, reinforcing their numbers, and the soldiers were emboldened. There were now more opponents than she had started with. Ryan took that moment to re-assess her situation. Her gaze fell upon the weapon of a nearby fallen enemy, and without hesitation, she flipped the blade upward, catching it in her free hand. She adjusted her stance, and with flowing grace, settled into a fighting style that favored the use of both swords. Her pleasure at the additional weapon was evident, her lack of fear pronounced, and at the intricate, skillful display, the expressions of the surrounding guards again fell.

The guards attacked, and Ryan should have been overwhelmed by sheer force, but somehow the flashing sword was always there, blocking an attack, deflecting a blow, or slicing outward with devastating effect.

Susan, clutched Drake, watching Ryan's lethality in astonishment. With the strength of these men and their overpowering numbers, Ryan should have long since fallen. Yet not only was she holding her own, she appeared to be winning. Soldier after soldier fell while Ryan, a study of concentration, slowly beat them back. With one last, great blow, Ryan decapitated the last guard on the terrace, and he fell to a kneeling position, then sprawled onto the heap of bodies.

Ryan turned back to Susan and took a few steps toward her. She heard footsteps and scuffling behind her, and Susan's expression told her all she needed to know. She stopped, heaving a sigh.

"There are a lot more behind me, aren't there?" Ryan asked.

Ryan did not wait for Susan's reply; she did not need to. She turned around, shifting her weight slightly as she assessed the new force.

It was easily twice the size of the previous. The soldiers crowded forward. Although the sight of their fallen comrades was daunting, the girl could not possibly prevail against such superior numbers. A simple all-out charge would suffice to take her down.

Ryan seemed to sense this as she gazed at the force, and she lowered her swords. The guards recognized the hesitation, and many grinned with predatory anticipation. Like a pack of wolves, they shifted forward slightly, awaiting only the signal from the alpha.

Although Ryan clearly communicated her negative assessment of the current odds, she did not evidence any concern. This gave the men pause, and they glanced at her uncertainly. Their uncertainty grew when she nonchalantly toyed with a sword on the ground in front of her, touching it with the blade of her own. She could not possibly utilize three swords.

Ryan carefully lifted the blade, balancing it on her own swords while elevating it to chest height. Although the sound of the battle below could be heard, the metallic noise of the blades sliding across one another seemed very loud. It was as if Ryan were mesmerizing the soldiers with some magician's trick, although in truth they really did not see the point of it. When she abruptly dropped her blades, then slapped the sword to the left before it could touch the ground, they saw no point in it at all.

The man who caught the sword, however, saw the point quite clearly. Kusunoki stepped from the shadows, his eyes on the troop of men. He swung the sword with pleasure and practiced ease. The same fierce light glowed in his eyes as the demon girl in front of them. The grins of the soldiers disappeared. The lithe lethality of this man was evident.

Ryan was not finished yet, however. She again flipped a sword upward, this time slapping it to the right. The soldiers knew enough this time to follow its flight as another man stepped from the shadows, a man with ice-blue eyes and a deadly expression on his face. Aeron caught the sword, appreciating its heft and balance. He swung it experimentally, and the soldiers shifted uncomfortably.

Ryan had not taken her eyes from the soldiers, knowing full well the positions of her allies without needing to look. Her tone was mocking as she addressed the soldiers.

"Allow me to make some introductions." She nodded in Aeron's direction without taking her eyes from the guards. "My beloved mate," she said, the endearment sarcastic but deadly. The guards shifted their attention to the blue-eyed man as the corner of his mouth twitched at the girl's dark humor.

Ryan nodded in Kusunoki's direction, again without taking her eyes from the guards. "My Master," she said with emphasis. The guards shifted their attention the other direction, toward the calm, Asian man with the gleaming eyes. This was perhaps even more disconcerting than an enraged mate; the one who had actually taught this demonic whelp to fight.

"And," Ryan said, flipping the final sword upward and to her side, "my father."

Victor caught the sword as he stepped from behind Ryan, appearing almost out of thin air. His eyes were fully on the soldiers as well. The guards in front took a step back as he revealed himself, even though their numbers still greatly exceeded the four standing in front of them. Something about this furious dark-haired, dark-eyed man seemed familiar to them. And the thought that this creature had actually sired the demon was immobilizing.

The four attacked and swiftly forced the guards rearward. Victor, Kusunoki, and Aeron quickly adapted to the deadly swords, and appendages began flying, most no longer connected to a torso. Victor, too, noted the strange burning sensation of the spattered blood from the enemy, but he pushed the distracting thought from his mind as Ryan had. He kept close to her, fighting back-to-back as they had for centuries. Aeron and Kusunoki created a similar pair, and when the four fought to the center, they created an impenetrable circle of flashing steel. They moved as one, each defending the other, attacking in the openings their companion swords created.

Victor was astounded at the strength of these men. Even he was beginning to feel fatigue at the tremendous strain of parrying the force of their blows. He glanced over at Ryan. He knew she had been ill, and she had been battling considerably longer than he had. Still, she was fighting with tremendous skill, her ineffable speed countering any strength advantage the enemy might have.

Kusunoki, too, was stunned at the physical power of the soldiers. And although the foursome continued to slay the surrounding forces, more and more guards began to pour onto the terrace. Obviously some signal had been given that the principle battle was here, and troops were being mobilized appropriately. Kusunoki glanced at Aeron, who was slaughtering the surrounding enemy with cold efficiency, then over at Ryan who was doing so with elegant grace. He was grimly pleased, but his countenance darkened as even more soldiers appeared. Although they had cleared an area around them, the sheer number of the enemy was beginning to press inexorably forward.

Ryan, too, glanced around her, with a quick look behind to ensure that Susan and Drake were still untouched. No one had broken their circle to reach her son and friend, although the battle was getting nearer to them. Ryan sliced through a nearby soldier, then turned to the entrance of the terrace. There was no way to stop the onslaught of soldiers pouring onto the balcony. She glanced around her, searching for any way out of their current predicament, and could see none. She glanced at her father, who caught her eye, and at Aeron, who looked to her with an equally grim expression. She thought furiously as her sword came up as if possessing reflexes of its own, blocking an incoming blow that she could not possibly have seen. She dispatched the owner of the attacking weapon with ruthless efficiency, still looking around her with studied concentration.

Ryan turned back again, this time making eye contact with Drake, who gazed at her somberly. Kusunoki glanced over, noting that Ryan seemed distracted. He felt a flash of fear as a sword came arcing out of the crowd toward her, but again, her sword came up as if of its own volition, swatting the offending weapon away and dispatching its owner.

Kusunoki turned and cut through two men who were pressing his corner, but again he had the urge to turn and look at Ryan. She had the strangest expression on her face, one of intense concentration, possessing an otherworldly quality as if what she was concentrating on was a long way away. Her swords continued to move as if they were alive, animated by some lethal force that required no effort from her. And stunningly, the swords began to move faster.

Kusunoki countered another slashing blow, but still his eyes returned to Ryan. They had sparred many times over the centuries and he was well-aware of her quickness. He had seen her move so swiftly she was an impression rather than an actual presence. But what she was doing now transcended even that. She was moving with such speed she seemed to be multiple images, with not merely two swords, but four, and then eight. Even with Kusunoki's preternatural eyesight, he was beginning to lose her in a blur. And even now, she gathered herself as if to move into an even higher gear.

And then something extremely strange happened. Some great shift occurred, rippling outward in a wave that overtook all who surrounded her. Ryan no longer appeared to be moving quickly, rather everything slowed down except her. She moved leisurely at normal speed. Everyone around her, however, was frozen or moving in very slow motion.

Kusunoki stared in wonder. As the wave rippled outward and overtook Victor, then himself, those surrounding him began moving in the same sluggish motion. The wave seemed to have no effect on him and Victor, however, and they were capable of moving at normal speed as well. A glance in Aeron's direction revealed that he, too, benefitted from whatever strange phenomenon was taking place. Victor glanced over at Ryan, still a study of concentration, but he did not hesitate to take advantage of the speed disparity. He began slicing at all of those surrounding him.

Kusunoki, too, began striking at the enemy around him. As they fell, one by one, he realized the soldiers were still moving at normal speed. It was the four of them that were moving at a speed beyond possibility, as if Ryan had taken all of them with her when she had shifted into that higher plane. Within moments, or perhaps seconds, hundreds of soldiers were dead upon the terrace.

A great thunderclap of noise stunned Kusunoki, and all movement shifted violently back to normal. Ryan had an odd look on her face, as if she herself was not certain what had occurred. Kusunoki was not sure if the clap of noise had been an actual sound or something that had occurred in his head. Aeron, too, shook his head as if to rid himself of mental echoes. Victor watched Ryan with some misgiving. He approached and put his hand on her shoulder.

"Are you alright?" he asked, concern in his dark eyes.

Ryan stared up at her father. "I am," she began, then paused uncertainly. "I am fine."

She glanced over at Susan, who was still clutching Drake tightly. The little boy watched his mother solemnly. Aeron, whose eyes had been on Ryan, followed her gaze. He froze at the sight of the small boy.

Drake turned his attention to the pale-haired, blue-eyed man on the terrace and examined him for a moment. He then smiled shyly and buried his face in Susan's shoulder. Aeron watched the small creature, a perfect little replica of his mother, and in that moment knew he was lost to both of them.

Ryan smiled at her son's antics, and it seemed to push away some of her disorientation. A strange flitting noise drew her attention as a silvery-blue arrow lodged into the marble at her feet. So strong was the material of the shaft and so sharp the arrowhead, it pierced the marble without cracking it, lodging firmly in the surface. A silvery, metallic rope was attached near the fletching, and Ryan recognized it as similar to her bindings, meaning it would be light and incredibly strong.

She glanced upward. Two terraces up, Kokumuo and several dozen of his warriors stood bearing wicked-looking weapons, swords, lances, and cross-bows, all of the same gray-blue metallic material.

"Ala's men have found the armory," Ryan said.

Victor immediately grasped the significance of the attached rope.

He snatched it and threw it over the side as several other arrows came flitting in. They now had an escape route.

Ryan took Drake from Susan's arms, hugging him tightly. She turned to Victor while gesturing to Susan, then bowed mockingly.

"Would you do the honors, dear father?"

Victor bowed, just as mockingly. "Of course, my liege." Without preamble, he picked Susan up, who could barely begin to lodge a protest before Victor was over the side and rappelling downward at breath-taking speed.

Ryan turned to Aeron. "Shall I pick you up, or do you think you can get down on your own?"

"Very funny, my dear," Aeron replied. He glanced over at the bundle in her eyes. "Try not to drop our son on the way down."

Ryan merely smiled, and Aeron noted as he went over the side that she had not corrected his use of pronoun.

Ryan turned to Kusunoki, prepared to make another joke when a look of concern passed over her features. Numerous footsteps could be heard in the long hallway approaching the terrace, but somehow he had the feeling that was not what attracted her attention.

Ryan moved to the edge of the terrace, still clutching her son. She glanced down at the battle that continued to take place, noting that the Others were beginning to turn the tide with the addition of the weapons that Ala's men had found. There were casualties on both sides, but the battle was definitely shifting.

Kusunoki watched Ryan closely. There seemed to be a pensiveness about her right now, a pensiveness that was turning into sadness and resignation. She glanced over at a spot on the wall adjacent to terrace opening, and when he followed her gaze, he was surprised to see the outline of a doorway, one he was certain had not been present before. He turned back to his beloved student.

"Ryan," he began uncertainly.

She reached up, placing her hand upon his lips to silence him. She looked down at Drake, who gazed up at her, his own expression far too enigmatic for one so young. She closed her eyes, holding her son tightly for a moment, then handed him to Kusunoki. The Asian man took the boy, but shook his head.

"Ryan, you cannot do this."

Ryan stared at the outline of the doorway. "She has awakened," Ryan said simply. She knelt down to pick up a bloodied sword, staring at the wicked blade. "And these will not harm her." She turned back to him. "If Madelyn takes the battlefield, all will be lost."

Kusunoki was insistent. "Ryan, you cannot go."

Ryan looked down, a deep sadness on her features. "No," she said, "I cannot stay." She turned back to him, her eyes burning. "Take care of my son." She pushed him toward the edge, her voice turning to steel. "You must go now. That is a command."

Ryan turned her back on him and began walking toward the outline of the doorway. As she neared, the stone doors whispered open. She stepped into the elevator and did not look back as the doors whispered closed behind her.

Kusunoki slid to the ground, holding the rope in one hand and Drake in the other. Victor, Aeron, and Susan were waiting in the shadows for them. Victor was impatient.

"Where is Ryan?"

Susan stared at Kusunoki. The minute she had seen that he held the boy, she knew something was wrong. Victor, too, quickly assessed Kusunoki's expression.

"No!" he cried, lunging for the rope.

Kusunoki handed the boy to Susan while making a grab for Victor.

"It was her wish, my lord," he said through gritted teeth, holding Victor by the shoulders, "and her command."

Victor took a step back. He, too, had felt the revival of Madelyn's presence, but he had hoped they could escape.

"Then all of this has been for nothing."

Kusunoki shook his head. "It is not over yet. Ryan must have some sort of plan."

Victor squared his shoulders, and Susan was reminded of how physically similar Ryan and her father moved at times. He glanced at Susan and Drake, then at Aeron. He then addressed Kusunoki.

"You and Aeron guard Dr. Ryerson and my grandson."

"And you?" Kusunoki asked.

Victor whirled on his heel and began stalking toward the open courtyard. "I am going to end the battle down here."

Ryan gazed at the intricate carving on the inside walls of the elevator. The markings again seemed oddly familiar, as if their meaning was elusively near. She did not have time to ponder this odd familiarity further because in a very short time the doors whispered open once more. She stepped out of the lift, unsurprised to find herself once again in Madelyn's chambers.

She gazed with some amusement at the gaping hole she had created earlier. It was a perfect outline of the geometric pattern she had endlessly traced during her confinement. The wind gusted through the opening, creating a low, mournful whistling.

Ryan took the stairs two at a time, pausing before the intricate carving on the doors to the inner chambers. She lightly pressed her hand to the surface, and with a quiet click, the door was released. She pushed the door inward and stepped into the inner chambers.

The room was empty. Immaculate and orderly as it had been the last time she had been in here. As the door whispered closed behind her, the chamber settled into a tomb-like silence. Out of curiosity, she placed her hand on the carvings on the inside of the door, and was not surprised when it did not respond. She would not get out as easily as she had gotten in.

Ryan turned back to the room, gazing up at the doors at its center. She remembered her last foray into the forbidden room and quelled the trepidation she felt. With a few strides, she was at the base of the stairs, and again took them two at a time. She paused at the top, staring at the engraved markings which now seemed to mock her. When she did not lift her hand, the door clicked quietly on its own and silently swung inward. Ryan took a deep breath, as always more from habit than need, and stepped into the room.

It took a moment for her eyes to adjust to the dimmer light. The room was warmer, far more humid than the outer chambers. Although none of the hideous apparitions of before were evident, the walls seemed to shimmer, shifting ever-so-slightly as if something was indeed trying to get out.

"That will not help you here."

There was a low, dangerous tone to the voice, yet a hint of pleasure as well.

Ryan glanced down at the sword in her hand, unaware she was still carrying it. "I know," she said simply, tossing the sword to the side. It clattered off into the shadows, then sounded as if it were dragged away by some unseen entity.

Ryan turned, taking a quick step back when she came face-to-face with Madelyn. She still could not accurately detect the woman's presence.

"So did you have some sort of plan in coming up here?" Madelyn asked mockingly. "Or were you simply going to sacrifice yourself in hopes I would let your precious father and son go?"

Ryan struggled to keep her tone even. "I did not really have much of a plan," she confessed.

Madelyn's eyes gleamed as she took a step closer. Her proximity would have taken all of Ryan's attention, but there was some skittering and scratching off in the shadows again, momentarily distracting her. Her attention was returned to Madelyn, however, when the women placed her hands about Ryan's waist, creating a teasing but very deadly intimacy.

"Let me guess," Madelyn said, mildly sarcastic, pulling her close "you were going to try and divert me, perhaps trapping me here long enough to create a permanent prison."

On this last word, Madelyn jerked her forward, not gently, so that they were fully pressed against one another. She now whispered in Ryan's ear.

"What is to stop me from killing you on the spot?" Madelyn asked, "then going down to finish off all that you love?"

Ryan gritted her teeth but said nothing as the dark-haired woman continued.

"Or perhaps paralyzing you, leaving you here to suffer while I destroy your father, son, your 'mother,' your lovers—all that you care about?"

Madelyn's tone was still entirely conversational. "Then I could return and kill you very slowly."

Ryan settled her hands on Madelyn's hips, surprising the dark-haired woman. She glanced down at the casually intimate pose Ryan had settled into. She gazed at the girl with suspicion, but was amused nonetheless.

"I have another suggestion," Ryan said thoughtfully. She examined Madelyn's perfect form, her eyes lingering so that Madelyn was further amused. "I can give you something you probably have not had in a very long time."

Ryan leaned closer to Madelyn, fully pressing against her. "And there is someplace I want to show you," she whispered in her ear.

Madelyn was guarded, but intrigued, and she hesitated just long enough for Ryan to attempt the impossible. Ryan's razor-sharp teeth whispered across Madelyn's throat, and although she was not certain her teeth would even break the skin, she was going to try.

Madelyn gasped and clenched Ryan so tightly there was an audible cracking of Ryan's preternaturally strong bones as they strained under the pressure. Ryan felt the wetness against her lips and immediately fastened on the wound she had opened. Madelyn's blood rushed into her mouth, burned its way down her throat through the bifurcation to her aorta. Her heart stopped instantly.

Ryan desperately tried to concentrate. The physical effect of the blood was devastating, destroying everything in its pathway. She felt capillaries burst, arterial walls strain against the liquid fire, venous pathways melt under the onslaught. It was as if the blood were part acid, part fire, leaving a swath of destruction as it rushed through her body.

Madelyn's first inclination was to rip the girl from her, tossing her aside like a rag doll. But the warmth that spread outward from the wound stayed the impulse. It was a pleasant flush, one that began to throb and pulsate as it spread to her extremities. She was astonished at the waves of pleasure that began to wash through her system. She glanced down at the girl, noting the great strain on her system.

"And are you trying to commit suicide, little one?" Madelyn asked.

Ryan continued to concentrate, ignoring the physical agony she was in. She leaned back only far enough to make eye contact with Madelyn, then leaned forward once more, slicing into the other side of Madelyn's neck. Madelyn again gasped with pleasure, amazed that the girl was even still alive.

Ryan's system again stumbled under the onslaught, the renewed flow of blood racing down already raw pathways. Her heart lurched at the attack, attempting to rip itself from her chest to escape the pain. Ryan pushed the agony from her mind, focusing with all of her mental ability. There was a pounding in her head, and a rushing flood that drowned out all light, all sound…

And then there was silence.

Ryan leaned back from the women who held her, slowly glancing around. The sky and mountains were blood red, and an infinite black lake lapped at the dark sand at her feet. Reddish light filtered through dark wisps of clouds. Other than the gentle flowing of the water, there was no sound, no breeze, no movement, all was utterly still.

Madelyn gazed at the blood-red world around her in amazement. She started to take a step back from Ryan, but Ryan easily held her, her strength as great, if not greater than the dark-haired woman's in this arena. She was no longer in any pain.

Madelyn continued to examine the scene in wonder and disbelief, but as time passed in infinite increments, Ryan sensed something else in the woman's demeanor. She sensed astonished recognition. Madelyn finally returned her attention to the girl in front of her.

"You know this place?" she asked, giving voice to her incredulity.

Ryan gazed at her steadily. "I rule this place," she said without a hint of boasting.

Madelyn stared down at her, myriad emotions on her face. Ryan sensed a reassessment, a realization, a touch of regret, and ultimately, a steely resignation.

"That is most unfortunate," Madelyn said.

Ryan felt a blinding pain in her midsection and she was instantly ripped from the blood-red world back into the real one, back into the inner sanctuary. Her hands were on Madelyn's shoulders and Madelyn's hands were about her waist, but it was not Madelyn's hands that now impaled Ryan. Ryan glanced down at the scaly, claw-like appendages that were thrust through her torso, appendages that were somehow a part of Madelyn. She felt the poison from the arachnid limb leach into her system, causing immense pain and unrecoverable tissue damage. Blood seeped from the corner of her mouth. Ryan slowly raised her eyes to look at Madelyn once more, and Madelyn was impressed that there was no fear, no revulsion, nor any real surprise in her steady gaze.

"I knew you were not my Kind," Ryan said.

Madelyn was intrigued despite herself. "And how is that?"

Ryan continued to gaze at her steadily. "Because I am not attracted to you."

Madelyn glanced down at the creature she held mortally impaled, amused. Even now, the girl entertained her.

"Liar," Madelyn said knowingly.

Although fatally wounded, Ryan merely smiled, the mischievous grin of a child caught in an untruth. And in that moment, Madelyn realized how completely dangerous the girl was. She leaned close.

"It is a pity," Madelyn whispered to her, "I think one day you could have been my consort."

Ryan again smiled, the light beginning to dim in her eyes. She struggled to swallow the blood in her throat. She gathered her strength, maintaining a steady gaze.

"No," Ryan said simply, "you would have been mine."

And with that stunning statement, Madelyn knew she could not let Ryan live. Not because the girl's words were insulting.

But because they were true.

Ryan groaned as Madelyn thrust the sharp claws clean through her body. Ryan felt the poison race through her system, and would have doubled up in pain were she not so impaled. Madelyn watched her for a moment, ensuring sufficient damage for death, then violently retracted the appendages.

Slowly, Madelyn stepped back. And slowly, the light fading from her mind, Ryan began to fall.

A great wind swept through the battle below. Fighting slowed, then stopped completely as men and women shifted uneasily in confusion. The bluish-skinned warriors sensed something they did not understand and felt the stirring of fear. That fear only grew when the great dark-haired, dark-eyed warrior, standing alone, untouched, cried out in agony from some unseen blow, then collapsed like a marionette whose strings had been cut.

Abigail rushed to Victor's side, disbelief and anguish filling every aspect of her being. She went to her knees, pressing her hand to Victor's chest. The disaster she sensed could not possibly be true, but she felt the girl's presence slipping away.

Kusunoki felt the fading as a physical blow, falling to his knees and holding his head in his hands. A grief the world could not contain overcame him and he pressed his forehead into the dirt in front of him.

Aeron stared upward, anger and denial filling him as tears of rage gathered in his blue eyes. Ala closed her eyes, turning away from a feeling that was present in every direction. Saladin pressed his fingers to his forehead in prayer and Marilyn openly wept.

Susan clutched Drake tightly, her young senses stunned by the shockwave that was traveling through the web of their Kind. Great strands were torn away, sections collapsed entirely, what remained violently vibrated. Susan looked down at the boy she held in her arms, fearful for the effect it would have on one who was more connected to Ryan than any other.

Drake, oddly enough, had an enigmatic expression on his face as he looked to the sky.

Ryan's body hit the stone ground hard, but she did not feel any more pain. Time seemed to slow as she stared upward at the vaulted ceiling. She could see her son's warm blue eyes, his beautiful little smile, could hear his irrepressible laughter.

Madelyn gazed down at the girl, suppressing any emotion she might feel. Blood poured from the wound in Ryan's torso, and Madelyn knew the poison would act far faster than Ryan's immune system could adapt. Still, as mortally wounded as she was, the girl gazed upward, a strangely peaceful look on her face. Madelyn again struggled with conflicting emotions, and spoke harshly as a result.

"You have failed," Madelyn said, a note of triumph in her voice, "in every way."

Ryan continued to stare up at the ceiling, unaffected by Madelyn's words. A pleasant fatigue settled over her. She could feel the darkness coming, and she closed her eyes, welcoming the warm blackness. She could almost let go, but something at the edge of her consciousness was rising to the surface.

Ryan reopened her eyes, but they were unfocused. Something was surfacing, something that had haunted her for a very long time. She closed her eyes again, relaxing. It would come to her if she did not search for it. Slowly, the presence came to her, something ancient, terrifying, something so powerfully malevolent it staggered her mind. Something that had threatened her endlessly, its voice echoing across space and time.

"I—" came the sibilant, hissing voice.

"–AM COMING–" the alien, prehistoric presence promised.

"–FOR YOU."

And Ryan at last understood. Her fear had caused her to misjudge intent. It was not a threat, it was a promise. The creature was indeed coming for her, not to destroy her.

But to save her.

Madelyn's eyes narrowed as she sensed some subtle shift she could not quite identify. She gazed down at Ryan. A deafening noise rumbled through the compound, and it took Madelyn a moment to realize it was not a noise at all but rather a mental shockwave. She glanced about her, trying to assess the presence. It seemed to have some great connection to the girl, and she glanced over at the dying girl, guessing at the identity.

"Your father is a formidable opponent, but he cannot save you now."

Ryan lay on her side, clearing the blood from her mouth so she could speak. Madelyn was impressed the fatally wounded girl could speak at all.

"If you think my father is formidable," Ryan paused, her words amazingly casual considering her mortal injuries.

"You should meet the rest of my family."

Blinding light filled the inner sanctuary as the rock wall split floor-to-ceiling. The wall did not break, but rather appeared to rip in two, as if matter itself were being torn apart. A great force shook the mountain as the energy the event produced shifted the very foundation. The blue light did not fade but rather gained intensity as it poured through the strange opening. Ryan shifted so she could see the extraordinary phenomenon, and was overcome by a reflexive, primitive fear.

She was not, however, as frightened as Madelyn, who had the disadvantage of understanding exactly what was happening.

"Oh dear god, no," Madelyn said, "this can't be."

Terrifying men began pouring through the opening, soldiers, all heavily armed and bearing a unique and intricate insignia. They had the similar, bluish tinged skin of Madelyn's men, but a deeper blue. Their expressions were grim, as if some great wrong had been committed that must now be punished. Madelyn recognized the fearsome insignia immediately, as well as its significance. She went to her knees.

Ryan felt the familiar sensation, but when the creature came through the opening, she had no way of preparing for the crushing weight of its power. Ryan could barely lift her head, so great was the force of the presence. The creature appeared to be a woman, dark-haired and dark-eyed, intensely beautiful but with a reptilian coldness about her that dropped the temperature in the room. She wore an elaborate headdress and robes both foreign and familiar to Ryan. The woman was extremely tall, but it was not her physical presence that was the most frightening. Ryan shivered uncontrollably, uncertain if it was because of the cold or her terror. The woman flowed into the room, surrounded by her escort, and she focused her attention with laser-like precision on Madelyn. Madelyn stood, resignation on her face.

"Your Majesty, I could not have known…"

The woman approached Madelyn, her fury evident. When she spoke, it was in an ancient voice, one that Ryan knew well. Although the language should have been unintelligible, Ryan understood her words clearly.

"There was a reason I put this world off limits, Madelyn."

Madelyn swallowed as the woman put her hand about her throat and leaned close.

"It is where I left my son," she said with the faintest hint of sibilance on the final word.

The woman paused, and for the first time, glanced over at the girl on the floor. She turned back to Madelyn, then said with significance.

"And my grandchild."

Ryan closed her eyes just in time to avoid the spray of blood that engulfed the entire room. She could not see what happened, nor did she want to. She kept her eyes tightly closed, still shivering uncontrollably. The shivering was taking what remaining strength she had, and she could feel herself again begin to slip into blackness. She was lifted, very gently, upward.

"Open your eyes, little one."

The words were whispered, surprisingly tender, from the terrifying creature holding her. She looked up into the beautiful woman's face who was looking down at her, assessing her injuries. It was evident she was not pleased with what she saw, but her anger was not directed at Ryan. Ryan was genuinely frightened of the creature, but this seemed only to amuse the woman who forcibly soothed her. Ryan felt the pressure like a powerful sedative and the tension drained from her body.

The woman stood upright without effort, cradling Ryan like a child. She shot a scathing glance to her chief soldier.

"Fix this," she paused, her disgust obvious, "this mess."

And with that, she strode through the rip in the space-time continuum, carrying her grandchild with her.

CHAPTER 33

RYAN WAS IN A TRANCE, half asleep, half dead. The rhythmic rocking motion of being carried added to her trance-like state, and she was only vaguely aware of her surroundings.

It was probably a good thing because what little she could see out of her peripheral vision was hideous. Scaly, clawed, tentacled creatures writhed in the shadows. Great fanged monsters snaked outward, then snapped back into their dark alcoves. The ground beneath her slithered in constant motion. When she turned to focus on something specific, however, reality shifted and all she could see were sterile walls that shimmered, then blurred.

Ryan closed her eyes for a moment, or what could have been many moments, or perhaps even a year. Their motion finally stopped, and Ryan felt the woman sit down, still cradling her. She opened her eyes.

They were in the blood-red world, although in this manifestation, it was considerably smaller. They sat upon a great throne that seemed to wrap itself about the two of them, enveloping them in a cocoon-like embrace. Ryan gazed about her in wonder. The room appeared to be alive, as if they were inside some great creature. Portions of it seemed to writhe and pulsate, more solid parts were covered with the intricate hieroglyphics.

"What is this place?" Ryan asked.

"You don't know?"

Ryan shook her head. "I thought I did, but apparently not."

"And where did you think it was?"

Ryan stared out into the darkness. "I thought it was the edge of death."

The woman laughed. "Well, for most it is." She glanced about the room. "This is my inner sanctuary."

Ryan felt a shiver of fear as the woman tightened her grip. She was stunningly beautiful, but her mannerisms were odd, almost animal-like. She would occasionally sniff the air, like some great beast picking up on signs and cues to which Ryan was oblivious. She even leaned down to sniff Ryan, like a lioness verifying its offspring. She moved with a reptilian grace, as if she had far more bones in her limbs than normal. She stroked Ryan's hair, but there was a predatory, possessive aspect to the gesture. Ryan knew whatever alien creature she was facing was not even close to being human, and just hoped it was not a species that ate their young.

The woman read her mind. "Actually, we do quite regularly. But I did not come across light years to eat you, my dear."

"Then why did you come?" Ryan asked carefully.

The woman was pleased by her boldness. "Let me show you," she said simply.

She leaned down, placing her lips on Ryan's throat. Ryan's skin split like tissue paper beneath her teeth, and Ryan shifted in pain. In her weakened condition, if the woman took even more than a single draw of her blood, Ryan was certain she would die. She was also certain she did not care, because she had never felt anything so extraordinary as the instant union with this creature.

The woman took only a single drink, leaning back with a look of intense pleasure. "Let us hope that at least one of us possesses some sort of discipline, otherwise my journey will have been in vain."

Ryan shifted once more. She was not certain she had any discipline at the moment. Fortunately, the creature holding her did.

"Here," the woman said, touching her fingers to Ryan's lips. Ryan grabbed her wrist, stopping the motion.

"That will kill me," Ryan said.

Ryan knew the woman was so immeasurably strong the Ryan was not restraining her in any way, but the woman did not force her.

"It might," she said, amused, "but I don't think so."

Ryan released the wrist, and the woman touched her finger to Ryan's sharp teeth. A tiny drop of blood appeared on the fingertip and the woman touched it to Ryan's lips.

Ryan's vision exploded, and had her consciousness not continued unabated, she would have surmised her head had exploded as well. Pictures, images, experiences all began to flood her senses. Instantly she saw and understood an extraordinary history.

The woman's name was Ravlen and Ryan's mind staggered to comprehend how old she was. The time scale by which she existed was foreign to Ryan, so it was impossible to know her exact age, but Ryan understood Ravlen was at least a hundred thousand of her years. As if that were not terrifying enough, Ryan grasped that this woman was far more than just the leader of her species. This creature was the undisputed ruler of an empire that stretched across the cosmos. Ravlen's power and control did not span mere planets, but entire galaxies.

Ravlen's history began to unfold before Ryan, rushing by with blinding speed. Ryan began to perceive Ravlen commanded an unstoppable predatory species, one that moved across worlds, subjugating, assimilating, or destroying everything in its path. It was a violent and powerful race, one without equal and possessing very little conscience, at least in terms of human understanding. It consumed, it absorbed, it obliterated.

The species was capable of extraordinary methods of reproduction, some sexual, some asexual, some so strangely foreign Ryan had no concept of. It appeared Ravlen's species was capable of exchanging genetic material with almost any other species, the results of which ranged from the monstrous to the sublime. The subordinate species had no say in the matter, experimented upon if Ravlen's species so chose. The results of that union might determine whether a world would survive, be enslaved, or be annihilated.

Ryan struggled to make sense of the images, shifting

uncomfortably in the woman's embrace. "And so you came to earth."

The woman smiled and Ryan realized she had Victor's perfect smile. Her smile. Her son's smile.

"Yes," Ravlen said with pleasure. "Oh, make no mistake. We had no hopes for such a small, backward planet. We thought to strip-mine it for raw materials."

"But something changed."

Ravlen again smiled. "I became quite intrigued by these fragile, bipedal, carbon-based life forms that were superficially similar to our own species. Specifically, I became intrigued by your grandfather."

The sibilance of the "s" in that semi-alliterative sentence distracted Ryan, but only for a moment. Ravlen's Memories flashed through Ryan's mind like a blinding light. Two images, separate until this moment, linked and became one. She saw the young Roman boy whose family was slaughtered by barbarians. She saw him meet Ravlen for the first time as a youth, then again as a man. She saw his actions, brave and strong, as he fought for decades to keep Briton from the Saxons. She saw him become a legend, and then a king. And Ryan saw that although he achieved almost everything in his life, the one thing he desired most eluded him.

"Ambrosius Aurelianus," Ravlen said, reliving the memories herself. "He was magnificent."

Ryan sorted through the Memories, both those of Ravlen and those of her grandfather. She felt a profound sadness and was uncertain if the emotion belonged to her or the man in her mind. "He loved you very much," she said quietly. She looked up at Ravlen, the creature she was just beginning to grasp was her grandmother. "Why didn't you Change him?"

Ravlen gazed down at the girl she held in her arms. Her tone was casual, noncommittal. "Several reasons. Our initial scouting parties 'explored' the possibility of reproduction with the human species. The results were disastrous."

Ryan had a flash of the hideous results, and blanked the memory from her mind as Ravlen continued.

"Assimilation was also explored. Absorption, or what you refer to as 'the Change,' was just as catastrophic. No one initially survived the transition."

Ryan again had a vision of the failed experiments, the pain and suffering of the chosen humans vividly clear. The attempts, both at reproduction and assimilation, had been horrific.

Ravlen's gruesome recount was still entirely conversational. "And so we thought to mine the planet, using the human species as slave labor."

"But then you met my grandfather," Ryan said slowly.

"Hmm, yes," Ravlen replied, enjoying the memory. "As I said he was magnificent. I think part of the attraction was the dominance of the human male, a very unusual occurrence. In the vast majority of species we encounter, the entity that bears young prevails."

This surprised Ryan only for a moment because she had the flash of insight from Ravlen's immense bank of knowledge. There seemed to be a pivotal moment in the development of any species in which the offspring-bearing entity acquired the ability to consciously control fertilization. Although the full effects might take decades or even centuries to unfold, at some point it became a zero sum game for the non-bearer. Without the option of forced reproduction, an organism's options for passing on genetic material became limited.

"In your species," Ryan said, searching the Memories, "the female is rare, but far stronger. And extremely dominant."

"Yes," Ravlen said, "although the human definition of female is not entirely applicable."

"The females bear young?" Ryan asked, still trying to understand.

"Yes," Ravlen said, "the females alone bear young. But we are capable of multiple methods of passing genetic material, not all requiring a male. And we give birth in multiple ways, not always bearing live young. So 'female' is not entirely an apt description."

Ravlen was thoughtful. "As I mentioned, we also occasionally eat our offspring, and generally kill our mates once we are finished with them."

Ryan shifted uncomfortably. What Ravlen was describing

reminded her of the black widow spider, or other, equally unsavory creatures on her planet.

Ravlen laughed at the mental characterization. "I already told you, little one. I am not going to eat you. And tell me this, did you not attempt to kill your mate?"

Ryan thought of Aeron and blushed. Although he had certainly given her good reason, she had in fact attempted to kill him. Not to mention her father. In light of the predatory species that had spawned them, Ryan suddenly understood a great many of the impulses of their Kind. In the nature versus nurture debate, nature was winning hands down. Which was a little disturbing since the "nature" that had produced them consisted of an extraterrestrial killing machine.

Ryan sorted through Ravlen's Memories. "But you did not kill my grandfather after you mated with him."

"No, I left so I would not." Ravlen's gaze grew distant. "I did not at first realize the mating would produce an offspring. First attempts had been so catastrophic it never occurred to me ours would be successful. And my gestation period was so long that your grandfather was dead from natural causes by the time my son was born."

"Victor," Ryan said slowly, "my father."

Ravlen smiled with pleasure. "Yes, my son. A perfect little creature, not quite human, but flawless. Weak and vulnerable, obviously, relative to my species, but still so compelling."

"So why did you leave him on earth? Why didn't you take him with you?"

Ravlen gazed at Ryan intently, and Ryan had a sudden vision of Ravlen's lineage stretching back eons through time. Thousands, if not hundreds of thousands of offspring, most pure within her own species, but with some hybrids scattered throughout worlds. Still, even in light of this, Ryan saw Ravlen's love of Victor. Ravlen sighed, sensing the girl's great perception.

"Victor would have been little more than a slave amongst my people. I did not take him for the same reason I did not take Ambrosius. On your world, they are Kings. Within mine, they would have been little more than chattel, their lowly stature exacerbated by the fact they were male. "

Ryan gazed at her astutely, sensing her pride in Victor. "You don't believe that anymore."

Ravlen again smiled at the girl's perception. "No. I think my son would have surprised many of my kind with his gifts, gifts that are rare even among my species. But I do not regret leaving him."

Something occurred to Ryan. "If the Change was so unsuccessful, then how are there any Others?"

Ravlen's gaze again grew distant. "When I contemplated Victor's impending birth, I decided to return him to your world. But I could not bear to leave him alone. I was determined he would have companions similar to himself."

Ryan did not understand. "But you said attempts at Change were unsuccessful, and breeding even less so. How did you achieve that?"

Ravlen smiled her predatory smile. "We destroyed nearly a hundred million humans to find the handful that would survive the mutation."

Ryan was shocked at the number, and searched her memory of human history to find such an event. It could not have possibly gone unnoticed, although it more than likely would have been misinterpreted.

"The Justinian plague," Ryan said slowly, "during the sixth century."

"Hmm, yes. That sounds about right." Ravlen said, unfazed by the horror she had unleashed. Ryan again had a terrible insight into her own Kind as Ravlen continued casually. "No additional attempts at breeding were successful, but several assimilations did take hold. Only two remain of that first generation."

"Aeron," Ryan said thoughtfully, "and Abigail."

"Yes," Ravlen said, her eyes gleaming, "one of my personal favorites. The others of that first generation were destroyed in internecine warfare, although many of their offspring live on."

Ryan was still deep in thought. "Kusunoki, Ala, and Marilyn are all second generation, Changed by One from that original Change."

Ravlen nodded. "Yes, all those you refer to as 'Old Ones' were within a few generations of that initial Change."

Ryan had a stunning, sudden insight into the interaction of her Kind. She understood the complicated politics, the hierarchy, the convoluted relationships, the predatory nature inherent in all of them. She understood her weakness toward Abigail, knowing now that no matter how powerful she herself became, the matriarch would always have a hold on her. She understood the magnetism between her and Aeron, realizing that together or miles apart, he alone would be her mate. She understood why only she and Victor were capable of sexual reproduction, the only direct descendents of Ravlen's species. And she at last understood why her power grew so exponentially relative to the Others.

Ravlen followed her thoughts, nodding. "Yes, Victor was first born. You are second born. And your son is third. But you are the only female in the direct line."

Ryan fell into a deep, contemplative silence. Unconsciously, she curled closer to the creature that held her, resting her head against Ravlen. The innocent gesture greatly pleased the dark-haired woman, who wrapped her arms about the girl. And as Ryan settled into the warmth of the embrace, Ravlen opened her mind to Ryan, offering her a vision as stunning as it was impossible.

Ryan again saw Ravlen's endless lineage, the hundreds of thousands of offspring spread across worlds and stretching backwards in time over eons. She saw their lives, deaths, failures, successes. She saw rulers, conquerors, the extraordinarily beautiful, the unbelievably cruel, the amazingly gifted. She saw an immense gathering of descendents, and in one, startling instant, saw the terrifying and unique place she occupied in that hierarchy, a position obtained only so recently in light of her youth and the encompassing span of time.

In case there was any misunderstanding on Ryan's part, Ravlen spoke to her, but did so without speaking. The phrase came in a rasping, alien language that Ryan somehow not only understood, but fully comprehended meaning, context, and significance.

"You are my beloved," Ravlen said simply, "the most precious of all my progeny."

Ryan gazed up at her, having no idea why she, the most insignificant of creatures in such a great web would occupy any such position of honor. And yet, gazing up at her grandmother, knew the stunning declaration was true.

Ravlen stroked her hair, again sniffing her with animal-like mannerisms. When she spoke, there was the faintest hint of sibilance in the "s."

"I wish you to stay with me."

At that moment, Ryan desired nothing else. She could remain in this creature's presence forever and she would be complete. But one thing held her, one thing she could not let go.

Ravlen assessed her thoughts. "You wish to return to your son."

Ryan's throat felt thick with emotion. "No," she said honestly, "I want nothing more than to stay here with you for all eternity."

This pleased Ravlen, but she knew better. "But…"

"But I cannot leave my son," Ryan paused, swallowing hard, "and he deserves to be raised with his own Kind."

Ravlen nodded. "I anticipated this." She shifted Ryan slightly, still holding her tightly. "I will allow you to return to raise your son. But when he is grown and successfully Changed, you will return to me."

Ryan gazed up at her grandmother. "I will. I promise."

Ravlen sat back. "Excellent. I will return you to your son. But for now you will rest with me a little while longer."

Ryan closed her eyes, feeling wonderfully drowsy. She wanted to memorize every aspect of the experience, wanted the moment to last forever, but she felt herself drifting off to sleep. She turned her head, opening her eyes as a though occurred to her.

"I'm not going to grow tentacles, am I?"

Ravlen quietly laughed. "I don't think so, my dear. I can't be certain, but it is unlikely."

Ryan again settled down, feeling lassitude creep over her. She was drifting off to sleep when another thought roused her.

"Ambrosius Aurelianus?" Ryan said, finally placing the name and its significance.

Ravlen followed her train of thought. "Yes. Your grandfather was a great man and a great warrior. He inspired legends on your world that live on even in the present. And although history gave him a different name, he will never be forgotten."

Ryan smiled to herself. She thought back to the very first book Victor had given her and wondered if he had any idea what a prescient gift that had been. And as she lay in the blood-red sanctuary in the arms of the alien creature who was her grandmother, this thought very pleasantly occupied her as she drifted off to sleep.

EPILOGUE I

VICTOR OPENED HIS EYES. Abigail, Kusunoki, as well as many others were leaning over him. The handsome Asian extended his hand, and Victor took it, pulling himself upright. He glanced about him in confusion.

"What has happened?"

It seemed everyone shared his confusion.

"We are not quite certain," Abigail said. She, too, glanced around. "Ryan's presence was fading." She stopped, trying to put into words what had occurred. "Then there was another presence." She stopped again. "An immense presence."

Victor glanced at the beautiful matriarch, then at those around him. "Madelyn?"

Kusunoki shook his head. "No," he, too, paused, at a loss. "This One dwarfed Madelyn."

Victor felt a cold chill as Abigail continued. "The men all stopped fighting and fell to their knees. They were obviously terrified. Other men appeared, similar in appearance, but not quite the same." Abigail contemplated the strange scene that had unfolded. "The new soldiers seemed to outrank the ones that were here, and for lack of a better description, they collected Madelyn's men and took them away."

"Took them away where?" Victor asked.

Abigail just shook her head. "I don't know. But they are gone, and they have left no trace."

Victor glanced around him. There were no fallen bodies, no weapons, no blood, not even a torn remnant of clothing that would indicate a scuffle had occurred, let alone the all-out battle that had taken place. He wondered how long he had been unconscious.

"How long did this take?"

Abigail looked to Kusunoki for confirmation, then to Aeron. Aeron nodded, and spoke for her.

"Minutes," he said in disbelief, "a matter of minutes."

Saladin and his chief Janissary also nodded. "They spoke not a word. I have never seen anything like it."

Ala and Kokumuo stood to Victor's right. "They collected all the weapons," Kokumuo said, "and emptied the armory. They have left nothing behind."

"But where did they go?" Victor asked in frustration, "and what happened to Ryan?"

Marilyn and Susan stood to his left. Marilyn glanced down at the child Susan held in her arms. The boy seemed remarkably unperturbed, his blue eyes calm as he solemnly sucked his thumb.

"At first, it felt as if Ryan were dying," Marilyn began slowly. She turned to Abigail, then to Victor. "But it did not feel as if she passed."

Abigail was also deeply thoughtful, agreeing. "It felt," she paused, struggling for words, "it felt as if just she went away."

Victor's frustration was at a maximum. He glanced around at his companions, searching for answers they did not have.

"Drake!"

Victor turned to the only one who had not spoken. Susan was now running down the toddler who had taken it upon himself to struggle free. It was incongruent to watch the boy scamper across the courtyard in such a solemn moment, especially since he was laughing joyfully. Victor was perplexed by the boy's unexpected behavior.

"Oh my god," Abigail said, pressing her hand to her chest.

A figure stepped from the shadows of the citadel, one utterly familiar and yet now completely foreign to them. The sun glinted off hair that was pure white and put a gleam in eyes that were now deep violet. Ryan smiled, her thoughtful expression containing both wonder and delight, the look of a child who has just been told a most miraculous secret. She watched her son run toward her, and as he neared, she bent low to grab his tiny, hurtling form. She lifted him high, tossing him into the air, grabbing him tightly as he came back to earth. He embraced her, his small frame shaking with the intensity of his joy.

Ryan smiled at her son, then turned to the Others. She was not surprised so little time had passed, although she felt she had been gone for weeks. She sensed their astonishment as they one-by-one reached out to touch her. She approached her father, gazing at him with deep affection. It was the first time she had been in his presence, not under duress, since he had awakened.

Victor looked down at his child, knowing something of great import had occurred. Something about Ryan had dramatically changed. She now possessed a presence similar to Madelyn's, not that it was malevolent or cold, but that its extent was difficult to grasp.

Abigail, too, sensed the great shift in the girl and inwardly smiled. Ryan turned to her and the two locked gazes. Ryan was not certain how much Abigail knew, how much she merely suspected, or how much was pure intuition. But Ryan now understood Abigail's hold upon her, and knew, regardless of her power, that it would continue unabated. She could tell by Abigail's expression that the matriarch knew this as well, and was greatly pleased by it.

"Are you alright?" Kusunoki asked, stepping forward. He hesitantly touched her sleeve as if to convince himself she was real.

"I am," Ryan said thoughtfully, "I am fine."

Kusunoki sensed a myriad of emotions in Ryan. Joy at seeing her son and her companions, relief that they were all safe, shock at what she had been through, which Kusunoki sensed was momentous. He also sensed the slightest trace of melancholy beneath these other emotions, as if there was something she was greatly missing.

"All in good time," Ryan said, sensing her master's questions. "It will take awhile to explain."

She began making her way through the Others, warmly

embracing Ala, bowing to Saladin with great respect, brushing a kiss on Marilyn's cheek. She stopped in front of Susan.

"Thank you for caring for my son," Ryan said.

Susan blushed under the warmth of Ryan's gaze, and Ryan leaned forward, brushing a kiss across her cheek exactly as she had done with Marilyn. Marilyn smiled at her flustered offspring, and in an uncharacteristically protective gesture, moved to Susan's side and placed her hand upon her shoulder. Susan was startled at how positively welcome the hand was.

Ryan again moved through the crowd, now stopping in front of Aeron. There was a slight tension about him, as if he was not sure how she would respond to him.

"You know," Ryan said conversationally, "I have recently learned a few important lessons."

"Really," Aeron said warily.

"Do you know the phrase 'big fish in a little pond'?" Ryan asked.

Aeron nodded, still cautious.

"I have learned," Ryan continued, "that there is always a bigger fish." She was silent for a moment. "And always a much bigger pond."

Aeron wasn't certain exactly what she was getting at, but he understood enough. Ryan handed him the blue-eyed toddler, and the boy went willingly to his father. Aeron held his son tightly for a moment, his emotion overwhelming him. When he regained control, his tone was casual.

"So tell me," Aeron asked, "will he also try to kill me when he grows up?"

"Hmm," Ryan said, "I am quite certain he will try to kill us both. It seems to be in our nature." This greatly amused Ryan as if it were a private joke. She paused as another thought occurred to her.

"What?" Aeron asked.

"Be thankful we did not have a girl," Ryan said, muffling her laughter.

Aeron did not understand her humor, but he was quite content just to hold his son. Ryan held Drake's hand for a moment, then released it to continue her walk. Victor fell in beside her. She paused looking up at the citadel.

"We should probably leave this place."

Victor looked to her for explanation and Ryan continued. "I don't think it will be here much longer. In fact, I am quite certain it will be gone the minute we leave."

Victor did not question her. He merely nodded, and gestured to the general assembly to begin departure. He again fell in beside his daughter. They began walking toward the courtyard entrance, enveloped in a comfortable silence. When Ryan at last broke the silence, her words were startling.

"You know," she said casually, "I met your mother."

Victor stopped in his tracks, stunned. Ryan did not stop, but merely glanced back, a darkly humorous look on her face.

"She wants to know why you haven't called," she said over her shoulder.

Victor's limbs were lead. He could not move. Abigail began to brush by him, but stopped, noting his ashen expression.

"Is something the matter?" Abigail asked.

Victor just shook his head mutely as Ryan's mischievous laughter drifted back to them.

EPILOGUE II

THERE SEEMED TO BE A GREAT PRESSURE in the Imperial Palace. Xvander watched the Empress with unease. Under normal circumstances, he would not dare approach her when she was in such a mood. But the stakes were too high for him to remain silent.

"I cannot believe you let the girl go," he said at last.

Ravlen's words were deliberately casual, disguising any underlying emotion. "It was difficult for me to release her for many reasons, and the one to which you refer was not chief among them."

Although Her Majesty seemed relaxed, Xvander could sense the great tension in her. A combination of many things, predominantly grief. Again, under normal circumstances, he would have taken his leave immediately, bowing respectfully upon exit. But these were not normal circumstances. He tried to control his tongue, but finally blurted out his concern.

"The girl controls time."

Ravlen appeared unfazed by the outburst. "Yes," she said mildly, "I noticed."

Now that Xvander had started, he could not stop. He paced about the chamber. "Granted, she does so indiscriminately, with no knowledge, understanding, or control of what she is doing, but still–"

"Still," Ravlen interrupted him smoothly, "she has displayed a gift that took me a full twenty thousand of her years to manifest."

Xvander calmed himself at the very dangerous tone in Ravlen's voice. But he could not relent. "I was thinking, Your Majesty, that she has displayed a gift that has the potential to rend the very fabric of the universe."

Ravlen smiled to herself, as if the thought gave her great pleasure. "Yes, there is that." She turned away from him, extending her senses across time and space. After a moment, she returned, and raised her eyes to her chief consort.

"The time it will take her to raise her son is but the blink of an eye. When that is accomplished, she will return and take her place at my side, and her gift will be contained."

Xvander gazed at his Empress, desperately wanting to believe her. "And if the girl chooses not to return at that time?"

Ravlen smiled, but there was steely glint in her eye. When she spoke, her words were gentle, but her expression not. "Do not mistake me, Xvander. When the time comes, the girl does not have a choice."

With those final words, the Empress gracefully moved up the steps to her inner sanctuary, her long robes flowing behind her. Xvander watched as she disappeared and the elaborately carved doors whispered closed behind her. He felt tremendous relief.

Now, he thought to himself, that was more like Her Royal Majesty.

And he smiled.

Made in the USA